The Jews of Donwell Abbey

An "Emma" Vagary

The Jews of Donwell Abbey

The Jews of Donwell Abbey

An "Emma" Vagary

Mirta Ines Trupp

Testimonials

"A creative, heartwarming take on a beloved story, *The Jews of Donwell* finally gives Harriet Smith her due."

~ Caroline Warfield, author of *An Open Heart,*
The Entitled Gentlemen series, *The Ashmead Heirs* series,
Children of the Empire series, et cetera

"Trupp has written a charming and entertaining novel with *The Jews of Donwell Abbey*. A captivating read!"

~ Meryl Ain, author of *Shadows We Carry* and
The Takeaway Men

"Blending *Emma* with a Jewish story line is an ingenious idea! Fans of Austen, and those who crave Jewish Regency stories rich in Jewish content, will find *The Jews of Donwell Abbey* an extremely satisfying read. L' chaim!"

~ Rabbi Jo David (aka Nola Saint James,
author of Regency Romances)

"The Jews of Donwell Abbey introduces a colorful dimension of minority identities in Jane Austen's *Emma*. Trupp's orchestration of history and mystery enriches the ongoing collection of stimulating rewrites of classical novels. A gift to Austen fans, it will interest all readers curious about the hidden facets of "proper" social intercourse in Georgian England."

~ Yael Halevi-Wise, author of *Interactive Fictions:*
Scenes of Storytelling in the Novel,
Professor of Jewish Studies and English Literature

"Who could have guessed that under the genteel veneer of Jane Austen's Regency England lurked secrets beyond what could have been openly addressed at the time? In *The Jews of Donwell Abbey*, Trupp brings sidekick Harriet Smith to the forefront, her mysterious origins are explained, and her ultimate happy ending turned into a lesson about tolerance, acceptance, and the miracles hidden within mundane lives. The perfect companion piece!"

~ Alina Adams, author of *The Fictitious Marquis,*
Romance Writers of America's first #OwnVoices
Jewish Regency Romance

*To my children
who inspire me each and every day*

"Seldom, very seldom, does complete truth belong to any human disclosure; seldom can it happen that something is not a little disguised or a little mistaken."

~Jane Austen, *Emma*

Chapter One

―――――∞⚜∞―――――

Surrey, England
August, 1812

Harriet Smith looked around the room she had shared with Miss Martin for these months past. She had been invited to spend the summer holiday with her schoolmates and was made to feel quite at home. Such a simple, yet evocative word. *Home.* It was the one thing she truly did not have of her own. It affected her keenly to leave just now, especially after the warm reception she had received; however, the circumstances surrounding her abrupt leave-taking were not of her doing. Harriet would have given anything to have remained for the three months complete, but it was a sorrowful event that had brought the visit to an end. The Martins had been thrown into a period of mourning.

Harriet had been roused from her slumber by foreign sounds, having grown accustomed to the natural cacophony of Abbey-Mill Farm. A messenger from the abbey had knocked upon the door, even before the family's favorite rooster crowed his first morning's call.

Wiping the sleep from her eyes, Harriet sat up and turned to her bedmate who had been awoken by the persistent rapping as well. Elizabeth bade her to be silent as they heard her brother's footsteps pass their chamber and down the stairs. The youngest family member, Judith, thankfully remained asleep. She would have caused a great commotion, as was her wont, and they would have been unable to keep their awakened state—and curiosity— unknown.

As it happened, the girls were unable to make out anything of interest, for only a mumbled exchange could be perceived. Elizabeth removed the counterpane and edged her way to the door, placing her ear against the thick wood in the attempt to hear below. Harriet waited abed, holding little hope that her friend's action would provide any clues. It was only when the messenger took his leave, and the front door was shut closed, that Mr. Robert Martin made his way back up the stairs.

Elizabeth scurried back to Harriet's side, and pulling the bedlinens back into place, the girls awaited for news of what was amiss. They shared a moment of disappointment when they heard Mr. Martin knock upon his mother's door. In truth, Harriet was more relieved than disappointed. She would have burned with embarrassment had Mr. Martin seen her in such a state—in her night rail and her hair rolled up in curling paper.

Elizabeth crept up against the door once again. The ploy proved more successful this time as her mother's chamber was down the hall, and the voices were easily discerned.

"*Baruch Dayan Emet*," Elizabeth heard her mother utter.

"Blessed is the Judge of Truth," Elizabeth and her sister repeated quietly.

"What is it?" Harriet whispered. "What has happened?"

Elizabeth brought her finger to her lips as she pried opened the door, and motioned for the girls to come forward. Huddled together, they peered through the opening and watched Mrs. Martin reach for a sewing kit that had been thoughtlessly discarded atop a chest of drawers.

Withdrawing a pair of scissors from its cover, Mrs. Martin took hold of her son's shirt collar and made a deep cut. Taking hold of the fabric, Robert deepened the cut with his own hands.

"A time to rend and a time to sew…do you know the verse, Harriet?"

"Yes, of course, I know it. It is from Ecclesiastes, but what does it signify?"

"Someone has died," cried Judith.

"It could only be one person for Robert to perform such an act," Elizabeth offered. "Grandpapa…"

Touched by this pronouncement, Harriet moved to embrace her friends, but Mrs. Martin caught sight of her daughters and called them hither.

"Mr. Knightley has sent word this morning," she began. "Your grandpapa, peace be upon him, is no longer with us—now, now girls—" Mrs. Martin tightened her embrace, "we have been prepared for this eventuality. I beg you, be calm. Grandpapa, no doubt, has been reunited with his son, your own dear father, and your grandmama."

Mrs. Martin brought a handkerchief to her lips and paused but for a moment. "We must dress and prepare the house. The rabbi will, no doubt, be visiting shortly."

The family dispersed, each quietly seeing to their morning ablutions. Once dressed, the girls made their way downstairs and looked to their mother for direction. Harriet wished to be of service, though she knew her best efforts would only cause her friends additional work.

During her six-week visit, Harriet had learned that the Martin household was like no other of her acquaintance. The pantry and cupboards, indeed, all kitchen matters, were governed by a particular set of rules. Food preparation was of the utmost importance, as was the observance of the Sabbath, which began on Friday evenings and lasted through dusk the following day.

Unable to control herself, Harriet had asked the girls to explain this strange practice. She smiled now, recalling how Judy had rolled her eyes upon hearing yet another question, but it could not be helped. Harriet had always been a curious creature.

"Mysteries are the bane of my existence!" she had declared on more than one occasion. How she came to live at Mrs. Goddard's school, she understood, was a mystery that could never be resolved. Therefore, at a very young age, Harriet determined that asking questions was her right—even if *impertinent Miss!* was often applied to her name.

Today, however, was another matter entirely. The household was in an uproar; the Martins were clearly distressed. Harriet would not add to their discomfort for the world, and so she sat quietly with her cup of tea and waited to be of service, and not a hindrance.

The cottage was not a grand home, not by any means, but Mrs. Martin had made it comfortable and had added feminine touches throughout. A framed mirror of respectable size had been placed by the front door where one could adjust one's wrap or bonnet. Nonetheless, this instrument of vanity was the first to be draped with linen. The girls covered their hand-held mirrors and placed them face down upon their dressing tables. One's *toilette* was not of importance on this sad day.

Mrs. Martin directed her son to gather as many small stools from around the farm that could be found while she swept the better of her two parlors. As mourners, the family would be seated low to the ground; those coming to condole would be offered the finer furniture—the upholstered chairs usually reserved to receive honored guests such as Mr. Knightley or his steward.

At length, Elizabeth put her friend to work, handing over a basket full of fresh eggs.

"Pray, set these to boil in the appropriate pot," she instructed. "You know which one by now, dear Harriet."

Before quitting the room, Elizabeth grabbed hold of her friend's hand. "I know you are bursting with the need to ask your questions, but now is not the time. I promise I will explain it all—perhaps you will not find it that much different from your own family's mourning rituals."

These words, no doubt, were kindly meant; nonetheless, Harriet could not help but feel her shame even more profoundly. Whatever was Elizabeth thinking?

Family rituals? She did not have a family—other than Mrs. Goddard and the girls at school. In truth, she was all alone in the world. But it was not her custom to be petulant or dreary, and certainly not when her friends were in crisis.

Harriet gently placed the eggs to boil and was quite pleased, knowing she had chosen the proper pot. Indeed, Mrs. Martin had instructed her upon her first day at Abbey-Mill. The kitchen had been carefully prepared to house two separate sections: one for dairy products and preparation, and another for meat. Explanations as to *why* had not followed, and Harriet had to tuck her questions away for another time. She had collected a great list of questions during her visit, and it would take another six weeks to address each and every one!

Harriet overheard voices from the parlor as Mrs. Martin sent Judith to find a small table to set outside the door. Elizabeth was to follow with a bowl and pitcher of water. The girls were heard scurrying about, when Harriet heard yet another knock upon the front door. Checking on her pot of boiling water, she wiped her hands on a borrowed apron and peered into the foyer as Mrs. Martin welcomed the visitor.

The gentleman was unknown to Harriet, having never made his acquaintance in Highbury. In truth, upon further inspection, she found him to be oddly fascinating.

Dressed in unrelieved black, his long coat reached down to his calves. His pointed beard, peppered with gray, reminded Harriet of the Martin's billy goat, and she nearly embarrassed herself by laughing aloud at the thought. She was unable to see the color of his hair, or if he had any at all, for he would not remove his hat—though he was in the presence of ladies. It was altogether strange to note that the man appeared to have ringlets on either side of his face!

Whatever could he be about?

Elizabeth and her sister had taken a seat by their mother's side and signaled Harriet to join them in the parlor. While Mr. Martin offered the guest their most comfortable chair, Harriet quietly crept in, standing behind the girls in silent solidarity. The man opened a book he had withdrawn from his coat pocket and, speaking in the language that Harriet had grown accustomed to hearing in weeks past, began chanting a mournful prayer.

"Thank you for coming to us so quickly, Rabbi Kolman," said Mrs. Martin after the family pronounced their *amens*. "We only just learned the news—you find us in quite a state."

"One is never sufficiently prepared for these events, Mrs. Martin. Pray, do not make yourself anxious. Doctor Martsinkovsky, of blessed memory, would not burden his family and friends by being ill-prepared—even for his own funeral." The rabbi allowed himself a slight chortle at his attempt at levity.

"My grandfather was known for his meticulous attention to detail," said Mr. Martin. "He was the best of men."

"Indeed. You will find that everything is in order, Mrs. Martin. The burial will take place this afternoon at three o'clock; our small congregation will accompany you during your seven days of mourning."

"What?" gasped Harriet. "So soon?"

Elizabeth glared at her friend, who immediately understood her blunder. Bowing her head, Harriet silently vowed to say no more.

"Robert," the rabbi continued, "you will want to unbolt the front door. It will be incommodious to be interrupted by visitors while at evening prayers. Whoever wishes to condole with the family will wash their hands before entering and come in quietly thereafter."

"Yes, Rabbi Kolman," replied Robert Martin. "I will see to it."

"And girls," the man said, addressing the Martin daughters, "make sure your dear mama does not tire herself with cooking and baking. The women of our congregation will fill the house with enough food to feed an army—certainly enough to last the week of mourning."

The rabbi rose and shook hands with the man of the house and made for the door. "Remember to exchange your leather boots for other footwear. The weather has been relatively pleasant of late. I doubt you will be plagued with mud or muck. And one more thing! There is to be no shaving nor hair cutting—you young men today seem to have a penchant for fashion rather than following our traditions—for the whole of the week, mind!"

He gave a short bow to one and all before declaring: "May the Almighty comfort you among the mourners of Zion and Jerusalem."

Taking to her feet upon the rabbi's departure, Mrs. Martin clapped her hands to rouse the party from their melancholy. "That's it, then," said she. "Let us finish preparing ourselves…"

Another knock upon the door, however, interrupted Mrs. Martin's directive. Harriet hoped whomever it was came bearing good news. She watched as Mr. Martin made for the door once again and was astonished to see Miss Emily

Bickerton, her classmate, standing there. Sitting atop the pony trap was Peter, Mrs. Goddard's manservant.

"Why, Emily!" cried Harriet. "Whatever do you do here?"

The young lady, known to Elizabeth and Judith Martin, for the foursome were at school together, was asked to enter and offered a glass of cool lemonade. This she was tempted to accept—the morning sun had taken its toll, even on the short ride—however, Emily Bickerton had been given a task, and she meant to discharge it with alacrity.

"Begging your pardon, Mrs. Martin," she began and offered a quick bob of a curtsey. "I should be happy to take refreshment with you and my friends some other time. Mrs. Goddard has sent this note for you, ma'am."

Having made her little speech, and handing over the missive, Emily turned to her classmates and took hold of their hands. "Harriet is to return with me," said she. "Word was received that the doctor had passed—Oh! Please accept my condolences—Mrs. G. thought it best that Harriet return home."

"Oh, no!" cried Elizabeth, her sister joining in unison. Even Mr. Martin seemed disappointed as his shoulders drooped even further, though he did not give voice to his objection.

Harriet felt herself blush. How kind they were to make such a fuss on her behalf. But she felt it only right to pack her things and return to school. Surely, she would only be in the way, and the family ought to have some privacy at such a time.

"Miss Smith," said Mrs. Martin, as Harriet made for the staircase, "our present circumstances must draw your visit to a close, but you are such a sweet, unassuming girl, I know you will understand."

"Pray, ma'am, be at ease. Naturally, I understand and should not wish to inconvenience you at such a time."

"Our tradition requires us to observe certain practices, my dear, beginning with the full state of mourning for a week complete. Perhaps, after the following thirty-day period, when our restrictions are lessened, you girls may make arrangements to meet—certainly, you shall see each on Market Day or a visit to Ford's."

"Robert, now *you* must say something," Judith decreed. "Lest Harriet feel she is not welcome by the whole family!"

Mr. Martin, it seemed, had no notion that he, too, was expected to add his farewell remarks. Caught unaware, he mumbled, "Miss Smith is always welcome at Abbey-Mill."

The girls tittered at their brother's lack of social graces as they accompanied Harriet upstairs to collect her things. The whole affair was handled in a matter of minutes, for she had not the heart to carefully fold and store her belongings as when she had set out nearly two months prior. When Mrs. Martin observed the girls descending into the parlor, teary-eyed and disappointed, she could not help but admonish the party.

"Such a display," cried she. "You shall all be reunited soon enough. Need I remind you—can it be that you've already forgotten—that we are burying your grandfather this day?"

"Of course not, Mama, but we shall miss our friend," said Elizabeth. "Surely, there can be no harm in expressing such sentiments."

"No," replied Mr. Martin, surprising one and all. "Elizabeth is correct. There is no harm, nor impropriety, in sharing such sentiments."

Harriet could not help but notice the change in Mr. Martin's countenance. He had taunted the girls with a sheepish grin throughout her long stay, but he had grown quite solemn, and she was not altogether certain that this sudden change in demeanor had anything to do with the loss of his grandfather. It was silly of her to think it, but it wounded no one to imagine that he might miss her company—as much as she would miss his.

Although she always had plenty of conversation, Harriet could not put two words together as Mr. Martin stared in her direction.

"Say your goodbyes, then," said Mrs. Martin. "Do not keep the driver, nor the poor horse, waiting out in the hot sun, mind."

With nothing for it, Harriet thanked her hostess once again, hugged her friends, and bobbed a quick curtsey to the man of the house.

Traipsing after Miss Bickerton with dampened spirits, Harriet was unaware that Mr. Martin had followed closely from behind. His actions were so swift she had not heard him approach as she handed her valise to the driver. Mr. Martin smiled at her gasp but held out his hand to help her board and take her seat. Miss Bickerton was handed up as well, while Elizabeth and Judith waved their final goodbyes.

Peter clicked his tongue, called out: "Gee up," and off they went, passing between the apple trees that bordered the broad, gravel walk.

Not wishing to sulk over having to leave the Martins sooner than expected, Harriet determined to be grateful instead. She had no business feeling sorry for herself! As the horse clopped along, tapping out a soothing rhythm, Harriet began reflecting on her many blessings and decided, then and there, to compose a list. She would keep it in her reticule as a constant reminder, and she knew precisely where she would begin.

First and foremost, she was grateful for Mrs. Goddard. More than her school mistress, Mrs. G.—as the girls had named her—had been more like a mother these many years.

Most young ladies, or even young girls, were sent off to

boarding school to receive a little education. But Mrs. G. had fashioned a home away from home, where her students were nourished and nurtured the whole year long. She even went so far as to teach something of worth, dabbling in a bit more literature, arithmetic, and the like, when other school mistresses remained fixed on hearth and home activities. This broadmindedness allowed for students of all faiths and denominations to be accepted. Schools for girls were few and far between outside of Town, Harriet might never have met the Martin sisters under other circumstances.

Mrs. Goddard had dismissed her students for the summer season, but Harriet was to remain as parlor boarder and instruct the youngest girls when they returned to school. Having completed their studies, many of the older girls went home to be married or to help their families on their farms or in their shops. There was no such plan for Harriet. No one would come to claim her, she had no home or family. Harriet was the natural daughter of someone. The question of who was that someone remained the great mystery of her life.

Harriet readily acknowledged that Mrs. G. had been mother, nurse, and teacher. She had received some education and a few homemaking skills, not to mention spiritual guidance and counsel. Mrs. Goddard was adamant that her boarders attend church and do their best to follow the precepts. For these reasons and more, Harriet would honor Mrs. Goddard as the top entry on her list of blessings. She would see to it this very afternoon! Indeed, she had numerous reasons to reflect upon her visit—not to mention the many questions that required resolutions.

Having shared hearth and home with a family of Israelites, Harriet was eager to discuss the many curiosities she had observed and pose as many questions as her lifelong mentor would allow. Day after day, she learned new words and melodies, tasted strange delights, and witnessed different practices. Still and all, Harriet had felt oddly at peace and wondered if her acclimation to these distinctive traditions must be considered sinful. Must Mrs. Goddard disapprove?

Ought she mention it to the vicar?

The question required further consideration, for just the thought of causing Mrs. G. any vexation made her anxious. However, as Peter brought the pony to a stop in the front garden, Harriet tucked these thoughts away, certain that Mrs. Goddard would soon make her feel at ease once more.

Shouts of joy greeted Harriet as she was handed down from the cart. Surrounded by her friends, happy tears were shed. Emily Bickerton clasped her hand in encouragement, and Harriet was heartened by this show of friendship. Dabbing at her eyes, Mrs. Goddard ushered everyone back inside, instructing Peter to go around to the kitchen for his meal and the girls to the parlor for tea and cakes.

Harriet was quickly relieved of her valise and brought to sit in the chair of honor, a pretty little chair upholstered with purple flowers and flowing green vines.

For the next quarter of an hour, the girls, ranging from six to seventeen, assailed Harriet with questions of every nature. She did her best to answer each one, but could not complete one sentence before another petitioned for her attention. Mrs. Goddard soon came to her rescue and sent everyone to see to their assigned tasks.

"It has been a busy morning, my dear," stated the matron. "I fear you must have experienced some distress at Abbey-Mill, under the given circumstances. Why do you not go to your room? You can resume your duties when you have had a chance to rest."

Another entry for her list of blessings.

"Thank you, Mrs. G. You are kindness itself." Leaning over, Harriet kissed the matron's wrinkled cheek before taking herself upstairs to the chamber she shared with Miss Bickerton.

Fresh linens and a cool, soft pillow beckoned. She made quick work of removing her outer clothing, tossing shoes and stockings beneath the bed. A moment later, Harriet gave thanks for yet another blessing as she closed her eyes and fell into a deep sleep.

It was several hours later when she awoke. Feeling refreshed, Harriet began unpacking and settling back into her room when she heard frantic footfalls coming up the staircase. Though accustomed to hearing the girls noisily traipse up and down the wooden steps, Harriet was startled when Emily Bickerton came bursting through the door with a pressing message.

She was being summoned to Mrs. Goddard's study at once.

"Do you know what it is all about?" asked Harriet. Had she slept overmuch? Did she abuse Mrs. G.'s kindness? Had something occurred with the Martins?

"I cannot say for certain," replied Emily, "but it must be something grand! A messenger has come from Hartfield—"

"It does not follow that it has anything to do with me!" Harriet was relieved. At the very least, it was not from Abbey-Mill Farm. The poor family had enough to deal with.

"You shall never find out if you do not attend the mistress...*immediately!*"

With a friendly push out the door, Harriet retraced her steps downstairs and found the matron was, indeed, waiting for her in the study. With alacrity, and not a little pride, Mrs. Goddard presented Harriet with the news.

"A gracious invitation has been delivered, my dear," said she, waving the missive in the air. "We are to call on Hartfield. Miss Woodhouse has specifically asked for your attendance."

"But why? Whatever could Miss Woodhouse want with me?"

"I suppose we shall find out soon enough. Mr. Woodhouse is the best of men, and his lovely daughter is a person of consequence in Highbury. It would behoove you, Harriet, to make a good impression. It is for certain that such a nod of recognition would serve you well!"

Chapter Two

Though she was but a girl of seventeen, Harriet Smith was well known by sight throughout Highbury. The townspeople could not help but know of Miss Smith. To be sure, they were not all of the same mind, for some folk were drawn to Harriet because of her beauty and gentility, while others solely held an interest in her provenance. Concerning Miss Woodhouse, Mrs. Goddard credited it to the former—with only the slightest underlying curiosity regarding the latter.

During her first encounter at Hartfield, Harriet was nearly overcome with a megrim, such was her anxious feeling. She had no idea what she had done to merit the invitation; but now here, she would have to—at the very least—attempt to impress her hostess with clever conversation. How was such a thing to be done? Harriet found that she could not put two sensible words together, though Miss Woodhouse was all assurance and kindness.

"Mrs. Goddard, she is quite enchanting!" cried Miss Woodhouse. "Indeed, Harriet, I would be delighted to know you better and—I flatter myself—believe that *you* would benefit greatly from our establishing a deeper acquaintance."

"I do take great pleasure in my friends," said Harriet, "and would be honored to count you among them."

"My dear, you ought not include Miss Woodhouse with your other acquaintances," Mrs. Goddard admonished, "for the young lady is quality, and your classmates are of a different sphere."

Miss Woodhouse smiled, dismissing the compliment with a delicate wave of her hand. "Tell me, Harriet, who *are* your friends? Would I know anyone by name?"

"There is Miss Emily Bickerton. She and I share a room, so naturally, I call her friend—all the girls at the school may be included. However, having just spent my summer months with their family, I would say that Miss Martin and her sister, Miss Judith, are my dearest friends. Are you acquainted with the family? They have suffered a loss just now. Their grandfather died very early yesterday morning, and I had to come away."

"Their grandfather? Dead, you say? I had no notion that his illness had progressed so severely—certainly, Dr. Perry had not said a word, and he was here, at Hartfield, not two days past. As to the Martins," said Miss Woodhouse, "I know the family by name and character, for they rent a large farm on Mr. Knightley's property. Very credibly, so I hear tell."

"Yes, precisely!" said Harriet. "I am pleased that you claim an acquaintance with them, for the Martins have become very dear."

"You have misunderstood, dear. I am *not* acquainted with Mr. or Mrs. Martin, for they are beneath my social standing. Though they are foreigners, I understand they are a very good sort of people. Tell me, are they very coarse and unpolished? Mrs. Goddard, I must insist on this point: Harriet is too beautiful, too sweet of temper to be wasted on inferior society."

"But I—I would not call the Martins coarse—nor foreign."

"You must know that the Woodhouses are the younger branch of an ancient family," Mrs. Goddard was quick to add.

"Indeed. We have been settled in Hartfield for several generations. Do the Martins have a similar heritage? Surely, they do not boast of their roots!"

"I know not, and I do beg your pardon," Harriet murmured. She was the last person who ought to speak on the subject, being in complete ignorance of her own family origins. "I am a person of no consequence!"

"Nonsense! You are far superior than you believe yourself to be. Mrs. Goddard has done wonders thus far. You only want for a bit of guidance and, possibly, a friend who may introduce you to a different society. I would be delighted to be such a friend."

Though she did not consider herself a clever girl—Emily Bickerton or Elizabeth Martin far exceeded her skills in arithmetic and geography—Harriet began to believe that, in this instance, she understood Miss Woodhouse very well. And, because she had recently pledged to count her blessings, Harriet conceded that she would, indeed, be inclined to socialize with upper echelons of Highbury society and accept whatever form of friendship was offered.

"If you truly are not offended by my…pedigree or lack thereof, Miss Woodhouse, I would be delighted to get to know you better."

"I do not care a jot, Harriet! Truly, I do not…but are you quite certain you know nothing about your origins? You are not withholding any information to make yourself more…*intriguing*, shall we say?"

"I would gladly tell you anything if it were in my power to do so, but I simply do not know." Her first recollections of childhood were vague and haunting—their very presence caused Harriet unyielding anguish. "Sometimes, I believe I can recall certain melodies—but then I realize I must have heard them in church. Other times, aromas seem to be familiar. Any real memories begin at school. Mrs. G.

explained everything to me when I was old enough to understand. I arrived with a few articles of clothing, a blanket, and a rag doll. Nothing more."

"How extraordinary! And how old were you? What of your name?"

"I was informed that the little miss was known as Harriet Smith," said Mrs. Goddard, "She was but three years of age."

"Yes, and I have been quite happy with Mrs. G. ever since. If God had wanted me to know my parents, He would undoubtedly have provided for different circumstances."

"You are too good, Harriet. With what you have shared just now, I am certain you must be the natural daughter of a gentleman of consequence. How else would you explain your board and keep? All your needs have been met; and, in some respects, they have exceeded expectations. Indeed, the evidence seems to speak for itself. The Martins of Abbey-Mill Farm will not do!"

"Oh, but Miss Woodhouse! Abbey-Mill Farm is quite lovely. Mrs. Martin enjoys two *very good* parlors, one quite as large as Mrs. Goddard's drawing room! She has kept an upper maid for five-and-twenty years. They have eight cows, two Alderneys, and one little Welch cow. I grew quite fond of that pretty little thing!"

"Is that so?"

"Yes! And they have a very handsome summer house in their garden—large enough to hold a dozen people!"

Mrs. Goddard believed Harriet had said enough about the Martins and attempted to draw her attention to the tea things, but Miss Woodhouse only wished to continue with the topic at hand.

"It seems Mr. and Mrs. Martin have done quite well for themselves. They may be very proud of their accomplishments; they ought to be grateful to Mr.

Knightley, for they owe everything to his benevolence and skill."

"Oh, dear! Pray forgive my impertinence, Miss Woodhouse, but I must correct you again. There is no Mr. *and* Mrs. Martin—well, I mean, there are two such people, but they are not a married couple—that is, I mean to say, Mr. Martin is deceased. Mrs. Martin, his widow, resides with Mr. Robert Martin, her son, and my friends, Miss Elizabeth Martin and Miss Judith."

"I stand corrected, Harriet. It seems the family has made quite an impression. Pray, tell me more about young Mr. Martin."

"Mr. Martin is everything respectable and agreeable," Harriet began. "He ensures his mother's well-being and that of his sisters and has also been very obliging *to me*!" She would not mention how struck she had been by his kind solicitude. The four together shared many merry evenings playing games and taking moonlight walks. These were treasured memories indeed. "One time," she continued, "I mentioned that I was fond of walnuts, and don't you know, Mr. Martin walked three miles to bring a bushel home!"

"That *is* impressive," Miss Woodhouse said, slicing another piece of cake and passing it to Mrs. Goddard.

"But that was not all. One night, he invited the shepherd's son into the parlor so that he could sing for our little party. I could not credit that Mr. Martin would do such a thing! I had told him that I was fond of music, and he provided the evening's entertainment to please *me*—his sisters' schoolmate."

"He sounds amiable, indeed, but how does he find time for these games and pleasantries? Does he neglect the farm? That would make him quite lazy."

"Oh, no! He has a very fine flock and tends them well. Indeed, while I was visiting, I overheard him say that he had been bid more for his wool than anybody in the county. Everyone speaks well of him in the parish, Miss Woodhouse. And his mother and sisters are naturally very fond of him, to be sure."

After sipping her tea, Harriet felt fortified to continue with her tale. She so enjoyed her time with her friends and could never tire speaking of it. "Mrs. Martin told me she had high hopes for her only son. I suppose every mother has the right to be proud. Mrs. Martin said he would make someone an excellent husband."

Miss Woodhouse's interest appeared to increase. "Do you believe Mrs. Martin has a match in mind?"

"She does not appear to be in any hurry to see him wed. In fact, Mrs. Martin was most emphatic on that score," said Harriet, recalling the very conversation where Mrs. Martin relayed sentiments that appeared to carry more weight than the question deserved. "Mr. Martin is in want of a particular wife, at least that is what his mother believes, and she hopes to be able to give any future match her blessing."

Miss Woodhouse acknowledged the statement with a brief nod before posing another question. "Is Mr. Martin a man of information? Did you ever discuss books during your visit?"

"Oh yes! Well—that is, I've seen books and agricultural reports by one of the window seats. He was diligent in recording daily entries and examining new methods or findings in his line of work. But sometimes, before we went to cards in the early evening, Mr. Martin read something aloud from the *Elegant Extracts*. He has never read *The Romance of the Forest*, nor *The Children of the Abbey*. I fear he believed me to be quite silly in asking if he had ever heard of such books, but he did say he would read one or the other now that I had made him aware of their titles."

"What sort of looking man is Mr. Martin?"

"Oh! Not handsome—that is, I thought him very plain at first, but I do not think he is so plain now. But did you never see him? He is in Highbury every now and then and he is sure to ride through every week on his way to Kingston. I believe he has passed you very often."

"That may be, and I may have seen him fifty times, though I did not know his name. Whether on horseback or foot, a young farmer is the very last sort of person to raise my curiosity. I hope to be useful in some way, you must understand. A farmer or his family could not require anything from me; therefore, in a sense, Mr. Martin is as much above my notice as in every other he is below it."

"Oh yes! I see…" Harriet replied, though she was not entirely sure that she could agree.

"I do not doubt his being a very respectable young man, and, as such, I wish him well. What do you imagine his age to be?"

"I know it exactly, Miss Woodhouse! He was four-and-twenty on the 8th of last June, and my birthday is the 23rd—just a fortnight and a day's difference."

"Only four-and-twenty?" Miss Woodhouse replied. "That *is* too young to settle. His mother is perfectly right not to be in a hurry. Six years hence, it might be desirable—if he could meet with a good sort of young woman in the same rank as his own and with a little money."

"Six years hence! Dear me! He would be thirty years old!"

"That is as early as most men can afford to marry, Harriet, especially men not born with independent means. Mr. Martin, I imagine, has yet to make his fortune."

"But they live very comfortably. A young lady would be hard-pressed to find a more agreeable situation."

"I mean to say, though I would not object to his sisters altogether—they seem to be educated and well-brought up girls—one cannot divine whom Mr. Martin may marry. It does not follow that his choice of wife would make a suitable friend for you. I pray you to take heed, Harriet, dear. You ought to take particular care with whom you associate. I believe in my heart that you are a gentleman's daughter. Your behavior and company must be beyond reproach to support that claim. Believe me, dear. This is a cruel world, particularly for young ladies with no means of protection."

Harriet recognized the truth of those words and took them to heart. With Miss Woodhouse as her champion, *she* could be a person of some consequence. And that, too, would be quite agreeable. "I believe," said she, "I better comprehend your meaning."

"Good girl! I would have you firmly established in good society, so that—even if you were not friends with a Miss Woodhouse of Hartfield—you would still be permanently well connected. That is why you must have as few *odd* acquaintances as possible. Try to limit your intimacy with those of little education or society. This Mr. Martin will surely marry a mere farmer's daughter, certainly not someone who ought to claim an acquaintance with *you*."

"I dare say that Mrs. Martin seemed exceptionally determined. Her new daughter will have a superior education and know a great many things. Oh, dear! I am being contradictory again. I beg your pardon, Miss Woodhouse. I do not mean to set up my opinion against yours—I am sure I shall not wish to claim an acquaintance with Mr. Martin's future wife—but I shall always have a great regard for my friends, Elizabeth and Judy. I should be sorry, indeed, to have to give them up."

"There, there now, Harriet," said she. "Let us not spend any more time discussing the Martins. Allow me to refill your tea—for you must be parched after answering my questions—and I will share a little bit about myself. If we are to be friends, you should also know about me. I am the youngest of two daughters; my sister has married and lives in London. My father is the very best of men, indulgent and most affectionate."

"And your mother? Oh, I beg your pardon—I have an inquisitive nature and often allow myself to voice questions without considering propriety!"

"Not at all. I interrogated *you* quite to my heart's content, did I not? Ask any manner of question. I shall do my best to satisfy your curiosity. As to Mama, she left this world when I was still full young. My memories of her have grown dim—it is disquieting, to be sure. The sensation can only be described as other worldly, would you not agree? It is as if one is gazing upon a beloved painting and having it suddenly begin to vanish, overcome by some fanciful mist. I fear you and I share that unfortunate connection, Harriet. Our mothers, both, are lost to us. You were raised by dear Mrs. Goddard, and I was well looked after by Miss Taylor."

Harriet carefully avoided the bit about the *lost mothers*. It was too painful a thought. She would continue on a different vein. "That lady must have been your governess," said she.

"That is correct, if one must be given a title. In truth, I have a great affection for Miss Taylor and have long considered her my dearest friend. Indeed, we are nearly sisters."

"But as your governess, were you not reprimanded or scolded?"

"No, indeed." Miss Woodhouse laughed. "Miss Taylor had a mild temper and was not one to impose her authority. Mr. Knightley has often remarked on that subject. I have been spoiled the whole of my life."

"It seems that life has been quite pleasant, though you have experienced sorrow at a young age," Harriet murmured with not a little envy. "A doting father, a family, and caring friends—you will forgive my little observation, I hope."

"There is nothing to forgive, dear Harriet. I wholeheartedly concur. However, there is another side to the story. While I do believe myself to be a fortunate creature, I pray you to take pity on me."

"I would gladly offer my support, in any form or fashion; but, Miss Woodhouse, why should you ask for my pity?"

"While you have a houseful of companions to share your days, I have only my father. He is a dear, sweet man but he often finds himself unwell or anxious. I dedicate myself to his comfort."

"Is Mr. Woodhouse so very old, then?"

"Harriet, child—" Mrs. Goddard interjected.

"No, pray, do not impede my friend's curiosity," Miss Woodhouse replied. "My father was not fortunate to marry young, you must understand, and certain events, such as losing my mother, have taken their toll. As time has gone by, I have come to terms with his limited conversation and his…peculiarities, such as they are."

"Mr. Woodhouse is a prudent yet *sensitive* gentleman," Mrs. Goddard offered. "Always, he is concerned with his health and the health of others. He is universally respected by all who know him."

"I cannot find fault with that description, madam. He has an amiable temperament and has only shown me adoration my whole life. But poor dear! He suffers greatly with any change whatsoever. He tires easily and seeks his bed soon after we dine. Most evenings, I am quite on my own."

"Certainly," asked Harriet, "you have family or friends for companionship?"

"Miss Taylor will soon be Mrs. Weston, and live but a half mile from Hartfield. However, it is not the distance that will separate us. Her new circumstance shall mean that I must content myself with tea in the afternoon or a walk into town to look at Ford's selection of bonnets and gloves—that is when Mr. Weston can spare his wife. My sister, Isabella, is settled in London, and while it is only sixteen miles away, she is wife and mother now."

We each of us are lonely; though she is enveloped within the loving arms of her father, and I am coddled within the shelter of the school.

Harriet's disposition was such that she was ready and fully prepared to enter into such an acquaintance. At the very least, it would be an adventure, something quite new, and with an open mind and an open heart, God alone knew what was in store.

Chapter Three

"I have not yet reconciled to my daughter Isabella's marriage," Mr. Woodhouse grumbled. "She has been away from this house so very long; I have lost count how many years have passed. Now, to part with Miss Taylor! Let me assure you, Miss Smith, it has been so very trying. I fear I do not have the fortitude to bear it."

Having just arrived at Hartfield, and being so recently introduced to the master of house, Harriet was at a loss for words. The gentleman's anguish over *losing* Miss Taylor seemed quite sincere.

"I am not convinced that poor Miss Taylor would not have been better off staying with us. We miss her company, Emma and I. It is as if Emma has lost another sister."

"Dear Papa," Miss Woodhouse cried. "You must not say such things. I have not lost Miss Taylor—Mrs. Weston, that is—and Mr. Weston is the best of men! So kind, so good-humored. Nor have I lost Isabella! Indeed, I have gained a brother in John Knightley. And what about the children? Am I not blessed by my nieces and nephews? I love them dearly, and they, in turn, love me—even with my odd humors."

"Yes, yes, of course," said he. "The children...but, my dear, you have never had any odd humors. Miss Smith, I pray you not judge us too harshly. Emma dear, what will your new friend think of us, I wonder?"

Dumbfounded, Harriet was unsure of her appropriate

response. Ought she agree with Miss Woodhouse or with the dear, old gentleman?

"Let us speak no more about it, Papa," said Miss Woodhouse, saving Harriet the worry. "What say you to a game of backgammon until we are called into dinner?"

But before the table could be prepared with all the necessary pieces, a gentleman was announced, and Harriet glanced at her hosts as the party stood to greet the newcomer. It was Mr. Knightley himself! She could hardly believe her good fortune.

"Good evening—I thought to come straight around to bring greetings from Brunswick Square," said the gentleman. "Ah, forgive me, Mr. Woodhouse, Emma—I did not realize you were entertaining this evening."

"Come in, come in, dear friend," cried Mr. Woodhouse. "Emma! Tell him, my dear."

"I shall, indeed, Papa, if you give me the opportunity!" Miss Woodhouse responded good-humoredly. "You are very welcome, sir. I should like very much to introduce my new acquaintance. Miss Harriet Smith, please meet an old and intimate friend of the family—Mr. Knightley. He is a frequent visitor—his home is just about a mile away—and the two of you are bound to run into each other here at Hartfield."

The gentleman made his bow, and Harriet could not help but notice his easy manner. Mr. Knightley was at home, sitting alongside Mr. Woodhouse in a worn leather chair. The footman offered him a glass of sherry, which he readily accepted without having asked or specifying his choice. Miss Woodhouse, it seemed, did not exaggerate this point. Mr. Knightley was, indeed, a frequent visitor.

"It is very kind of you to come to us, sir, so soon after arriving from London," said Mr. Woodhouse. "But you must take better care. The trip is tiresome, and one always seems to catch cold when one is away from home. And to walk all this way! It is late, and you must be chilled to the bone!"

"Not at all, sir. The evening is so fair I must draw back from your great fire. How fortunate that Miss Taylor enjoyed such fine weather on her wedding day! Nary a cloud in the sky!"

"No, indeed, sir! We have had vast deal of rain of late—tell Mr. Knightley, Emma! I was certain the bride would catch cold, never mind the rest of us who accompanied her to church. I had hoped they would put off the wedding, but I would not be heard!"

"Naturally, everything was just as it was supposed to be," said Mr. Knightley. "Allow me to extend my congratulations to you both, for I have been remiss in wishing you joy. Although the bride is not a blood relation, I know what Miss Taylor has meant to Hartfield. Tell me now. How did it all go? How did you all behave? Emma—I know I can rely on you for the details. Who cried most?"

"Ah! poor Miss Taylor!" Mr. Woodhouse shook his head. "I dare say I witnessed a few shed tears. I pray she has no regrets with this sad business."

"I cannot allow such melancholy, sir! While I understand that you and Miss Woodhouse may suffer from this new arrangement, I cannot agree with your sympathy for 'poor Miss Taylor.' She has come up in the world! A home of her own and a doting husband. And now," said Mr. Knightley with a bit of a mischievous tone, "she need only worry about pleasing one family member rather than two."

"Say what you mean," teased Miss Woodhouse. "If my father were not seated by your side, you know very well that you would have the temerity to say, 'Especially when *one* of those two is such a fanciful, troublesome creature.' I know you well enough, sir."

"I believe you have the right of it, my dear." Mr. Woodhouse sighed. "It is too true; I am sometimes quite troublesome, what with my disquieted nature."

Of all the ungrateful…!

Never could Harriet have imagined speaking of one's father in such an accusatory manner! It was only when Mr. Knightley raised his brow in concern that Harriet recognized the misunderstanding, and all was put to right when she witnessed Miss Woodhouse fall to her father's feet.

"Dearest Papa!" said she. "Of course, we do not mean *you*! It was a joke, one of many that Mr. Knightley and I lance at one another. I was referring to myself, sir. I know that Mr. Knightley finds *me* troublesome. It was all playful banter. No offense was meant."

Mr. Woodhouse seemed to ponder the remark, but Harriet was made uncomfortable by the overall feeling in the room. Not having had the pleasure of such discourse amid her own family, she did not have the ability to understand the seemingly sibling-like teasing, nor how the head of the house would react.

Miss Woodhouse seemed to be penitent, but ought she have been so careless to prompt such feelings in the first place? Harriet was grateful for the clarification that followed and began to hold Mr. Knightley in high esteem.

"My intention was not to accuse, Mr. Woodhouse," said he. "I only meant to point out that while Miss Taylor was in residence in Hartfield, she needed to please two people. Now, as mistress of her own home, she need only please one—Mr. Weston. Therefore—if one were keeping score—it would seem that Miss Taylor, ahem, I mean Mrs. Weston, is ahead of the game. Now, then, do not keep me in suspense! Tell me about the wedding, if you please."

Mr. Woodhouse appeared to be soothed by this comment. Miss Woodhouse patted her father's knee as she regained her own seat and leaned towards Harriet's direction.

"Never let it be said, Miss Smith, that ladies alone enjoy some good tittle-tattle. As you see, the gentlemen are just as inclined to gossip!" said she. "I will tell you all you want to know, Mr. Knightley. We all behaved charmingly. Everybody was punctual, everybody in their best looks."

The gentleman laughed as the young lady fluttered her eyelashes and adjusted her skirts.

"As you say, however, I am certain that you, Emma, were a veritable watering pot. How did you manage without me at your side? I've never known you to have a handkerchief on your person when required."

"Not a tear was shed, sir!"

"Were you not saddened to be parted with your friend, Miss Woodhouse?" Harriet asked, still unable to ascertain the level of sincerity in the conversation. "It sounds as if the two of you were inseparable."

"Saddened?" Miss Woodhouse cried. "Not I! We shall only be half a mile apart, and I arranged the match, if truth be told. Mr. Knightley would be right to call me foolish if I regretted my achievement—and I could not bear to concede to his judgment."

"You, Miss Woodhouse? You arranged the match?" Harriet was genuinely surprised to learn such a fact.

"Indeed, I did. It must have been nearly four years ago, but I knew the two would suit, even though the general public declared Mr. Weston would remain a widower forevermore. I could see that their future together would bring glad tidings to all concerned."

"How clever you are, Miss Woodhouse, and how generous too! You thought only of Mr. Weston's loneliness and Miss Taylor's benefit—never a thought for your own comfort."

Harriet stopped at this, noting Mr. Knightley shaking his head and failing to hide a crooked smile. Mr. Woodhouse became unsettled once more, entreating his daughter to cease making matches and attempting to look into the future. He was adamant in his belief that whatever his dear Emma predicted, came to pass and the gentleman could not tolerate any further upheaval to his comfortable arrangements.

With eyes fixed upon Miss Woodhouse, Harriet wondered at her response. Surely, such a direct command ought only to result in an obedient daughter's acquiescence. She was taken aback when the young lady would not vow to heed her father's decree.

"I promise you to make none for myself, Papa, but I must, indeed, for other people. It is the greatest amusement in the world! And I have so little entertainment these days—"

Oh! That is cheekiness!

"I plan not to make a match for myself, mind you," Miss Woodhouse continued, "but where others are concerned— why, it is nearly my duty!"

"You count yourself successful as a matchmaker," said Mr. Knightley, "when, in fact, you have only been lucky. More to the point, I believe it was simply coincidence; the marriage would have occurred with or without your little games and interference."

"I pray you, daughter, no more matches! The gentleman is correct, and one must not tempt Fate!"

"I refuse to engage in a battle of wits with Mr. Knightley. He only wishes to goad me into a further quarrel. However, I do have one more match in mind, Papa, and it is for poor Mr. Elton. He has been in Highbury for a year complete, all alone in his parson's house. He is in need of a wife; you must agree."

"Surely you jest, Emma!" Mr. Knightley grumbled. "Elton will not thank you for your meddling—"

"What is your opinion, Miss Smith?" asked Miss Woodhouse. "Oughtn't the parson be wed? Is that not what any congregant would expect of their church leader?"

"I have not given the matter much thought, Miss Woodhouse. It would never have occurred to me—indeed, it is not my place—"

"Well said, dear girl," Mr. Woodhouse decreed. "There's no need to speak of it any further, Emma. I cannot help but think what other family circle will suffer the effects of your interference. Pray, no more talk of marriages!"

"Here, here!" said Mr. Knightley. "Depend upon it, a man of six or seven-and-twenty can care for himself. Find some other means of *entertainment*, Emma, but for heaven's sake, do not try your luck again. You will rue the action; I am sure of it."

The conversation was cut short when the butler announced dinner. The party arose, Miss Woodhouse taking her father's arm and Harriet timidly taking Mr. Knightley's. Understanding the order of things, Harriet felt the honor immensely. Only Donwell Abbey surpassed Hartfield in the vicinity. Tonight, she was not a lowly miss sharing her evening meal with a houseful of girls. Tonight, Miss Harriet Smith was dining in a grand estate accompanied by the notable families of Surrey.

As they took their seats, Mr. Woodhouse appeared low-spirited once more. The table settings were of the finest quality, and the room was aglow with many candles that flickered prettily. Harriet wondered if she ought to attempt to say something witty to combat the gentleman's gloom, but Miss Woodhouse already had the matter in hand.

"Papa, dear, what say you to inviting the Westons on Tuesday next? Mr. Knightley will surely condescend to join us again, and of course, Miss Smith, you shall come as well. We do so enjoy having company in the evenings, do we not, Papa?"

"Yes, yes, that would do nicely. Perhaps you should ask Mrs. Bates and Miss Bates—Mrs. Goddard too. Now that Dr. Martsinkovsky is no longer with us," Mr. Woodhouse said with some regret, "I would have my old friends about the place."

"I didn't realize you were at all acquainted with the doctor," said Harriet. "But then again, how would I—" she paused and felt herself blush.

"He was my physician and great friend," replied Mr. Woodhouse. "He was taken from us too soon, another loss I must suffer—"

"But we are fortunate, Papa, to have so many others to hold near and dear. I will make certain to invite everyone just as you proposed. We shall have cake and set up the card table."

Mrs. Bates and Miss Bates were well known to Harriet. However, both mother and daughter were well past the age of being of any use to Miss Woodhouse. They certainly could not replace Mrs. Weston in the young lady's affections.

In their brief time together, Harriet had had the opportunity to glimpse at Miss Woodhouse's daily life. She was certainly a young lady of leisure. Her position within good society was accompanied by a certain power. With alacrity, Harriet began to understand that Miss Woodhouse had singled her out for a purpose. To be sure, until this very moment, Harriet had failed to comprehend the full measure her good fortune.

I am to be her next project.

Rather than take offense at the notion, Harriet was gratified. More than that, she was delighted. Miss Woodhouse had treated her with great affability that evening. She would gladly accept her solicitude, for though Mrs. Goddard and the girls at school were kindness itself, they did not equal such a personage as Miss Woodhouse.

Chapter Four

Harriet felt welcome at Hartfield, and her intimacy was such that all expected, and accepted, her presence in that grand estate. Miss Woodhouse had made it known that Harriet had an open invitation, and she encouraged her to come to call often and without ceremony. Harriet understood that accompanying Miss Woodhouse on her walks or errands accomplished various useful tasks, but, most importantly, their mutual satisfaction with one another was free to grow and become a settled thing.

She understood that losing Mrs. Weston had proven to be difficult for Miss Woodhouse. Harriet tried to make herself always available, always grateful—always as clever as can be. Though this proved to be tiresome at times, the acquaintance was mutually beneficial. There was no artifice here. The truth of the matter was that Miss Emma Woodhouse needed to be useful and Harriet wished to be needed.

In this light, Harriet prepared for an evening's entertainment at Hartfield. She could not hope to replace a Miss Taylor, now a married and respectable lady of some fortune, but she could be the young friend that Hartfield seemed to require. It was not an unfamiliar role. Indeed, Harriet had been playing the part, in some form or fashion, the whole of her life. Not for her were Shakespeare's words: *Speak what we feel, not what we ought to say*. At school, at church, or amongst friends, Harriet understood what was expected of her—and what could never be borne.

Mr. Woodhouse was in mid-speech as Harriet and Mrs. Goddard were shown into the drawing room that evening, apparently the last to have arrived.

"Papa is feeling a bit melancholy this evening," whispered Miss Woodhouse as she greeted Harriet at the door. "Pray, sit by my side. I shall need your cheerful disposition."

"I am thankful you have come," said Mr. Woodhouse to one and all. "I am missing my good friends this night. The Colonel, as always, and now, Doctor Martsinkovsky. We at Hartfield will feel his loss. I am not at all certain how we shall get along…"

"We shall get along splendidly, Papa. Mr. Perry has been to visit," said Miss Woodhouse. "Surely, he will do just as well, if not better. A true Englishman, he is sure to understand your every concern."

"Emma, what nonsense is this?" cried Mr. Woodhouse. "Foreigner or not, the doctor understood me perfectly! And do not forget the great service he rendered my dear friend and neighbor, Colonel Knightley."

"I did not mean to offend, Papa, it is just that Mr. Perry is—"

"Mr. Perry is a country apothecary," supplied Mr. Knightley. "Nothing more. Martsinkovsky was a physician, educated on the continent, and with knowledge that Perry would never hope to assume, even if he lived another hundred years."

"Why, Mr. Knightley," said Miss Bates. "I have never heard you speak so passionately about such things. I have little knowledge of physicians, surgeons, or apothecaries, so I appreciate when others comment on the subject. Do tell us more, Mr. Knightley, as only you can."

"I know for a fact that Mr. Martin—that is to say—*the Martins* feel the doctor's loss greatly," Harriet murmured. "I was at Abbey-Mill Farm when they received the news." Acutely aware of the sudden attention she garnered, Harriet felt the need to qualify her statement. "Naturally, at the time, I was unaware that the families were related…"

Miss Woodhouse raised her brow, and Harriet was made uneasy.

Oh, dear! I have caused offense!

Unable to interpret her friend's meaning, Harriet made another attempt to rectify her blunder.

"Pray, if Dr. Martsinkovsky was not an Englishman, how *are* the Martins related?" She risked another look at her hostess only to confirm that she did, indeed, make matters worse.

"The matter does not signify," said Miss Woodhouse. "Robert Martin is a farmer of no more consequence than his sire. Dr. Martsinkovsky, himself, very likely descended from Russian serfs or some such."

"You are grievously mistaken," replied Mr. Knightley. "Your father ought to take Mrs. Weston to task for not having lectured you on foreign affairs with more care."

"Emma, my dear!" Mrs. Weston cried. "Pray, do not embarrass me before my new husband and your guests. Indeed, we have spent hours and hours studying the atlas…"

Harriet wished the floor would open and swallow her up whole! Such a fuss over her impertinent question!

"Pay me no mind, sir," said she. "My query was of no great importance, and you certainly do not owe me an explanation, to be sure."

"The mistake can be clarified quite easily, Miss Smith. Mr. Martin's grandfather had been a physician of some renown—even in his own country. He hailed from the

Grand Duchy of Lithuania, an area tragically conquered and partitioned by the Kingdom of Prussia and the Russian Empire."

"Minor details, I am sure," said Miss Woodhouse.

"Not *minor* to my mind, especially when you erroneously equate Robert Martin's grandfather with a serf."

Aghast, Harriet observed the two go to battle, with no one brave enough to intercede. She sunk deeper into her chair.

Oh, the shame of it all!

"All of Highbury heard the tittle-tattle about the Jew living at Donwell," Miss Woodhouse retorted. "All these years later, it provides our neighbors with sufficient fodder for speculation. Why, I even overheard Mr. Elton mention the matter while greeting the congregation after services."

"Anyone who cared to know the truth ought to have asked the Colonel, when he lived, or myself. Let me, now and forever more, clear up any misconceptions. No doubt, *all of Highbury* will soon hear of it, thanks, in no small part, to your childish machinations."

"I refuse to argue with you, Mr. Knightley. Pray, do continue. Amaze the party with your soliloquy."

Mr. Knightley began to pace, attracting the company's full attention. "My father, the Colonel," he declared, "owed his life to Doctor Martsinkovsky."

"You have the right of it, good sir!" cried Mr. Woodhouse.

"Oh, dear! I do hope you will spare us some of the details, Mr. Knightley," cried Miss Bates. "Pray remember we have yet to dine. Is that not right, Mama?" she said, patting her matriarch's wrinkled hand. "Would that you could save the details for when you and the other gentlemen are enjoying your port and cigars. We are rather delicate, are we not Mama, and do not wish to hear that which might ruin our appetite."

Mr. Knightley did not offer a reply, though he did perform a curt bow. Harriet felt a great story was about to unfold as the gentleman began his discourse, inviting one and all to recall the summer of '57.

He asked the party to recall how great armies had been on the move, not only on the continent but across the ocean in the Americas. Complex strategies had moved the King's men like chess pieces upon a checkered board. Mr. Knightley reminded those old enough to remember how Austria united itself with France and how Frederick II, in turn, aligned his kingdom with the English Crown.

"And with that, Prussia's invasion of Saxony brought the leading nations of Europe to war," said Mr. Knightley. "Frederick not only required English funds to support his campaign, he required English troops."

"How could anyone of us forget, sir?" asked Mr. Weston. "Only think of the men we lost—just in this parish alone—I will never forgive the king's own son for causing so much pain. The coward!"

"Do allow Mr. Knightley to continue, dearest," said Mrs. Weston, laying a soothing hand upon her husband.

"It is true; the Duke of Cumberland was sent to command the Hanoverian Army. His regiment, the 1st Battalion of Grenadiers, included my father. The Grenadiers were sent to support the Hanoverians—nearly 40,000 strong—to prevent French troops from crossing the Weser River. My father proposed that men be strategically placed to defend the Rhine; however, the duke rejected the plan!" Mr. Knightley's fist came crashing down upon a side table. "This miscalculation cost them the day and much more."

"Mr. Knightley, you are not yourself," said Miss Woodhouse. "I insist you sit down and have a cup of my father's good wine. If you need to hear my capitulation, sir, here it is: *I surrender*! There is no need to continue in this manner—all to explain how a foreigner of no consequence came to live among us."

"Emma, my dear!" cried Mrs. Weston. "That is badly done!"

"How do I offend, Mrs. Weston? As hostess, is it not my duty to see to my guests' comfort? Why spoil Serle's dinner with all this talk of war?"

"I fear Harriet has asked one too many questions," Mrs. Goddard supplied. "Perhaps it would be best, dear, to refrain from posing another."

"Not at all, Mrs. Goddard; however, in the interest of time, I will endeavor to measure my words and bring closure to the tale," Mr. Knightley said and bowed to Miss Woodhouse. "The Duke of Cumberland's hapless orders did indeed lose the battle at Hastenbeck. His retreat, as Mr. Weston intimated, was a matter of shame and needless casualties—among the wounded, of course, was my father."

"Were his injuries severe, sir?" Harriet asked, unwittingly prolonging Miss Woodhouse's vexation.

"To be sure, it never fails to astonish how my father survived that day, shattered and beaten as he was."

"It was all due to the good doctor," cried Mr. Woodhouse. "I may be in my dotage, but I know what I have seen and the healing I have personally experienced by that man's hand."

"Now, Papa, there is no need—"

"Miss Smith," Mr. Woodhouse continued, "if only I could make you understand the consideration given to cleanliness—the rituals observed by his people. Tell them, Mr. Knightley! Tell them, for my proclivities must always appear foolish to one and all."

"Oh no, sir!" cried Miss Bates. "That we cannot allow! Is that not so, Mama?" She enunciated loudly into her mother's ear, though the lady was beside her. "Mr.

Woodhouse says he is *foolish*. Such condemnation of a gentleman we hold in high esteem—why the idea...*no*! Never that!"

The gentleman waited until the lady had done. Harriet could only admire Mr. Knightley's patience and solicitude, knowing that the party intended to hear the full of the story and that the gentleman was inclined to comply. In an effort to acknowledge Miss Bates' protest, Mr. Knightley offered her a brief smile before continuing with his explanation.

"Thanks must be given to the good men who carried their injured to the nearest military outpost, marching across blackened fields littered with the remnants of the battle. When my father awoke, he found himself being prepared for the surgical theatre, such as it was. He noted a surgeon washing his hands as he moved from one patient to the next. The Prussians mocked the man, making gestures and smirking behind his back as he approached my father's gurney. He, in fact, was not a surgeon, as my father surmised. Yosef Martsinkovsky introduced himself as the physician assigned to the British troops. The Prussians preferred to be attended by their own kind."

"I do not understand, sir," said Harriet. "Was he not Prussian, himself?"

"Indeed," replied Mr. Knightley, glaring at Miss Woodhouse. "He was Prussian by birth; however, the doctor was considered a foreigner because he was an Israelite in faith."

"Good God!" Mr. Weston exclaimed. "Were they not all trapped in that hell together?"

"My dear—" his wife gently called attention to his language.

"I beg your pardon," the gentleman bowed his head towards the ladies in attendance.

"But *that*, sir, was the exact term used by the physician.

Indeed, my father vividly recalled the remark. In the middle of the mud and—let us say, in the thick of things, Doctor Martsinkovsky quoted from a sacred book of his people. He said: 'The very best of doctors go to hell.' He vowed that he would endeavor to keep my father—and himself—away from its fiery gates."

"And how did Colonel Knightley fare?" asked Harriet, unable to help herself from interrupting and fearing that she had become quite like Miss Bates.

"The procedure was a success, and—well, perhaps I ought to leave it at that. Emma will never have me to dine again if I said much more."

"No, indeed. Pray, continue," said Miss Woodhouse. "You must not keep the party in suspense."

"Very well," said he. "My father was ordered home to convalesce; however, due to his injuries, it was thought he would require medical care for the journey. Naturally, no one else would do other than Doctor Martsinkovsky. After several weeks under the doctor's care, the two had exchanged many stories, you must understand. They became friends—in truth, it was more than that. My father believed he was given a second chance and he could do no less for the man who saved him."

"Was the doctor's life in peril, sir?"

"Perhaps not due to the ongoing battles, but certainly because of the ceaseless persecution his people endured. Doctor Martsinkovsky's homeland had changed hands from one tyrannical power to another. The Israelites often found themselves trapped in the game. The doctor had lost the majority of his family on one occasion in a brutal attack known in their language as a *pogrom*. When my father proposed that he come live at Donwell, Doctor Martsinkovsky took him up on the offer."

"To lose one's family is a tragedy," Harriet murmured.

"I concur, Miss Smith, but once in England, the doctor rebuilt his life and career. He lived in the abbey at first. My father required constant care, as you may well imagine."

"I believe Mr. Elton had a comment or two on the wisdom of granting such luxuries to one's physician," said Miss Woodhouse.

"Perhaps Mr. Elton ought to consider that the man saved my father. The Colonel was able to live a full life; he saw his son marry and produce another generation of Knightley children. Would the vicar not think the doctor merited our gratitude?"

"*I* would agree, sir; however, Mr. Elton observed it was an odd arrangement. Hebrews living in an abbey, or some such."

"There are times, Emma, that I truly have to restrain myself..."

"Children, children! I pray you desist!" cried Mr. Woodhouse. "Emma dear, Martsinkovsky deserved every praise—just think of what he has done for me. No other physician understood my needs!"

Disquieted by the turn in the conversation, Harriet threw herself back into the fray, hoping Mr. Knightley would appease her curiosity. The gentleman was about to explain familial relationships. She risked further admonishment and encouraged him to continue his discourse. Mr. Knightley was only too happy to oblige.

"As time went on," said he, "the doctor wished to marry, but sadly, it seemed there was no one eligible in Highbury..."

"Did you hear that, Mama?" Miss Bates interjected. "Mr. Knightley said that no one was eligible to marry the doctor. What say you to *that*?" The older woman waved her daughter away, but Miss Bates was not deterred. "I do believe there is a tale to tell, but it is not my tale, so I may not tell it! Pray, forgive the interruption, Mr. Knightley."

"Where was I?" He had been interrupted on so many occasions it was becoming disconcerting, to say the least. "Oh, yes—the doctor contacted the Israelite community in London, and a few weeks later, he traveled there—only to return a bachelor. All were surprised when the gentleman contracted marriage with a young lady of a small congregation here in the village."

"I never knew!" Miss Bates exclaimed. "I never knew she was not from London. Did you hear, Mama? The doctor had asked for a young lady's hand—here, in Highbury. Were you aware of it, Mama? I certainly was not. Heavens! I never heard that story. I thought she had come from London, but how was one to know—those people keep to themselves…"

"It was *bashert*." The party was stunned when Mrs. Bates uttered her first words of the evening. It was lamentable that no one other than Mr. Knightley understood her meaning.

"Precisely, Mrs. Bates, the match appeared to be preordained—but how did you know?" asked the gentleman.

The lady, it seemed, did not hear the inquiry, or she did not care to respond. Mr. Knightley did not press the matter and continued.

"The doctor always said that one oughtn't question Providence. They married, and when their first son was born, the couple moved into Donwell Cottage. They named the child Yonaton in honor of my father," said Mr. Knightley. "As the child grew, he became greatly attached to the Colonel, and it was clear soon enough that the boy was a farmer through and through."

"I recall seeing the lad traipsing after your father," said Mr. Woodhouse. "He soon went from young Yonaton Martsinkovsky to being known as Jonathan and then, simply, Mr. John Martin."

"Indeed, sir." Mr. Knightley replied. "And when he was of age, he too traveled to London to find a bride. Unlike his father, the young man was successful and brought his wife home to Abbey-Mill Farm. Robert Martin and the girls followed soon after."

"If I am not mistaken," said Mrs. Goddard, "the doctor often observed that immigrating had saved the future generations of his family. Heaven knows what awaited his people if they should have stayed in their native country."

"Oh my!" said Harriet. "Mr. Martin and his family are truly blessed. I understand so much more now. Mr. Martin tried to explain, but I could not comprehend..."

She would have completed the thought; however, upon observing Miss Woodhouse's keen gaze, Harriet felt the blood rush to her face. It was apparent that her comment had struck a wrong note! Certainly, there could be no harm in mentioning Mr. Martin *now*. Her countenance, Harriet was convinced, did not betray any wrong feeling; however, Miss Woodhouse seemed able to see beyond her indifferent façade and would want a full accounting in the following days.

Once again, the dinner bell served to curtail further dialogue as the party entered the dining room. Harriet surmised that her exoneration, as it were, would be of a short duration.

Chapter Five

"I am so happy you were able to join me on my long walk, Harriet. My father never goes beyond the shrubbery, you know. Depending on the time of year, he may take the shorter path if the weather is cold, or it is determined to rain. If it is a pleasant day, such as today, he may take the longer, winding path, but that is all. I could not be satisfied with so little exercise though it serves Papa well enough."

Harriet could not help but admire the old gentleman. He was so kind and devoted to his daughter. Even when they disagreed, Mr. Woodhouse did not reprimand or threaten to put her aside. Though on the surface, these reflections were lighthearted and innocent, Harriet could not help but wonder what she had done to her *own* father to provoke such a cruel abandonment.

Mr. Woodhouse appeared to suffer from some sort of ailment, though what it was, Harriet was sure she did not know. How hard it must be, she thought, to always be ill or uneasy, but with no outward sign of injury or malaise. Perhaps her father suffered a similar affliction. Perhaps that was why he felt it necessary to leave her alone in the world. She posed the question to her friend as they walked down Donwell Road one afternoon.

"Dear Harriet!" Miss Woodhouse cried in response. "Would that I could find your father and demand that he explain himself to one and all! The matter regarding my father is one of a delicate nature. We tend not to speak of it amongst the family. We find it makes things harder to bear."

"You need not say anymore. I fear I forget my place. My impertinence shall be my undoing."

"No—you do well to ask. Had I not promised that we should be intimate friends? How can we be as sisters if you do not know the life we have led at Hartfield."

Harriet lowered her gaze as her friend began to speak. Sometimes, it was easier not to look at someone in the eye when sharing something deep and profound. She knew not why. Perhaps it was true what they said about the eyes being the window to the soul.

"Mr. Knightley spoke of war the other evening," began Miss Woodhouse. "My father alluded to similar events…"

"Indeed, I recall the conversation well."

"I will speak plainly, then. You see, Papa also served the Crown. He was a young man, no more than four and twenty, but he was present at the Fall of Minorca. I know not the full horror of what surpassed, Harriet. In truth, much of what I learned was never meant for my ears. I am not one to admit to wrong-doing, but in this instance, I will own that I trespassed on my father's privacy."

"Oh, Miss Woodhouse! I cannot believe it to be so!"

"There was nothing for it. Necessity drove me to break with the niceties of proper protocol. When I was but a child, I could not recognize the difficulties my father battled. His mannerisms were all the more endearing; my adoration was complete. Too soon, however, Isabella and I found ourselves motherless. We had no notion of how deeply our father relied on her strength, until he began to falter."

"You were fortunate to have had your family intact, Miss Woodhouse, even if it was for a brief moment of time. How did you ever manage afterward? You and your sister, Mrs. Knightley, were both so young."

"I am not altogether certain—we had Miss Taylor, of course, and our dear friends. Nonetheless, we soon began to recognize our father's decline—not only physically but mentally as well. It was not deemed sensible to speak of the matter with Isabella or myself, though we frequently heard the allusions to his prior character. '*Henry Woodhouse was so witty in his youth,*' they would say. *Or 'Would that you could have known him back then. He was full of life!'*"

"It must have been dreadful to hear them speak of your father in such a manner," said Harriet. "To speak in terms of *was* and *back then...*"

"After a while, we grew accustomed to the physicians with their daily visits and their unending poking and prodding. They would apply leeches to balance Papa's humors, bleed him to improve his miasmas—starve him to avoid a derangement of the intestines. They taxed his body and spirit until my poor, dear papa could stand no more! One afternoon, the Colonel came to pay a call. I helped bring in the tea things, and when the housekeeper disappeared down the hall, I hovered around the door and listened as my father wept."

"Dear friend, my heart breaks for you!" cried Harriet. "What did you learn? What is the cause of his affliction?"

"I learned the truth. I learned what should have been plainly disclosed but, instead, was disguised as the anticipated grief of a widower or the gentle decline into *Amentia senilis* as one physician prognosticated."

"I cannot fathom why the older generation believes it is necessary to protect the younger generation in such a manner. Oh, how I despise concealment of any nature! It is altogether too cruel, is it not? Indeed, I believe it is a *kindness* to be blunt and precise and to say what is what—Forgive me, Miss Woodhouse! I fear I share the same trait as Miss Bates, going on and on without taking a breath. I shan't interrupt you again. Pray, continue. What did you discover that afternoon?"

"Only that my poor dear father had been taken prisoner many years past. It was during the siege of Fort St. Philip. I heard my father recall the battle, the death of his compatriots, and the cruel treatment of the injured by their French jailers at Gibraltar. I cannot comprehend how they— how *he*—managed to live with so little food or medical attention. It was no wonder that Papa buried those memories! To endure such suffering, in addition to witnessing my mother's demise, well—in my mind, it explains his...his..."

"*Peculiarities.*" She would not have used such a word, but since it had been uttered by Miss Woodhouse herself on another occasion, Harriet believed herself to be safe.

"Precisely. Exactly, so. I became the lady of the house at the tender age of twelve. Upon my honor, Harriet, I *have* attempted to keep him content, to see to his every need, and to ensure that he is kept cheerful and occupied. When Isabella married and went away, I thought the burden would be too much. I was fortunate to have Miss Taylor with me—and Mr. Knightley, who has been so kind and considerate."

"Even though you bicker like two magpies."

"*Especially* because we bicker." Miss Woodhouse said with a becoming smile. "In truth, I owe him an apology for the other evening. I said some dreadful things and was too eager to share thoughts that were not my own. I regret my outburst. I failed to behave in accordance with my personage as the lady of the Hartfield. I failed to set a good example for you, my friend!"

"Not at all, Miss Woodhouse. I have only admiration for you and Mr. Woodhouse, and all your guests. I was certainly out of my element in such company."

"That will not do at all. You were exactly where you were

meant to be. Mark my words: I mean to see you well ensconced in our little society."

The two young ladies continued their walk in companionable silence. Passing a copse of trees that had obscured their view, they spied a young man walking in their direction.

It was Mr. Martin!

Harriet immediately took notice of his appearance and was glad to see him looking neat and sensible. She noted that Miss Woodhouse took the opportunity to survey the young farmer and could only wonder at her estimation.

Harriet smiled first at Mr. Martin and then at her friend, who suddenly bent down to fix a shoelace.

"Go on, speak with your friend. I will just be a moment," Miss Woodhouse said, waving Harriet down the lane.

She and Mr. Martin took a few steps together, stumbling over words, starting and stopping as they interrupted one another. They laughed at their silliness; such awkwardness amongst friends who lived under the same roof for six weeks seemed unwarranted—but could not be helped. It seemed they only managed to conquer their timidity when it was time for Harriet to come away. She bid Mr. Martin send kind regards to his family, though she nearly lost her footing bobbing a final salutation. Mr. Martin—ever attentive—booted the culpable rock from her path.

"Pray watch your step, Miss Smith," said he. "My sisters would have my hide if I allowed you to come to any harm."

And with that, he bowed and continued on his way.

Harriet turned to find Miss Woodhouse approaching. With her spirits all aflutter, it was difficult to contain the smile that spread across her face. She prevailed, however, and soon found herself somewhat composed.

"Imagine running into Mr. Martin!" Harriet exclaimed. "He told me he never came this way and was quite surprised to see us—he supposed we would be for Randalls. Oh! He apologized for not having the opportunity to read the book I had previously suggested. He has been busy on the farm, but that is neither here nor there. Tell me, Miss Woodhouse, what did you think? Did you find him plain?"

"He is very plain, indeed; I did not doubt he would be. He appeared clownish, dear—so totally without air. A gentleman—or someone a degree or two nearer gentility— would not carry himself in that. I believe I have never witnessed such a silly grin! Such an earthy laugh!"

"To be sure," said Harriet, mortified. "He is not so genteel as a *real* gentleman."

"I am gratified that you can recognize the difference. Now that you have been in company with men of quality, Mr. Martin cannot seem as agreeable as before. Hold him up in comparison with others of your acquaintance. Think of Mr. Weston. Think of Mr. Knightley."

Harriet allowed herself to imagine Mr. Knightley's countenance. He did have a fine air about him, a certain way of walking, an elegance…an easiness.

"Indeed. I can see the difference between one man and the other, but is it fair to make such a comparison? Mr. Knightley is so very fine a man, but he has had every opportunity afforded him; his life is one of leisure."

"A man of leisure? I do not believe Mr. Knightley would agree with your choice of words. He would not see himself as such, but I understand your meaning. Very well. Let us not compare Mr. Martin to the landed gentry. Let us compare him to another gentleman. What say you to Mr. Elton? Can you imagine Mr. Elton traipsing about the wood in such a foolish, awkward manner? Would Mr. Elton suspend the pleasure of a young lady?"

To be questioned in such a manner, so soon after coming upon Mr. Martin, was almost too much to bear. All the pleasure of the unexpected meeting was cast away, to be shadowed instead by censure and judgment. Harriet struggled to respond without appearing too ridiculous.

"I am not qualified to speak on Mr. Elton's character, Miss Woodhouse. I cannot claim an acquaintance on such an intimate level."

"Then let me assure you," Miss Woodhouse was quick to reply, "the vicar would seek the lending library post haste! He would demand Ford's procure a copy of the title that any young lady of worth might recommend. Gentility would demand that he display a true sense of liberality. Mr. Weston ought to be considered as well. Surely, you have noticed how solicitous Mr. Weston is towards his wife. That shows good breeding. *That* shows him to be a gentleman."

"Mr. Weston? But he must be nearly fifty years of age. Why, he could be my father! Would you encourage me to take such an old man for husband?"

"It is not his age that I recommend, but rather his mannerisms. Perhaps Mr. Martin's awkwardness may be disregarded now. He may be tolerated and made acceptable due to his young age and lack of worldly experience. But tell me this, Harriet. What shall he be like in a few years' time—when *he* is an old man of nearly fifty?"

"I cannot say, Miss Woodhouse. I doubt he will change so very much, not if he continues to work so hard and never has the opportunity to read or travel."

Not everyone is able to spend their days at their leisure!

"I am happy that my point is understood, but I would go further. I would wager Mr. Martin would not stay much the *same* but would allow himself to decline even further! His livelihood would demand it of him, to be sure, and in giving himself to the land, Mr. Martin will become inattentive to his appearance. He will be nothing but a vulgar farmer. And, if Mr. Elton's philosophy is to be believed; as an Israelite, Mr.

Martin would think of nothing but profit and loss!"

"I cannot credit Mrs. Martin would allow her son to become so slothful, so insensible to the rules of good society. Indeed, when she spoke of the requirements of his future bride, Mrs. Martin declared that propriety and concern for one's reputation were of top importance."

"Harriet, just think of his current frame of mind. Mr. Martin himself declared that he was kept 'too busy' with his business. He quite forgot to look for the book you had so highly recommended. I am certain that he will see his mother right, not to mention his future wife. The Martins will undoubtedly thrive, but that success will come at a price. He will remain unworthy of your attention."

She could not answer. Miss Woodhouse would have to interpret her silence however she pleased, for Harriet was lost in her thoughts and did not have the desire to speak. She recalled her emotions upon hearing Mr. Martin admit he had not read her favorite book—the one she had *so kindly* recommended. He ought to have said the one she *courageously* recommended, for he knew not what it had cost to make the suggestion in the first place! On the other hand, he did make an effort to bring her a gift of walnuts, and she could not forget that kindness.

"Mr. Elton and I have become more acquainted of late," Miss Woodhouse continued. "I was not all too sure what to make of him when he came into Highbury, but I must admit—and you may not repeat this, Harriet—there are times when I believe that Mr. Elton's manners are superior to Mr. Weston's or even Mr. Knightley's."

Harriet was not prepared to entertain such a comment. *Whatever could she mean by it?*

"Mr. Elton is neither too brusque or jovial, compared to Mr. Weston, nor is he as imposing or gruff as Mr. Knightley. No—Mr. Elton is rather obliging, I dare say. He has been altogether easy of late, very pleasing indeed. I would not be surprised if this improvement in essentials has not come about thanks to you!"

"*Me*?" Harriet was suddenly ready to have a share of the conversation. "That he would wish to please me would be extraordinary, indeed, Miss Woodhouse. How could I have drawn his interest?"

"Why would you question such a natural thing? You are, after all, a singularly attractive young lady with many notable qualities. I would be surprised at the man if he did not notice! It would be an excellent match if I dare say so myself—and I do!"

"But Mr. Elton is a gentleman. Surely, his situation in life would require a wife of equal standing."

"Just so. His situation *is* most suitable. He has some independent property and must earn well enough to support a wife and any future children."

Harriet felt her face burn at the insinuation, but could not give credence to her friend's expectations.

"Surely Mr. Elton's family or…or perhaps, even the church, would object to the connection. How could they approve a match with someone who knows nothing of her own family lineage?"

"Oh, Harriet! You are a charming, beautiful creature. You *must* be a daughter of a gentleman. I know it! And regarding any familial objections, I do believe Mr. Elton answers only to himself."

"I would have never dared to think so high! He is very handsome. Everyone at school admires Mr. Elton, to be sure."

"You must learn to think yourself worthy, Harriet. You are *my* friend, after all. Would I choose to acquaint myself with just anyone? Surely not! I urge you not to settle for a gift of walnuts and evenings spent talking of crops or livestock. Trust me. You were meant for more than that."

Chapter Six

"She is a beauty, Robert, and I think very well of her sweet temperament," said Mrs. Martin while folding a basket of laundered bed linens. "She has a strong and healthy disposition. She would be of some help on the farm; a man could not ask for more."

"We are not discussing a new workhorse, Mama. I am certain you have observed Miss Smith's fine qualities. Pray do not confess to finding her wanting."

"Fair is fair, my son. Miss Smith is not without some refinement. She would make someone a fine wife. And now, under Miss Woodhouse's wing, Miss Smith will be schooled in all the essentials. I would have your sisters take note of her accomplishments. Perhaps they too could aspire to such a friendship. Having said as much, you know my objections. I do not question the girl's manners or intelligence. It is solely a question of her upbringing. She is not one of us."

"I believe Miss Woodhouse would be mortified if she spent any length of time with Elizabeth or Judy. She can barely condescend to look me in the eye. Would you have us behave towards others as the gentry treats the yeomanry? Do you care so much about what the gossips may say about the match?"

"Careful now. I would have you mind your manners. I care not about the tittle-tattle that spreads throughout our little congregation. Heaven knows that every family of our acquaintance has dealt with this dilemma or, in some cases, even more compelling situations. I try to follow what the prophet Samuel said: *'For a person sees the eyes and God sees the heart.'* I cannot judge or envy my neighbors, for I know not their troubles. I am only concerned with me and mine."

"But you *know* Miss Smith. She is kindness itself. Already Elizabeth and Judy welcome her as a sister, and having not known her own mother, Miss Smith would cherish your guidance and care."

"I cannot deny what you say; nonetheless, I would have you marry a Jewess. I would have you take a wife who knows our traditions, someone who—God willing! —will raise your children in the faith of our fathers." Mrs. Martin put aside her basket and took hold of her son's hands. "Tell me this: have you declared yourself to Miss Smith, even before speaking with the rabbi?"

Robert Martin shook his head in silence. He had not met with the man, fearing what the rabbi would decree. It was not much different from what his mother said, but his judgment would carry more weight. The rabbi's word was the law for their small congregation—so far away from London, the rabbinical courts, and those advocating for reform.

"I have not yet addressed the matter with Rabbi Kolman," he replied. "I will, however, speak with Mr. Knightley on the subject. I believe he would approve the match—"

"I have no doubt that he would, but tell me, what does the gentleman know about our ways?"

"Mr. Knightley knows the scriptures, and due to the liberality of his upbringing, he has never shown any prejudice or disdain for our faith. He is a man of integrity and good morals. I do not doubt that he may have reservations about this union, but once I explain —once I have had the opportunity to express my hopes for the future—I believe Mr. Knightley will support my choice.

While he is not the rabbi and has not the authority to speak on the matter, Mr. Knightley will be hard-pressed to convince me to do otherwise."

"Again, I ask you, son: have you spoken with Miss Smith? Are you certain that she would accept an offer of marriage from a farmer, let alone a Jew?"

"My livelihood may be a point of contention, especially now that Miss Smith is under Miss Woodhouse's patronage; that much I will allow. But I cannot believe she would reject me based on spiritual convictions. She has lived with us, she has witnessed our faith in how we break bread, in our observation of the Sabbath, and even in the treatment of our animals. I am certain that she would have me, she may even consider conversion—"

"Oh! You men are all alike! Why is it that a man always imagines a woman is ready to accept an offer of marriage from anyone who happens to ask? I fear this is my own doing. I have praised you too much; I have made you believe you are a great *tzaddik*!"

"That is utter nonsense, Mama. I am neither sage nor righteous master! I have never besought that title. I have one grand illusion: that Miss Smith would find me a respectable young man—a man worthy to be her husband and father to her children."

"But is she your equal, Son? We know nothing of her birth or her connections. She is the natural daughter of nobody knows whom! She is a parlor boarder with no more education than your sisters. The match would be completely to her advantage, for she would be well settled in a comfortable home and have a suitable income. I cannot imagine that Miss Smith would receive many other offers, even with the help of the likes of Miss Woodhouse. Who, in their society, would marry such a girl without a dowry, connections, or family background?"

"You paint a dark picture of degradation and illegitimacy, Mama. Though her father is unknown, there could be no doubt that he must be a gentleman of some means. Think upon it. She has been well provided for all these many years. Nothing has been begrudged in the manner of her improvement or comfort. Miss Smith must not be held accountable for the offense of her parentage. She may be called Nobody in society, but she is not that to me."

"Whoever might be her parents, Robert, they appear to have washed their hands of the girl! What will you say to your children? How will you explain that Grandpapa and Grandmama *Smith* will not join us on holy days or family celebrations? Son, living amongst Gentiles—separated as we are from our vibrant community in London—is not always an easy task. When your father, may his memory be for a blessing, decided to farm this land, he had to make certain alterations to his religious practice. We found ourselves bending the rules, so to speak, out of necessity…"

"Precisely!" Robert was quick to agree. "Our practices have evolved, centuries of living in the diaspora have made it so. You allow the girls to attend Mrs. Goddard's school— tell me how *that* is not an abomination?"

"Your sisters require an education, I will not debate that point. They are village girls and ought to make friends with their neighbors—Christian and Jew alike."

"Then you agree we must intermingle with the Christian majority?"

"Are you trying to convince yourself *or me*? Son, you have yet to answer my question. Have you declared yourself to Miss Smith?"

"It is not that simple. I fear I have given rise to false hopes, but I have not made an offer of marriage. I cannot reconcile my beliefs with my heart."

"Oh, my dear boy! At the very least, I am thankful that

you consider our traditions. A prudent man would be anxious about entering such an unequal match, especially when the mystery of her parentage is yet unresolved. Miss Smith would be safe with you, Robert, respected and happy forever. But, what of you? What of your children?"

"There is no use in discussing it further. My feelings were—*are*—sincere and just. It is a personal matter, Mama, between myself and our God."

The men had set aside their plans and reports, having completed their customary meeting. Mr. Knightley's steward, William Larkins, begged to leave, for he had other matters to attend that morning. Robert Martin appreciated the opportunity to speak with Mr. Knightley alone, for he had some concerns that weighed heavily on his conscience.

Robert Martin had had the good fortune of being blessed with strong men of integrity and scruples to guide him the whole of his life. Following his father's footsteps, he had an innate respect for the land. He saw himself as an instrument of the Lord. *He* was not the one that brought forth the fruit of his toils, for he could not fully comprehend nor control the ways of nature—Robert Martin saw himself as working in partnership with the Master of the Universe.

Being a tenant farmer, and not a landed gentleman, Robert held much esteem for his employer and terrestrial master. Working for the owner of Abbey-Mill Farm was an honor and a privilege, for Mr. Knightley was a man of his word. He was fair and honest and never flaunted his importance over those who worked his lands.

Still, it was not an easy task to see oneself as an equal— to speak as if one was not in a position of subservience. In this frame of mind, Robert addressed Mr. Knightley that afternoon.

"I happened upon Miss Smith and Miss Woodhouse the other day, sir," Robert began. "They were on Donwell Road, just where the path divides to the east. Such was my surprise —I hadn't expected to find them there, you see—that I neglected to warn the ladies of something I had recently come to discover. You will pardon me, sir; perhaps it is not my place—"

"Not at all, Robert," replied Mr. Knightley. "Speak your mind."

"There has been word of gypsies in the wood, sir. I have not encountered them myself—if I had, I should have said something sooner. It is just—Miss Woodhouse ought not walk so easily without a groom in attendance. Two ladies, alone, may be seen as easy prey."

"I quite agree. I had no notion of these persons making camp on Donwell land. Larkins will see to it. But what of you? Found yourself tongue-tied in front of the ladies, eh?" Mr. Knightley laughed. "No shame in that, my friend! It happens to the best of us."

"I do not understand it, sir!" Robert slapped his hat against his leg; such was his humiliation. "Miss Smith spent six weeks with my family. We were all at ease with one another. I suddenly come upon the young lady, and every sensible thought is lost! What she must think of me, I cannot know."

"Come, come now! It cannot be as bad as all that."

"'Twas worse, sir, and I am ashamed. Miss Smith had mentioned a particular book, a favorite of hers. I promised to read it so that we could discuss it together. When she asked about my progress, it was if all time stood still. I could not string two words together! I uttered the first thing that came to mind and immediately saw how it pained her."

"Well—what did you say, man?"

"I said…I said that I was too busy. I said that a farmer's life is not his own. I said the animals, the crops—the land must come first."

Mr. Knightley could not help but laugh at the young man's blunder. "Forgive me," said he. "I do not mock you, nor do I wish to appear callous or cruel. I have stood in the same predicament on many occasions, Robert. You are not the first man, nor will you be the last to find himself in that uncomfortable state."

"There is more, sir. I feel it is far worse. While Miss Smith visited us this summer, my behavior was not as it ought to have been; I must own."

"I cannot like the sound of that, sir!"

Robert was quick to explain himself, not wanting to tarnish the man's good opinion. "I was foolhardy and insensible, Mr. Knightley, allowing myself to imagine a future with the young lady; but it was my heart alone that was in danger, sir. I would not intentionally harm Miss Smith or her reputation."

"But, if your actions raised her expectations, that would be a cruelty."

"Indeed. I have come to recognize my blundering ways. And now it seems she has become Miss Woodhouse's particular friend—I know not what to make of it."

"Yes—I am aware of their developing friendship, and truth be told, I am not altogether surprised by the association. Just now, Miss Woodhouse is in need of a companion, and I do not doubt that Miss Smith will fulfill her responsibilities to admire, concur, and condole with her…*patroness*."

"Therein lies my concern," said he. "While Miss Smith was at Abbey-Mill, we enjoyed easy conversations. We laughed together and took pleasure in the simplest of things. My fear, sir, is that Miss Woodhouse may attempt to influence Miss Smith in a different direction."

"What *direction* is that? Certainly, you cannot believe Miss Woodhouse would negatively influence a young lady."

"No, sir. But what should happen if they undertake a course of study?"

"My good fellow! Since her adolescence, Miss Woodhouse has collected titles that would be the envy of any gentleman's library and has drawn up lists to satisfy the matriculation requirements at Cambridge or Oxford. That being said, she lacks the patience; she will not commit the time nor the thought to the practice! Mrs. Weston, Miss Taylor as was, attempted to entice her student with the classics to no avail! Where Miss Taylor failed, Miss Smith surely would not succeed. Undoubtedly, the ladies will chat about bonnets, tea sandwiches, and Highbury gossip. Nothing too deep, to be sure."

"I would never insinuate that Miss Woodhouse is ignorant, sir—"

"No, nor I. Miss Woodhouse is too clever for her own good, I have always said. In many ways, she was very much like her mother. Her elder sister was never as quick or self-assured as her sibling. It is no wonder that Emma has Mr. Woodhouse wrapped around her little finger!"

"Miss Smith will be her next conquest then," said Robert Martin. "She will feel inferior, sir. I know it for a fact. She will revere Miss Woodhouse for condescending to offer friendship to a simple parlor boarder."

"How do you mean?"

"Miss Smith does not hold a high opinion of herself. She will feel unrefined and uncomfortable in your society. It will be all gratitude and devotion for the lady of Hartfield. I cannot favor such an acquaintance. What will happen to

Miss Smith once Miss Woodhouse tires of the charade?"

"Have a care, Robert," Mr. Knightley admonished. "I am a partial, old friend of Miss Woodhouse. Where I can happily enumerate her imperfections, I cannot condone anyone else to point out her faults. She is a beautiful young woman with a good heart and a sound mind. She is not vain and will not lead a friend astray. Not by design, at any rate. Miss Smith will simply have to prove her mettle and show she has a mind of her own—unless *you* wish to be the only one who receives Miss Smith's gratitude and devotion."

Robert Martin tugged at his shirt sleeves, removing an imaginary piece of lint. Unable to look at Mr. Knightley, he murmured his soft reply.

"I do…that is, I would be honored…that is—I *would* offer for Miss Smith, but there are certain obstacles that I cannot deny. My mother has made her objections known as well. What is your opinion, sir? I value your friendship and advice in all things."

"Well, now—"

"Would it be imprudent to settle so early? I have not seen much of the world, but I know what I want in life."

Robert Martin did not hesitate or stumble now as he found just the right words to lay his plans for his future and the farm. He spoke of his apprehensions and his mother's objections and explained how deeply they had affected him.

"You do well, Robert, in seeking counsel from your elders. You must know that I think you are an excellent young man, a fine son and brother. I do not doubt that you would be an excellent husband to Miss Smith. The young lady is to be praised, for she is lovely as she is dutiful. That being said, I pray you take notice of your own concerns and your mother's words. I cannot know what it would mean to her and—dare I say—you as well, if you were to marry a young woman not of your flock. Does not the Bible say this very thing: 'Do not give your daughters to their sons or take their daughters for your sons'?"

"Indeed, it does, sir. However, Proverbs says: 'He who finds a wife finds a good thing and obtains favor from the Lord.' If my people found their way to this country, where we live and pray in peace, perhaps it would not offend the Lord if I take to wife one who I know to be sweet and good."

Robert fixed his gaze upon the great man who stood before him. The Knightleys had always been fair and honest with his family. Having lost his own father at a young age, Mr. George Knightley represented all that Robert respected and admired. He was more than a landowner and his superior—Mr. Knightley was the sort of man Robert wished to be. It was, therefore, difficult to observe his mentor struggling to reconcile the matter. Robert had hoped to be more convincing.

"In bringing your plans to my attention, you have proven that you are prepared to take on responsibilities of husband and father," Mr. Knightley began. "However, I cannot advise you on the more consequential issue, which is on the point of your faith. Evidently, you have been contemplating the matter, for you have answers at the ready!" He laughed and kneaded his forehead as if the motion would clear his thoughts. "Let us not have a battle of proverbs. Instead, I propose we cut to the chase. It matters not what I believe or how anyone else feels about your decision. You alone must make the determination and be at peace with the consequences."

"That is just it, sir," replied Robert. "If it were only a question of my love for Miss Smith, I would be on bended knee, offering my heart and my hand. But our union would have broader implications. My children would no longer be considered Jews—my line would come to an end. This marriage would affect my sisters, for the *taint*, as it were, would deter their suitors. There also is the matter of Miss Smith's faith. Will she be shunned by her friends? I cannot take these things lightly, sir."

"As long as I have known you, Robert, you have proven yourself to be a man of integrity. With your father's passing, you assumed the role of provider and protector, and I admire your great sense of responsibility toward your mother and sisters. I see now that this profound sense of duty extends to your people. I cannot know how you will resolve this dilemma, but whatever you choose, I will champion your cause."

Chapter Seven

Having had, for some time now, received proper guidance from Miss Woodhouse, Harriet was nothing if not grateful and feeling a great deal more sensible in the matter of all things—and in particular, in the matter of agreeable men.

She had pondered her circumstances often enough in years gone by; the thought of her family, her origins, and her prospects had never been far from her mind. What a fortunate creature she was in knowing Miss Woodhouse. The lady was unlike anyone Harriet had ever known; it followed that Miss Woodhouse's acquaintances were of significant consequence and of equal import.

It gave Harriet pause to think more about Mr. Elton. That he was a handsome man, there could be no doubt. His manners were agreeable, for he was always eager to please and spoke with such solicitude. And Miss Woodhouse—so amiable! Harriet had no compunction to believe she was the envy of all the girls at school, for no one else could call Miss Woodhouse *friend*. Certainly, no one had such a personage to care for her, to advise her, or to ensure she was fit for good society.

As she made her way to Hartfield, Harriet felt she carried herself with just a bit more aplomb. She was still quite the product of Mrs. Goddard's instruction, but she no longer giggled like a schoolgirl or thought so meanly of herself.

She heard voices as the Hartfield butler led her to the drawing-room, and much to her surprise, Harriet felt her heart begin to race upon recognizing Mr. Elton's strong voice.

"Miss Smith was a beautiful creature when she came to you."

Harriet overheard a snippet of his comment before the butler announced her entry. Her face was on fire as she made her curtsey.

"Harriet!" exclaimed Miss Woodhouse. "You have come at last! Mr. Elton has joined us, as you see. We shall make a merry party indeed."

"To be sure," added the gentleman. "I am fortunate to be in such exalted company—such beauty, such grace!"

"Very prettily said, sir. Do you not agree, Harriet? You might have come on time if you knew you would be admired and showered with such praise."

"Oh, Miss Woodhouse. I *would* have come sooner, but…" Unsure how to respond to the compliment *or* her friend's raised brow, Harriet sought to invoke something of relevance that would excuse her tardiness.

"'Charm is deceptive and beauty is fleeting; but a devoted woman is to be praised.'"

"Proverbs 31:30, I believe," said Mr. Elton. "The wording may differ here and there, but I shan't correct you, Miss Smith. Well done, indeed."

"Why, Harriet. Are you quoting the Good Book? You shall put me to shame!"

It seemed she did not handle the situation as cleverly as she had hoped. Ill at ease, Harriet struggled to appease the vicar while reassuring her friend.

"Never that, Miss Woodhouse!" said she. "I simply intended to use a phrase I overheard at the Mar—while visiting a schoolmate last summer. I thought it would address the issue of punctuality in conjunction with duty. Pray understand, I was helping Mrs. Goddard and—"

"All is forgiven, Harriet. I see you meant no harm, and you have sufficiently acquitted yourself. Your devotion to Mrs. Goddard is certainly praiseworthy. And, perhaps, quoting that precise verse from the Bible was providential, for beauty *is* fleeting. Here, Mr. Elton and I were discussing the merit of portrait painting. Harriet, what say you? Will you allow me to attempt to paint your likeness?"

"Let me entreat you, Miss Smith," cried Mr. Elton. "Pray allow Miss Woodhouse to exercise her charming talents. I have noted her drawings in this very room. Certainly, you are not ignorant of her work?"

"Ignorant?" Harriet repeated. "No...no, I do not believe I would say that I was ignorant of Miss Woodhouse's talents, sir, but a portrait...of *me*?"

"I have not had the pleasure of taking a likeness in several years, although several of my friends have encouraged me to do so," said Miss Woodhouse. "Ever since my last attempt, I have kept to drawing landscapes and flowers, such was my exasperation at the fastidious commentary of some family members. I had thought I had captured my brother, Mr. John Knightley, very well—it was certainly well enough for my limited talent. But Isabella insisted that it was *little like* him. I had made him too handsome! Such a critique is not to be borne!"

"No, Miss Woodhouse. I cannot allow it," cried Mr. Elton. "I have seen your work, and though I am not an expert, I do believe you capture your subjects with great success. A portrait of your friend would be an exquisite possession for any collection."

Miss Woodhouse smiled at the compliment but appeared more concerned with securing Harriet's approval. She promised to do her very best if Harriet would only promise to sit patiently and endure whatever position or form of torture she may devise.

"I shall not attempt to deceive you," she said. "*I know* my talent and do not fear for my reputation. I shall not worry overmuch as long as you are pleased with the results."

"If you insist, Miss Woodhouse, and I promise to be the very best of subjects. I will praise your work and choose my words wisely. Not for you shall I say *little like* nor *too this* or *that*. After all, there are no husbands or wives here to cause us to be anxious."

Mr. Elton applauded Harriet's speech and added a few words of his own. "Exactly so. No husbands and wives at present," he said.

Harriet spied Miss Woodhouse's smile and, once again, felt herself blush.

The sitting only wanted for Miss Woodhouse to determine which instruments would be put to use. Pencils and watercolors were her preference, for she feared other mediums would require more time and, above all, more talent. She enlisted a footman to help organize the room and sent Harriet upstairs to her chamber, in order that she may change her gown.

"I have just the right costume," said Miss Woodhouse. "I had it made for a Twelfth Night masque—though I never wore it. Papa feared I'd catch my death in such a light, ethereal thing. It will suit you very well, I should think!"

When everything was just so, Harriet took her pose under the direction of Miss Woodhouse. Though she was anxious, and her nose suddenly began to itch, Harriet did not move or change her countenance. Mr. Elton, however, was another matter.

He began to pace immediately after Miss Woodhouse completed her first brush stroke. Harriet saw, at once, that his anxious behavior was not the catalyst that one required when in a creative state of mind. She assumed a bit more tranquility would have been preferred, perhaps listening to a soothing piece of music being played on the pianoforte or hearing birdsong fill the air. Harriet was not, therefore, surprised when Miss Woodhouse gave the vicar an occupation with which to pass the time.

On a side table nearest the window, there lay a book of Shakespeare's sonnets that Miss Woodhouse had abandoned the night before. At her request, Mr. Elton began to read aloud, resolving many grievances with one stroke, as it were. The vicar remained seated and composed, Harriet no longer fussed, and Miss Woodhouse concentrated without fear of Mr. Elton's foot coming into contact with her delicate vials of paint.

A short while later, Miss Woodhouse threw her brush down and professed her arm grew tired. There had not been any consideration for Harriet's arm, which held up an urn much like a Grecian princess, but that hadn't concerned anyone of the party.

Miss Woodhouse declared that she would continue the following day, for the lighting had changed, and she was concerned that she would not do justice to the color of Harriet's eyes. She requested Mr. Elton return for the sitting, and he agreed with great alacrity.

"Nothing shall keep me away, so enthralled am I in this creative process of capturing Miss Smith's likeness for all eternity!"

The following day's events followed much the same path. The three exchanged civilities and courtesies as Mr. Elton chose his seat and found the marker where he left off in the book. Harriet changed her gown and patiently endured Miss Woodhouse's manipulations as she was repositioned on the divan once more.

The day's work proved more successful than before, and Miss Woodhouse declared that she had done as the sun began to set. Before Harriet could move—her extremities had begun to prickle, and she required a moment or two—Mr. Elton had already made his way to the easel. And so, his raptures began.

"It is heavenly, Miss Woodhouse! It is a work of art like no other I have seen!"

Miss Woodhouse smiled and bowed her head to acknowledge the pretty compliments. If she agreed with Mr. Elton's estimation, she would not say. Harriet was unsure how to approach the matter, for it was her own likeness on the canvas.

How does one compliment the artist without seeming vain?

"I do not know how you manage it, Miss Woodhouse," said Harriet. "I have no such accomplishment. Such a steady hand! Such an eye for detail!"

Miss Woodhouse nodded her gratitude and murmured her thanks. With her next breath, she invited the vicar to dine, adding that Mr. Knightley and the Westons were expected as well.

"I shall need your support, Mr. Elton," said she with a coy laugh, "for I cannot be assured that the others of the party will find favor in my work with such enthusiasm."

Mr. Elton could do no less than accept the invitation. He pledged to tell one and all that it was at his suggestion that the portrait was undertaken, and he was very pleased with the result. Very pleased indeed!

After the company completed their meal later that evening, and the gentlemen reunited with the ladies once more, Miss Woodhouse called for a footman to carry her easel into the room. It was deposited alongside Mr. Woodhouse, and Harriet watched with not a little trepidation as the others circled to inspect the work.

Her nerves were on edge, for she feared someone might cause Miss Woodhouse distress. What if they found the style wanting? What if they found the subject lacking in beauty? Such mortification could not be endured!

Mrs. Weston was the first to speak, and though she was kind, her observation inadvertently criticized Harriet's features.

"Emma, you have captured Miss Smith's expression very well, indeed, but she has not those eyebrows nor such long eyelashes," said she. "It is a shame, for they would suit her countenance very well."

Mr. Elton, however, would not hear such censure. "We must allow for the effect of shade, Mrs. Weston," said he.

Mr. Knightley came around with his teacup and saucer, observing the image with great care. Upon taking his measure of the work, a pronouncement followed that failed to surprise most of the party but certainly disturbed one.

"You have made her too tall, Emma," said he.

"Oh no, sir," said Mr. Elton. "The *artiste* preserved all the correct proportions. One must recall that Miss Smith was seated."

Mr. Woodhouse was most appreciative and provided his approval in his usual manner; however, the gentleman focused on Harriet's bare shoulders and feared for her comfort as was his wont.

"She ought to have worn a little shawl, Emma, dear. I look upon her countenance and can only believe she was cold."

Miss Woodhouse quickly reassured her father that Miss Smith had been warm enough as the work was done indoors, and that the young lady was seated by a low fire all the while.

"It was supposed to have been a summer scene, Papa. You see, there are the trees and flowers that border the drive."

"I, for one," said Mr. Elton, "am quite astonished. I count myself fortunate for having been able to witness this work of art come to life—to see Miss Smith's countenance, her every expression memorialized for all time to come—it truly has been one of my life's greatest pleasures."

"It only wants for a frame," said Mrs. Weston. "It shall look lovely in your sitting room, Emma."

"Oh yes!" said Miss Woodhouse. "Perhaps I shall send it to London and commission Isabella to see it done. She knows all the best places—"

"No, not Isabella," cried Mr. Woodhouse. "It is far too cold—it is the dead of winter, Emma! She might catch her death or slip on an icy cobblestone..."

"There is no need to ask Mrs. Knightley to venture outside her comfortable home," said Mr. Elton. "I should be most pleased to take on the task. Do you trust me, Miss Woodhouse, with your work?"

Miss Woodhouse could think of nothing better, or so she said. She embraced Harriet and expressed that she had been an exemplary muse. She gave Mr. Elton a pretty little curtsey to show her gratitude.

"I shall write down some suggestions as to color and nature of the wood for the frame, Mr. Elton," said Miss Woodhouse. "I am certain that you will manage very well."

"Thank you, sir, for undertaking this task," said Harriet. "I am sure I have never had such attention paid to me before."

"It is the very least I can do." Mr. Elton smiled and performed a courtly bow. "The very least I can do in the face of such beauty."

Chapter Eight

The daily visits to Hartfield, along with the various activities and the stimulating conversations proposed by Miss Woodhouse, had given Harriet a taste of a very different lifestyle. It was all go in Highbury these days!

The girls at school, particularly Emily Bickerton, were astonished when Harriet let it slip that she was the subject of Miss Woodhouse's painting and that Mr. Elton had gone to London to see it framed. Even Miss Nash—who was not much older than some of the students—had appeared a bit jealous of the attentions and honors being bestowed on one of Mrs. Goddard's lodgers. Harriet had always been sensible to the strain between herself and the head teacher. She did not care to examine it too closely, but it hovered over the relationship like a dark cloud threatening to let loose at any given time.

Emily and Miss Nash had been her daily companions for as long as Harriet could remember. Indeed, Emily Bickerton was a boarder, just as she, though her circumstances in life could not compare. Emily *knew* her mother and father. Her roots were firmly established in Surrey and the surrounding towns and villages. It was only due to her mother's passing that Emily came to live with Mrs. Goddard. Mr. Bickerton, though a laborer, would come to visit the school when he received his wages and always took his daughter into Highbury for tea or a trip to Ford's.

Miss Nash—a young woman of some independence and

knowledge—had always championed the girls and encouraged them to excel in all things—until the day she realized Harriet would remain at school and would be given a class of her own to lead. Though she was in position of authority, Miss Nash *could* be kind and generous. Harriet had come to believe that the fault lay in the head teacher's insecurities—so familiar to her own—and learned to turn the other cheek. Still, Harriet was nonplussed at the thought of her friends being envious. It would never have occurred to her that they would not be happy for her little jaunts and experiences with Miss Woodhouse.

As it was, she was expected at Hartfield for breakfast—it was a standing invitation, and Harriet was determined not to break the commitment. Gathering her things, she bid everyone a good morning and continued her day as scheduled.

She was warmly received at her friend's house; Mr. and Miss Woodhouse awaiting Harriet at their breakfast table. The room was happily situated with a wall full of mullioned windows facing full east. Harriet always admired the room and had been equally impressed when told that Miss Woodhouse had seen to its décor. It was a cheerful location; full of sunlight and flowers, it inspired one at the start of a new day.

While Mr. Woodhouse read his paper, and occasionally let out a gasp or a *tsk-tsk*, Harriet paid close attention as Miss Woodhouse listed her plans for the upcoming week. They were to take baskets around for the poor and to check on Mrs. Turnbull, who had turned her ankle and was abed.

Mrs. Turnbull was a favorite seamstress in Highbury. Miss Woodhouse thought it would be a kindness to drop in with a jar of homemade marmalade and fresh scones. And if Miss Woodhouse were to leave behind a pelisse that required mending while paying that call, it certainly would be seen as a generous gesture—for Mrs. Turnbull would appreciate the custom and the means to help pass the day.

The next call would be paid to Mrs. and Miss Bates. However, Miss Woodhouse insisted it would have to be paid before Tuesday afternoon, for the women would not have received their customary letter from their niece. Listening to Miss Bates read the letter, Miss Woodhouse explained, was to be avoided at all costs!

Harriet nodded and agreed with all that had been proposed, and in this manner, the morning hours leisurely slipped away. When Mr. Woodhouse began to yawn and allowed his daily paper to slip from his hands, Miss Woodhouse called forth a footman to assist. Harriet recognized it was time for her to take her leave.

Mr. Woodhouse was escorted to his favorite chair for a quiet coze, while the morning mail was set out for the lady of the house to review. Miss Woodhouse would busy herself with missives from her sister and invitations to dine. No doubt, she would busy herself overseeing the evening's menu with the housekeeper. Other than that, Harriet was not altogether certain what else Miss Woodhouse would do when she was on her own. She decided these ponderings were none of her concern as she thanked her hostess and said her goodbyes. Harriet walked back to the school satisfied and ready for a quick catnap herself.

The comfort of withdrawing to her bedchamber—at least until the girls were called to tea—was summarily denied, for the moment Harriet crossed the Mrs. Goddard's threshold, the lady fell upon her, just bursting with news to share.

Mr. Martin had come to call while Harriet was out, and finding that she was not home—he was adamant that he was not expected; therefore, he would not accept Mrs. Goddard's apology—Mr. Martin left a small packet that had been conveyed by his sisters.

Harriet thanked Mrs. Goddard and went directly to her room, noting the kind woman's disappointment in not sharing the contents but wishing to inspect the items alone. Closing the door, she whispered a prayer of gratitude for Emily Bickerton was otherwise engaged; Harriet had the room to herself as she carefully unfolded the coarse paper.

She was not surprised to see the musical scores she had lent Elizabeth to copy, accompanied by a letter from her friend. This she tossed aside and trembled at the sight of another packet. It was a letter from Mr. Martin. Upon reading the missive, and then reading it again and again, Harriet became increasingly distraught.

Ought I be pleased or—ought I take offense?

It suddenly occurred to her that only Miss Woodhouse would know how best to act, and though she had just returned home, Harriet collected her bonnet and her wrap and made her way to Hartfield with nary a word to Mrs. Goddard, who now sat with her cake and tea by the fire.

At Hartfield, Harriet was shown directly into the morning room where Miss Woodhouse still reposed. Unable to keep from smiling, Harriet waved the letter about.

"Mr. Martin has declared himself!" She exclaimed. "Well, he has shared his feelings—no, he..."

"Dear Harriet, do stop rambling. You seem not to know whether you ought to laugh or cry! What is this all about?"

"Pray, Miss Woodhouse, read the letter and tell me what you think, for I cannot trust my own judgment."

"Very well, but you must sit and settle down. You will make yourself ill!"

The letter was handed over, and Harriet sat on the proffered chair, accepting a fresh cup of tea though she hadn't the fortitude to drink it.

Dear Miss Smith,

Our meeting, by chance the other day, has been the impetus of much contemplation. Pray forgive my impertinence in communicating with you in this manner, but, selfish creature that I am, I beg to be permitted to ease my conscience. You are all that is good—generous, cheerful, and loving. Nonetheless, I have imposed on you, Miss Smith. I have abused your friendship. I thought only of my heart and was careless with yours.

Proverbs speak of a woman of valor, a woman who is worth more than rubies. Though you are yet full young, you are that woman in my eyes. Your behavior has been unreproachable; the blame, if the word may be applied in this circumstance, is mine alone. I believe I have given rise to precious hopes and have allowed feelings to develop where they ought not have taken root. In seeking happiness, both mine and yours, I was insensible to the impediments we must face—impediments that I must not neglect.

You have lived with us and know something of our ways. Our traditions and rituals are ancient and revered. Though we are a displaced people, living in a land not of our own, we have learned to bend, very much like a sapling in the wind. In order to survive—and for future branches to thrive—we may adapt, but we must not break. In this, I admit, I am culpable of being blind to my own true feelings, for I must agree with this axiom. As to your own familial relations, condemning a child for sins not of her own doing seems a ruthless act. Deuteronomy provides much thought on the matter and, in doing so, contradicts itself! If the Author of the text was unable to make a determination on such a heady subject, a simple farmer ought not be judge, nor jury.

Like my father, I know the worth of rich soil and deep roots. I am profoundly connected to my past, though my heart had fixed itself to the future—one shared with you. I plead for your forgiveness, Miss Smith. I had no right to dream this dream. I was foolhardy; I fear my naïveté in matters such as these has harmed us both. I pray that God bless you and grant you, in future, a worthy husband and a happy home.

I remain your servant.
Robert Joseph Martin

Having read the letter several times, Harriet had committed it to memory. She mouthed the words as her friend's eyes swept across the page. She knew exactly when Miss Woodhouse read the final word but was unable to determine her assessment of the whole of the document. After what seemed to be an unbearable length of time, though only seconds passed, Harriet insisted on hearing the decree.

"Tell me, Miss Woodhouse, tell me at once, if you please! What are your thoughts?"

"I must admit, I can hardly believe the author of this letter is the same person we met the other day on the road. He could not speak nor formulate a sensible sentence if memory serves, but Harriet—whatever does he mean by sending this missive? Had you come to an understanding with Mr. Martin?"

"No!" cried she, "I had no notion that *he* liked *me* so very much. Nothing was said in so many words. But, his actions, Miss Woodhouse—"

"What of his actions, dear girl? Have you been

compromised in any way? I shall have to speak with Mr. Knightley directly!"

"No—please do not. I am utterly ashamed! Mr. Martin was always a gentleman—well, he was to my way of thinking. He was so attentive, Miss Woodhouse, not unlike a hero in a novel. That is…his smile, Miss Woodhouse, his mannerisms…"

"You imagined yourself to be in love? Harriet, I thought we decided—that is to say, I thought you were of another mind."

Harriet held her tongue for a moment, unsure how to express herself.

"Oh, Miss Woodhouse! I am such a silly girl. What do I know of flirtations or coquetries? I had no idea that Mr. Martin's affections were so engaged," said she. "Now he writes to beg *my* forgiveness but then continues to outline the reasons why we would not suit! Am I to blame for allowing such liberties, though they were innocent enough, *or*—ought I be insulted? Pray, do advise me!"

"I shan't, Harriet. You are capable of expressing yourself intelligently. If you wish to offer your forgiveness, then, by all means, do. If you wish to express your grievance, I would only remind you to command your temper."

"Then, you do believe I have been insulted by this slight."

"Harriet, do not put words in my mouth. I said no such thing. *You* said 'insulted,' not I. In any event, I find that I am just as confused on the matter as you are. Am I mistaken? Had you not decided to pursue another path?"

"But that was only after I made your acquaintance," she cried. "While I was at Abbey-Mill Farm, the alliance felt perfectly acceptable—"

"Whatever his past actions, Mr. Martin has now made himself quite clear. He is unable to marry, however eloquently he describes his affection for you—perhaps one of his sisters came to his aid, though it is not written in a feminine style. It is obvious that you would not suit. Would you always be uneasy with his family? Would you always be reminded that you are lesser than they?"

"No! I cannot believe that of the Martins! I do not know how I must act. Must I believe that our affections would be offensive to one and all?"

"We each of us need to find the strength to make up our own minds when presented with these questions. It is not my place, nor my desire, to have such influence over your thoughts. I encourage you to assess the entirety of the situation. Mr. Martin is a tenant farmer. He is descended from foreigners and is an Israelite, no less! Do you consider that you and Mr. Martin are in the same social sphere? Do you share the same history, the same traditions, or even the same aspirations?"

"I have not given it much thought. Oh! I had no idea that love and marriage were such complicated matters. If only I had a mother or father. Never have I wished for their guidance more than this moment! And if you will not advise me, I will have to do for myself. I shall not hesitate…I have decided…I am convinced that it is for the best for all parties that I put aside my silly infatuation of Mr. Martin."

"If you are certain," said Miss Woodhouse. "I only want the best for you, Harriet, but you must judge for yourself. The fact that you are now questioning your feelings tells me that perhaps there *is* someone else. You are blushing, my dear friend. That proves my suspicions."

"It is solely because I am overwhelmed with gratitude. I would have never dreamt of having a choice, not with the questions regarding my ancestry. What right do I have to expect any offer of any kind?"

"I cannot allow you to continue with such dark thoughts. If there *is* another gentleman—you needn't mention his name aloud—I simply wish you to believe in your worth."

"Thank you, Miss Woodhouse. Given the circumstances, I believe I shall make a wise decision—I shall reply to Mr. Martin at once, advising him that there is no question for forgiveness because no harm has been committed. Perhaps you may help with the wording?"

"Harriet, I would not have influenced you for the world, but now that you have decided, I will happily lend a hand in penning your response. And what's more, I can now reveal a secret I was keeping until I knew your heart."

"A secret? What would that be? Oh, dear! Tell me quickly!"

"I understand perfectly, dear Harriet, how you loathe mysteries and such; therefore, I shan't keep you in suspense. *If* Mr. Martin had offered and, *had you accepted*, I would have found the need to break our acquaintance. I could not have visited Mrs. Martin of Abbey-Mill Farm, nor would that lady have expected an invitation to Hartfield."

Harriet was aghast. The idea had never crossed her mind, but considering the matter closely, she now realized what she had been spared. Naturally, a farmer's wife could never be a proper companion for the lady of Hartfield. Having such a friend as Miss Woodhouse had afforded her some distinction. Truth be told, Harriet was not ready to renounce the acquaintance.

"I had not thought I would have to give you up," said she."

"And you shan't, Harriet. Now that you are determined to seek a more prodigious match, our friendship is secure! You no more belong to Abbey-Mill Farm than a donkey belongs in Donwell's stables!" Miss Woodhouse exclaimed. "The nerve of that young man! The cheekiness! I know Mr. Knightley thinks very highly of him, but—"

"Oh, no! Pray do not disparage Mr. Martin so. Do not

think unkindly of him," cried Harriet. "Should he be faulted for not being Mr. Knightley's or Mr. Elton's equal?"

"As if he ever could!"

"I have had the great pleasure of becoming acquainted with many people since you have befriended me, Miss Woodhouse. It is inevitable, I suppose, that one would make comparisons. Mr. Martin is so very amiable, and I will always treasure his letter—for it was the first such letter I have ever received—but I am under no obligation to him."

"You have made a wise choice, and a wise observation. Just because a man writes a tolerably good letter to a young lady, it does not follow that she is obligated to fall at his feet!"

Harriet laughed. "And it was not that good of a letter, at any rate. Will you help draft a reply that is ten times better?"

The two put their heads together and began composing a missive that would be delivered directly. Miss Woodhouse insisted on not holding the pen; however, she had no qualms in dictating nearly every word. Now and then, she would refer back to his letter and use his phrasing or expression to help formulate the proper reply. Harriet was concerned that it may be too harsh and reminded her friend that Mr. Martin may allow his mother or sisters to read her response. It made her uneasy to think she would lose their acquaintance, as well as his. Surely, there was no need for that!

At length, the letter was completed and sent off with a messenger boy. Miss Woodhouse expressed relief that her friend was finally safe from Mr. Martin, but Harriet could only respond to this sentiment with a brief smile and a pitiful shrug of her shoulders.

"I suppose I shall never receive an invitation to revisit Abbey-Mill again," she murmured.

"But you shall be at liberty to spend more time with me, Harriet—here, at Hartfield."

"But—I was just thinking—what do you imagine Mrs. Goddard would say about today's events? Would you suppose that she would have sanctioned the match…I mean to say, if Mr. Martin had indeed offered for me? Marriage is always a topic of conversation amongst the girls at school. Miss Nash would have approved, for she thinks very highly of her sister's match and she only married the linen draper."

"I would not be surprised if Miss Nash, or even Mrs. Goddard, would have supported your union. They may have even envied your position as Mrs. Martin of Abbey-Mill Farm. This must appear as a position of consequence for a schoolteacher, would you not agree? However, they are unaware of the new acquaintances you have formed since coming to Hartfield. They do not yet know that there may be *another* potential candidate for your hand."

The image of Mr. Elton came to mind, and Harriet felt herself blush.

"As you say, Miss Woodhouse, though I hope Mr. Martin is not very hurt. We had become such good friends, and he had been ever so attentive and considerate of my feelings the whole of the summer! I wonder if he has received the letter, I wonder what he will do—if he will tell his sisters…"

"Now, Harriet, let us turn our thoughts to our other friends," said Miss Woodhouse. "Just think, Mr. Elton may be gazing at your portrait at this very moment, meditating on the fact that the artist did not do justice to the original. And he would be correct in that estimation!"

Chapter Nine

Mr. Elton closed the door of his abode and made his way down Vicarage Lane, carrying a worn carpet bag in one hand and a fine leather satchel in the other. The lane had been laid out with great precision by some meticulous engineer who, no doubt, had hoped his right angles would disguise the irregular and serpentine-like fashion of Highbury's main road.

Mr. Elton kept a steady pace, neither looking to the left nor the right, for he did not care to lay his eyes upon the inferior dwellings that were unfortunately situated near his own home. He could not help but flatter himself that, within the last year of his occupancy, the vicarage—an old and not very good house—had undergone some improvement. As its present proprietor, Mr. Elton felt it was money well spent. The future Mrs. Elton would surely approve of it. With this thought, a small smile graced his countenance, and he held the satchel with a firmer grip.

Turning the corner, however, Mr. Elton's jovial mien was transformed. To his chagrin, Mr. Perry had caught sight of the vicar and hailed him from across the way with a wave of his hat.

"Well met, Mr. Elton!" said he upon reaching the vicar's side. "Where are you off to this fine morning? I hope you have not forgotten we are to meet tonight for whist!"

"You will forgive me, sir, I shan't be able to attend. I am for London. Pray give my regards to the others of the party.

As you see," said Mr. Elton, lifting his bag in proof of his travels, "I will not be back until tomorrow, that is, if my business goes as planned."

"Why! You have never missed a night of whist, sir. It is very shabby of you to absent yourself, Mr. Elton, for you are our best player. Can I not persuade you to put off your journey for a later date?"

"No, indeed, Mr. Perry. You may call me names or think poorly of my behavior, but nothing you may say would induce me to rearrange my plans! I am on an enviable commission, if you must know," said Mr. Elton, bringing the satchel closer to his person," and am the bearer of something exceedingly precious."

It was then that Miss Nash came upon both gentlemen with quite a look of despair. "Oh! Mr. Perry!" she exclaimed. "Thank the good Lord, I have found you, sir! Mrs. Goddard has need of you. Will you come straight away?"

"Certainly, my dear. Is it Mrs. Goddard herself or one of the girls?"

"One of the youngest, sir. She is burning with fever! Might you come?"

"You better go, Perry. I am off to catch the mail coach," said Mr. Elton bowing to the pair. "I shall pray for the little girl, Miss Nash. Forgive me, but I shall be late!"

And with that, the vicar made way for the town square, where he would await the coach in peace. He recognized the look upon Miss Nash's face, however, and knew she would question the apothecary endlessly. His traveling plans would be discussed and pondered this night when their little group settled down to the cards table. Mr. Elton could not be bothered with their curiosity. He would allow them to come to their own conclusions, certain they would be kept engrossed until he returned. He had enough to worry about without concerning himself overmuch about the town's gossips.

Therefore, the sixteen miles to London were endured quite easily as Mr. Elton contemplated the obligation he had undertaken. He had no prior knowledge of how to get the thing done, but thankfully, Miss Woodhouse had provided some guidance as to color and style, and he could not help but flatter himself that she characterized him as a man of taste.

He, of course, had no scruple in applying for the commission. In fact, Mr. Elton had feared for a moment that he would be overlooked for the task. In assuring Mr. Woodhouse that Mrs. Knightley need not stir from the comfort of her home, the vicar felt quite confident that he had pleased, if not his employer, then the man who provided his living. It was a gallant gesture, one that Miss Woodhouse was sure to appreciate as well.

Mr. Elton had set forth to Town with precious cargo in his charge, but the question still remained: Where did one go for a picture frame? He knew nothing of such commerce or trade. It was not until arriving on the busy streets of London that Mr. Elton decided on the proper course of action.

Gathering his personal equipage, the vicar followed his fellow travelers as they made their way to the coaching inn. The Rose and Crown seemed to be a reasonably well-run establishment, and Mr. Elton did not hesitate to order some refreshment. While waiting for his meal, he sought the proprietor and asked for directions to the nearest shop — one that specialized in works of art. Not that he thought Miss Woodhouse had produced a work of art per se, but he had pledged to complete the task, and he would see it done properly.

The information was happily provided, so much so that Mr. Elton wondered if the two merchants had not put together some sort of scheme for mutual benefit. In either case, Mr. Elton was directed to Bond Street; the proprietor had given him the name of a particular merchant and expressed that he should ask to speak with a Mr. Benjamin Deutsch.

Navigating through the streets of London brought no pleasure to the vicar, so accustomed had he become to his country life in Surrey. He had begged pardon to countless people as they made their way hurriedly hither and thither, the weight of his baggage began to tire; he could no longer bother tipping his hat as the ladies walked past. Mr. Elton found that he would be quite happy to be relieved of the satchel and no longer fear damaging its contents.

At last, he spied a storefront window with an intricate display. *Deutsch & Lipovetsky ~ Frame and Furniture Makers* read the sign, and Mr. Elton could not restrain himself from sighing in relief.

Crossing the threshold, he witnessed a woman attending a customer at a wooden countertop of superior design. Though she wore a matron's mob cap and her wedding band shone in the sunlight, she was young and fair. Mr. Elton stood to a side and observed the interaction. The gentleman had a detailed list, two pages long. The woman seemed to be quite capable of handling the order; however, Mr. Elton grew impatient while the pair completed their business.

He looked about the place, hoping to spot Mr. Deutsch or even Mr. Lipovetsky, but they were not to be found. Eager to return to his room at the inn, the vicar approached the woman in hopes of garnering some attention.

"Pardon me, madam," said Mr. Elton. "I have come from Surrey in a matter of urgent business. Is Mr. Deutsch available to attend me?"

The woman looked up from her ledger and smiled. "Pray, forgive me, sir. My husband, Mr. Deutsch, is not available; however, I shall be happy to assist you. Would you care to take a seat? I shan't be a moment."

Unwilling to leave the shop in search of another qualified craftsman, Mr. Elton removed his hat and found a serviceable, round table with two equally serviceable, yet comfortable, chairs situated in the corner.

The woman—or rather, Mrs. Deutsch—completed her journal entry and provided her customer with a receipt, while somewhere in the hidden recesses of the establishment, a clock noisily ticked the minutes away.

Situated in this manner—with his vision unimpaired— the vicar looked upon the woman's face with some curiosity. He thought how odd it was to see a woman alone in such a shop. Though she was not full young, she could not be more than five and thirty. Something about the shape of the eyes and the lines about the mouth caught his attention. Her delicate features were striking, in truth.

When, at length, he saw that the proprietress was at liberty to wait on him, Mr. Elton approached the counter and began opening the clasp of the pouch. His eyes, however, remained firmly on the woman's face.

Where had he seen her before?

It would torment him all the way home to Highbury; he would rack his brain until discovering the answer. It was one of his faults; or possibly, a virtue—if seen in an appropriate light. He would not admit defeat until the goal was achieved.

"How may I assist you, sir?" Mrs. Deutsch asked, bringing his attention back to the matter at hand. "I thank you for your patience. As you see, I am short-handed today, and we have been quite busy."

"That is a shame," Mr. Elton replied, "for my business in London cannot be delayed. Who shall complete the work, madam? You cannot be here alone."

"We have several men in our employ, sir. They wield their hammers and their saws, while my tools are this pen and measuring instrument. Unfortunately, my husband and his partner, Mr. Lipovetsky, are traveling. You shall have to deal with me. I am quite competent, I assure you."

"Very well, I suppose I have little choice in the matter. This shop comes highly recommended—though it serves me right coming to a Hebrew merchant," Mr. Elton added under his breath.

The lady, unfortunately, heard her customer's remark and was not of a mind to countenance it.

"*Hebrew merchant*, sir?" she said.

"Very well, then—*Israelite*." He retorted, with some annoyance.

"I am sensible enough, sir, not to take umbrage at your choice of words. It was the fault of Shakespeare and Chaucer and Dickens who sullied the word Jew, though Jew is what I am, and proud I am of it!" Mrs. Deutsch paused a moment, fearing her passions were getting the better of her. It was not the man's fault that he was ill-informed. "It is your tone, sir, that offends," said she, smoothing out the wrinkles of her apron as if the action would mollify the conversation. "This shop is known and respected; my husband has worked diligently to ensure its reputation. I put it to you, sir. Shall you transact your business here or elsewhere?"

She had had her say and was prepared to show the man to the door; however, he removed the canvas and laid it upon the counter for her inspection, offering no further word of apology or contrition.

"I have been commissioned to have this portrait framed…" Mr. Elton began but could not continue.

The woman had lost the color in her cheeks. Her fist pressed against her lips as if to hold back a cry or a shout—he knew not what.

"Are you quite well?" The room grew silent, except for the ticking of the clock that marked the passage of time.

Mrs. Deutsch came from behind the counter and, gently picking up the canvas, walked to the window and allowed the sunlight to properly illuminate the delicate lines of the young lady revealed there.

"Madam? Whatever is the matter?"

"Who is she?" asked Mrs. Deutsch. "I mean to say, what is this girl's name?"

"Do you know the young lady? She is Miss Harriet Smith of Highbury—in Surrey," replied Mr. Elton, having no compunction of withholding the information.

"Surrey." Never letting go of the canvas, Mrs. Deutsch began to sway.

Mr. Elton quickly took her by the arm and led her to a chair. "Madam, are you acquainted with Miss Smith?"

"Yes, that is no—"

"Mrs. Deutsch, it is obvious you know the young lady. The very sight of her has caused you great distress. Pray, tell me, for I must know. What is the nature of your relationship with Miss Smith? Is she in any danger? Are you?"

"I have pledged never to speak of it. I dare not—too many innocent people would be made to suffer," she cried.

"My name is Mr. Philip Elton, madam. I am the vicar at Highbury. As a man of the cloth, you may confide in me."

She remained silent, her eyes never moving from the young woman's countenance.

"Almost immediately upon entering your shop, madam, you appeared quite familiar. Is it possible that you are somehow related to Miss Smith, or am I completely mistaken?"

"You are not mistaken, sir. But, if I should tell you, you must vow never to say a word of it to her. Miss Smith must never know."

"Know *what*, madam?"

"That I am her mother."

Placing the canvas gingerly upon the table, Mrs. Deutsch came to her feet. Although Mr. Elton attempted to assist her, the proprietress waved his hand away. Her motions appeared ethereal, as she seemingly floated across the floor towards the entryway. She pulled down the shade and locked the door. There would be no further business transacted this day.

Returning to her seat, she lifted her eyes to face the vicar, but Mr. Elton could not like what he saw there. Her dazed countenance set him on edge, and he feared for the story that she would relate.

"Pray, sir, tell me first…is she well? Is she happy?"

"She is in the best of health. Indeed, she is very well and under the protection of Miss Woodhouse of Hartfield."

"I suppose that is all I need to know…or rather, all that I deserve to know. I shall tell you my tale and take you at your word, vicar, that my daughter will not learn it from you."

"You have my pledge, madam. Miss Smith shall not learn a word of it from my lips. My only request is that the framework be completed so I may return to Highbury as scheduled. Any delay may cause alarm, and I would not care to explain myself to Miss Woodhouse."

"Well then, shall I begin at the beginning? Before I came to be known as Mrs. Deutsch, my name was Hannah Weiss…"

It was rare occasion that Philip Elton found himself to be utterly spellbound. But such was the case. His gaze would not stray from the woman's countenance, though her own eyes closed as she began to relate her story. Many a time, he had been called upon to listen to a penitent congregant, many a time he had provided council, direction, and absolution. This *confession* was nothing like the others for this penitent was a nonbeliever and, in the act of listening to her admission, Mr. Elton felt transported to another time entirely.

           ~

It was September 1794. Hannah Weiss, a young woman who had not yet reached her majority and had no real knowledge of the world beyond the four corners that united her neighborhood, believed herself to be in love with Yaacov Kupperman. Left quite unrestrained by parents who were otherwise engaged in rebuilding their lives in a foreign land, Hannah and Yaacov's childhood friendship blossomed.

They shared the love of the written word and the love of adventure. Stolen moments were spent sharing tidbits of knowledge, whether acquired from the streets teeming with intriguing activity or from passages within a tattered book. Whispered promises and fanciful dreams became woven into their very existence. It seemed so natural a thing. They spoke of their future lives with the same assurance that their mothers would bake sweet challah for the Sabbath and their fathers would sleep through the rabbi's sermon the following day. It was inevitable. It was bashert—it was meant to be.

On a cool, temperate evening, unencumbered by chaperones or naysayers alike, the besotted pair anticipated their wedding vows. Yaacov murmured his pledge to be Hannah's knight in shining armor, such as the men from days of yore. He vowed to protect her, to provide for her. There would be no more talk of the Judengasse, of poverty, or fear. They were English now, and their lives would be the stuff of fairytales.

"You will speak with my papa?" Hannah whispered. "You will come by us for Shabbes?"

Yaacov gently tugged on a golden curl. "Do not speak in that foreign manner, my sweet one. Instead, you should say: Will you come to our house for the Sabbath? We are native Londoners, even if our parents were born in Frankfurt. Let us not speak as if we were still in the ghetto."

"You would admonish me now?" she bristled. "After we— after just—"

"You are such a little girl! See how you blush!" Bringing her closer, Yaacov whispered, "Never fear, my dear heart. I will speak with your papa and should be pleased to share the Sabbath meal with your family. How else will I earn my mother-in-law's favor?"

Hannah smiled at his teasing but persisted with her train of thought. "What of your papa? Oughtn't you speak with him first? Perhaps now, you may become his partner!"

"Perhaps," he chuckled. "My father certainly has high hopes for the family business. I will speak with him on the morrow after he has broken his fast. Rest assured, my love. We shall be wed before Chanukah."

Later that evening, Hannah peeked out her window and gazed into the heavens. She sent up a prayer asking for forgiveness. She was not so ill-bred that her earlier actions did not cause her some shame. Perhaps they ought to have waited until after the words had been spoken—after they had stood under the wedding canopy and the rituals had been commemorated.

I shall be married soon enough, and all will be well!

Hannah murmured another grateful prayer, for her dreams would soon be fulfilled. By December, she would recite the blessings over the chanukkiah, the precious heirloom that had been in the family for generations. It would soon be passed on to the newest bride.

September went by in a flurry. October and November, although bathed in vibrant hues of red and gold, foreshadowed the bitterness that was yet to come. Hannah could not take pleasure in the riot of colors that fell upon the city, not when her eyes were clouded with remorse.

Yaacov had not come for Shabbes that Friday evening. Indeed, he had not been seen for many months past. Hannah considered asking for him at synagogue after services or when she encountered Mrs. Kupperman at the butcher, but the unspoken words stayed upon her lips. How would she respond if they questioned her? It was not becoming for a young, unmarried girl to ask after a young man, even if they had been friends and neighbors throughout their youth. People were certain to talk. To be sure, in this matter, there was no distinction between the ghetto of Frankfurt and the streets of London.

And then, quite unexpectedly, Yaakov Kupperman appeared at the Weiss' door. Begging for a private audience, he suggested a walk to the park square. Hannah took his arm as he quietly escorted her down the street. Moments passed, and no words were exchanged until Hannah heard him draw a breath. He shuddered as if it pained him to speak. She could not countenance his prevarication and determined, then and there, she would have the first word.

"It has been weeks and weeks since we...since we were together. Nay! It has been closer to months! Where have you been, Yaakov? Did you have words with your father? Did he turn you out? Naturally, I have said naught at home..."

"I am glad for that, at least," he softly replied. "It was difficult for me to stay away, dearest. You will never know how much. Nevertheless, now may not be an opportune time to speak of our— our understanding. Mayhap, we can discuss it again in another twelvemonth. We need not rush; we are both very young."

"Are you in earnest?" she cried. "Have you had a change of heart—"

"No, no," he said, unable to look her in the eye.

"Then, at the very least, you owe me an explanation! You are nearly of age, and I will soon be eighteen. We are well-matched, and I—I do not wish to wait. What has happened?"

Taking her hand, Yaacov led them to a nearby thicket. The trees were nearly bare, but they was secluded enough; few people braved the chill.

"Dearest, I have been away on business—on business that Papa contracted on my behalf without my knowledge. He has arranged for my advancement concerning my profession, and Hannah—oh, but this is difficult! I do not wish to cause you any pain—"

"I beg you. Be straightforward and be done," she groused. "We have never withheld anything from one another."

With this, Yaacov spat out the words he had long dreaded to voice. "Papa will not countenance a match between our families. As the eldest son, he insists on a more prodigious union when I finally contract marriage."

"Pray forgive my ignorance," cried Hannah, withdrawing her hand. "My father is a tradesman, as is yours. Are you not meant to follow in your father's footsteps? Since when has keeping books for other merchants required a wife from the aristocracy?"

"It pains me to speak to you thus, but I have no other recourse at this time—other than to do what Papa has arranged. I may, yet, be able to make him accept my choice of wife but for now..."

"Yes, go on."

"I am for Hertfordshire to apprentice with a Mr. Phillipson— or Phillips rather—it does not signify. The man is willing to take me on as an articled clerk. And, there is more, Hannah. I am to be known to the world as Jacob Cooper. This Phillips fellow knows I am a Jew, but he seems to believe that I will fare better with this Anglo moniker, though I will be able to practice law without taking a Christian oath of faith."

"Hertfordshire? So far a distance?"

"You are little aware of your surroundings, sweetling," Yaacov replied, unable to hide his grin. "It is merely four and twenty miles—and good road, at that."

"As you say. If such is the case, then it would not be inconceivable for your betrothed to visit and stay by you..."

"Please understand my situation. I am not at liberty to proceed with an engagement. And truthfully, Hannah, you ought to say, 'with you, or near you—not by...'"

"I speak well enough! Must you continually draw attention to my grammatical ineptitude? Is it not enough that you think me a kurveh? And before you reprimand me further, allow me to exchange that distasteful, antiquated word for one you may approve. What think you of light skirt? Or, perhaps you prefer ladybird?"

"You are no such thing in my eyes! Do not speak as if I haven't treasured every moment we have shared together. Try to understand. This man, Phillips, is connected to notable people. My family is relying on my ascension in this new world. We did not leave one ghetto to live in another! Here is a great opportunity. I may be a solicitor or a man of business for a great estate. It was never my intention to dishonor you—pray, believe me— nonetheless, it will be years before I am able to marry. I am penniless, Hannahleh. My life is not my own to command."

"Years, you say? I cannot afford the luxury of time," she wept. *"I—I am with child."*

Mrs. Deutsch opened her eyes at the conclusion of her soliloquy, fixing her gaze upon a nonconsequential object just beyond his person. Mr. Elton saw at once what the recollection of the events had cost her. She was spent.

"The intensity of your memories appear not to have faded, madam," said he."

"How could they, sir? They are my constant companions. They haunt me when I seek refuge in my sleep and torment me each day with the rising sun."

"Have you confessed your sins?" Mr. Elton asked. "Is such reconciliation a common practice in your faith?"

"Though my God is forgiving, sir, I shall carry this pain until my dying day. I care not for absolution, for it will weaken my only connection to *her*."

Chapter Ten

Class had been dismissed nearly an hour ago, but Harriet remained seated, drumming her fingers on the tabletop and flipping through nearly three hundred riddles and puzzles of old. Miss Nash had compiled the lot of them and tasked Harriet and Emily Bickerton to complete the collection. It was meant to encourage the younger girls in their literary pursuits, either by having them invent their own or by citing other works of prose. The challenge, happily accepted by Miss Bickerton, was one that Harriet loathed above all things.

Her friends teased her incessantly, for she could never find the resolution. There were not many things that Harriet found disagreeable, but charades or any manner of guessing games were at the very top of her list! How would she be able to supervise the assignment? Harriet was nearly in tears when Mrs. Goddard found her thus, staring at the page with a broken quill in her hand.

"Harriet, dear," said Mrs. Goddard. "You are sure to stain your fingers, not to mention your gown, if you do not mind the ink dripping from your pen! Whatever are you about? Did Emily not come fetch you to tea?"

"I sent her away," cried Harriet. "She and the others will excel on this assignment!" She did not want to give credence to a growing—and quite disturbing—notion that Miss Nash knew exactly what she had done. "I cannot even solve the first riddle, let alone think of writing one of my own!"

"You are clever enough, my girl."

"I do not care for mysteries! They breed an anxious feeling in my breast, one that surpasses any pleasure that may be achieved by finding their resolution."

"My dear girl, there are many things in life that we may not care for; nonetheless, if we are pledged to it in some form or fashion, we must see it through. Once a commitment is made, one must keep one's word."

"Life asks too much of us, Mrs. G. Perfidy and obscurities abound—it is all too cruel! What if we never can decipher their meaning? What if there are missing pieces to the puzzle, or worse yet—what if the pieces do not fit? What then?"

"I fear we are no longer speaking of Miss Nash and her assignment," said the wise woman as she settled her skirts across Harriet's bed.

"I *detest* this assignment! There! I have admitted as much and will not recant! My entire life is a riddle, with so many unknown variables that it is impossible to resolve. The other girls have families and happy childhood memories to sustain them through dark times. They cannot know my shame—to be abandoned, to be tossed out like a tired piece of ribbon or an unwanted pair of gloves!"

"Now, now, dear. You know very well that every girl under this roof has her own story to tell. We each of us have our history, our burdens."

"Miss Nash never reveals anything personal of her own, yet she is the first to examine and disparage," Harriet accused, though she cringed at the harshness of her own words. "And, Mrs. Goddard," she added, a bit softer now, "I have never heard *you* speak of such things."

"Naturally. That is the way it should be. What would become of us if we spent each day grieving about the past, lamenting some injustice committed against us? It is a precious waste of time."

"But is it not right to spend *some* time in introspection, to reflect on our lives and ruminate on how we came to find ourselves in our present circumstances?"

"I should say, Harriet, that the good Lord does approve of a little self-examination—now and then, of course—but that act differs from brooding, my dear. Some memories are deep and painful. To recall them may cause more harm than good. Some memories lighten our spirit and allow us to seek future opportunities that may mimic those pleasures. One must be sensible about such things."

"Do you have painful memories? Do you bury them so that they can do you no further harm, or do you sometimes allow them to surface so that, even if it pains you, the recollection somehow defends the solemnity in your soul?"

"Oh! My dear!" cried Mrs. Goddard. "Heed me well! Neither you, nor I, nor any of us can understand the workings of the Lord. What we can do, what we *must* do, is use these teachings, lovingly given, to endure our trials. Throughout my many years, I have, naturally, suffered disappointments and experienced many sorrowful events. I choose not to look backward. I choose to be grateful and know that the Lord has everything in hand. Can you try, Harriet? Can you place your faith and trust in the Lord?"

"I *am* trying, but I shall endeavor to try harder," said she.

"There's my girl! And I shall help in any way I can. Why, think! We are our own little family of sorts. The girls at school, Emily Bickerton and the Abbots, are very much like your sisters. Never mind the Martin girls who love and admire you and wish you well."

"About the Martins—"

"Oh! And let us not forget Miss Woodhouse!"

"I fear that Miss Woodhouse is simply a spoiled young lady who is bored and seeks to do a good deed every now and then," Harriet murmured. "She believes that my absent father is a gentleman—though I cannot call a man who abandons his daughter *a gentleman*—and wishes to witness an improvement in my essential social graces."

"I would not have you speak so. Miss Woodhouse is a genteel young lady. Whether or not she is restless or lonely, as you say, does not signify! No one else can claim such a friendship in this household, other than my own longstanding acquaintance with dear Mr. Woodhouse. You should be delighted for her interest. Why not take Miss Nash's book along with you to Hartfield? Miss Woodhouse is very clever. I am certain she will be of great assistance."

~ ~

There it was. The picture. *Her* picture. Elegantly framed and hung over the mantelpiece in Hartfield's sitting room. Harriet was beside herself. She had not seen it at first. Why would she? One does not stroll into a room and begin looking about to see what is new or has been replaced. But there it was. There *she* was. And Mr. Elton, who sat beside Miss Woodhouse, could not help himself. He would offer his praise for all to hear. The vicar clasped his hands as if in prayer, gazing at the portrait from afar.

"Never I have seen such…" Mr. Elton began. Coming to his feet, he strode up to the portrait and turned his head this way and that. "The lines, the details, the refinement …"

Seeking his chair once again, he began uttering half sentences of admiration, never quite completing a full thought but certainly conveying sentimentalities at the image before his eyes.

He truly must be in love with me.

It was difficult for Harriet to believe, but the vicar would not possibly act in such a manner otherwise! Miss Woodhouse had understood his true feelings at once, but she was so very good at affairs of the heart. It must be true.

And if Mr. Elton had allowed himself to form such a strong and steady attachment, it oughtn't be that difficult for her to do the same. She *would* come to feel the same for the vicar, would she not?

A deep and obstinate sensation, something quiet, yet profound planted a seed of doubt within her soul. The feeling she hoped would start beating in her breast was not quite there. That sweet emotion inspired by Mr. Martin being near, that first blush—that skip of a heartbeat when their fingers accidentally touched as they reached for something across the table—it was not quite *there*.

Perhaps, now that she had matured a bit under Miss Woodhouse's care, those sentiments were also meant to change. Perhaps what she would grow to feel for Mr. Elton would represent her growth as a woman of quality—refined, elegant, and demure—with nary a skip of a heartbeat.

However much she wished to delay the work, these meandrous thoughts could not suspend the inevitable. A task had been assigned, and Miss Nash would expect Harriet to see it done. And, after all, the purpose of coming to Hartfield that afternoon was to beg for Miss Woodhouse's assistance.

To Harriet's surprise, not only did her friend readily agree to help, but Miss Woodhouse also engaged Mr. Elton to join his intellect in the project. The vicar, who happened to be paying his patron a call, happily agreed to contribute any good enigmas and puzzles that he might recollect. Miss Woodhouse was delighted by his generosity and insisted that Harriet demonstrate her gratitude by solving the vicar's first entry, a rather well-known conundrum that Mr. Elton recited with much sentimentality:

> *My first doth affliction denote,*
> *Which my second is destin'd to feel*
> *And my whole is the best antidote*
> *That affliction to soften and heal.*

Hearing the words caused Harriet's head to ache—it was an immediate response. Any attempt to decipher the riddle's meaning increased her discomfort; her vexation grew when Miss Woodhouse urged the vicar to try his hand at writing a riddle of his own.

"I am not certain I am capable of such a task," said Mr. Elton. "Truly, as much as I would be delighted to contribute to the collection, I fear it would be impossible. Never have I been inspired to do such a thing in the whole of my life!"

The gentleman turned to Harriet and begged her pardon. She did her best to smile and nod, but the very movement seemed to cause her megrim to worsen.

"The act of writing sermons is taxing enough," he continued, "but you, Miss Smith, surely you are clever enough to complete this assignment on your own."

Miss Woodhouse could not contain her smile as she proposed a new solution. "Why not write one together?" said she. "Mr. Elton, what was that you spoke upon last week in your sermon? Something from Ecclesiastes…"

"Oh, Miss Woodhouse! How astute you are to think of it," said the vicar. "You honor me, madam."

"And might you share a portion of it, sir, in your own, powerful voice?"

"Miss Smith," said he, clearing his throat. "I believe Miss Woodhouse, in her infinite wisdom, has recalled just the right verse for our current predicament: *'Two are better than one, since they have good reward for their toil.'* Perhaps we do have the means to see you through this problem, for I am well-read, after all, and you, Miss Smith, are…youthful and given to imagining. I do not doubt that we shall impress Miss Woodhouse—and, of course," he quickly added, "your Miss Nash."

Chapter Eleven

Christmastide celebrations, not to mention long-observed traditions, kept the Hartfield family and staff on their toes. There were breads and meats to be given out to the poor. Mulled wine, rich with winter fruits and spices, to be made ready for sharing with those who braved the cold and came a-wassailing. For Emma Woodhouse, it had always been a time of great joy.

She spent months selecting gifts for family and friends—not to mention the staff who saw to their every need throughout the year. Their Christmas boxes had been prepared and stored away for weeks now. The main hall and drawing room had been decorated with holly and ivy, and when her father looked the other way, Emma brought in a bit of mistletoe and rosemary.

The final touches had been completed, and all that was left to do was to enjoy the season. Soon, the Knightleys would arrive from London with their brood, and Emma's heart would be full. There was nothing like being with family for the holidays. The halls of Hartfield would, once again, ring with laughter and the joyful voices of her nieces and nephews.

If only Isabella and John would be as accommodating!

Mrs. John Knightley, Isabella Woodhouse as was, had always been gentle and restrained compared to Emma's quick and confident nature. She was the model wife to a London lawyer and the mother of five children. Her happiness revolved around ensuring their happiness and pleasure. Much like their father, her tenderness of heart made Isabella generally beloved by all who knew her. She found fault in no one, having the ability of always finding at least one good thing to focus on—unlike Emma, who was always sure to be quite the opposite.

These characteristics were made clear almost as soon as the Knightleys arrived. Isabella was eager to hear the news about her Highbury friends and acquaintances, knowing, even before a tale was told, that she would be gladdened for their triumphs or saddened for their disappointments.

"How delightful to know that sweet, amiable Jane Fairfax shall be in town," said Mrs. John Knightley. "Her family must be overjoyed with the news, and Emma, what a fine time to improve your acquaintance!"

Mr. Woodhouse agreed wholeheartedly, always most happy with his own family reunited.

"I thank you for the favor, Isabella, but I have made a new friend in Miss Harriet Smith," said Emma. "I could not have a better companion."

"That is all very well and good, Sister, but what is Miss Smith compared to Miss Fairfax? We know her to be so very accomplished and superior in all the essentials."

Emma was spared any further commentary as the children's nurse suddenly appeared with a list of questions and concerns that needed her sister's prompt attention. As mistress of the house, Emma would have liked to have been consulted if there had been any issues with the nursery—the children's comfort was surely just as much a concern to her as their mother's—however, she was delayed from intervening with the arrival of a piece of mail delivered on a silver salver.

The missive was directed to Miss Woodhouse, Hartfield, from Mr. Philip Elton, Vicarage Lane. Emma slipped the letter from the tray and quickly quit the room to find a bit of privacy.

Oh, dear! The house was full of activity!

Rather than attempting to escape to her bedchamber—no doubt, one little imp or another would run and tug at her skirts—Emma collected her wrap and bonnet and braved the cold out of doors. Then, once situated on the bench in the folly, she carefully unfolded the document only to find…a charade? Mr. Elton had declared that he was incapable of writing such a thing; nonetheless, here was evidence that proved otherwise. Emma's smile increased as she read each line.

> *Dear Miss_____,*
> *My first displays the wealth and pomp of kings,*
> *Lords of the earth! their luxury and ease.*
> *Another view of man, my second brings,*
> *Behold him there, the monarch of the seas!*
> *But ah! united, what reverse we have!*
> *Man's boasted power and freedom, all are flown;*
> *Lord of the earth and sea, he bends a slave,*
> *And woman, lovely woman, reigns alone.*
> *Thy ready wit the word will soon supply,*
> *May its approval beam in that soft eye!*

This was evidence, indeed. It was practically a proposal of marriage! Emma could only think of her friend, for Harriet must be informed at once. A Christmas wedding would not be possible—there was little time to prepare—but a Twelfth Night ceremony might do just as well!

Wrapped up warm, Emma left word with a footman that she had been called away to Mrs. Goddard's house. Though the air had a bitter chill, the snow had yet to fall; and, even if it had, a few flakes would not keep her away from Harriet—not at this moment of crisis!

Emma had read the riddle with alacrity, never once supposing that its meaning would not be easily resolved. She had not counted on two essentials, however. Harriet was utterly unskilled in solving riddles—even in the best possible circumstances, and this particular moment did not qualify as such, for Harriet was abed, having contracted some sort of malaise.

"It is no use, Miss Woodhouse," said Harriet, clutching the bed linens. "I have read through it twice, but cannot guess its meaning. Will you not help me? What does Mr. Elton mean by *kingdom*? Do you find it to be a good charade? Shall I include it in my book? Will it help me find favor with Miss Nash?"

"Harriet, dear! Read it again, slowly this time."

"I have read it slowly, Miss Woodhouse, to be sure! *A lovely woman reigns alone*. Can it be Neptune? A mermaid?"

"No, no! Harriet, please try to consider. It is from Mr. Elton. He sent it to *you*, dear."

"To me?"

Emma was quickly losing patience and murmured a prayer for strength.

Oh! To have Isabella's serenity! How does she manage with the children?

"Harriet, dear, Mr. Elton speaks of courtship. It is a proper compliment. It only wants your reply. Shall you make him the happiest of men?"

"Do you mean to say this is an offer of marriage?"

"There can be no doubt!"

"But Mr. Elton sent it to you, Miss Woodhouse."

Emma had not thought of that point but dismissed it with a wave of her hand.

"Naturally, he would. Mr. Elton knew that I would act as your intermediary. You were supposed to have worked together on a riddle but you had a terrible megrim. Do you not recall? Then you came down with this wretched cold! It appears that Mr. Elton grew inpatient and took matters into his own hands!"

"Can you be certain of it?" asked Harriet, holding a handkerchief to her red nose.

"He has been attentive beyond measure, has he not? Think of how he read to you while I painted your portrait. Think of how happy he was to champion a commission on your behalf!"

"I suppose—"

"Now, with the holidays upon us, we shall be a gay and merry party—and we shall have a wedding breakfast to plan as well. What say you to a Twelfth Night celebration?"

"Oh, Miss Woodhouse, must it be so soon?"

"Harriet! Why would you wish to delay?"

"To begin with, Miss Woodhouse, I am not in my best looks! I am ill, and Mr. Perry has yet to see me. Perhaps you oughtn't remain in my chamber. I would not wish to ruin your Christmas."

"Do not worry about me, dear friend. I am hale and hearty! But tell me, how did this all come about? You seemed to be in good health just the other day."

"I always come down with something this time of the year," Harriet admitted. "The girls have gone home; it shall only be Mrs. G., Miss Bickerton, and Miss Nash at the school."

"But what does that signify?"

"Holidays have always been a difficult time for me. Families with ancient traditions, everyone gathering together. Yet, I have none—"

"You shall spend Christmas with us at Hartfield, and we shall make our own traditions. And when you marry, Harriet, you shall be mistress of your own home and direct the celebrations to your liking."

When Harriet's response was swept away with a resounding cough, Emma thought only to hasten her friend's recovery.

"I *must* have you well!" Emma declared. "Your timing is unfortunate, dear. Miss Jane Fairfax is in town, and all of Highbury is aflutter. I shall need you—more than ever!"

"Why is that? What is all the fuss about Miss Fairfax?"

"Oh—it is always the same!" Emma exclaimed. "Jane Fairfax has been away for quite some time, living with a family named Campbell. Jane has been a companion for Miss Campbell, you must understand, but now that the young lady is to marry, Jane must come home to live with her grandmother and aunt—the Bateses."

"Oh!" Harriet said as she began to sneeze. "I hadn't realized the family connect...connect...*connection.*"

"Jane was the only child of Mrs. Bates's youngest daughter." Emma retrieved a fresh handkerchief from the bedside and handed it to her friend. "When she became an orphan, Jane was blessed to be the recipient of the Campbell's kindness. She has received every advantage thanks to them but remains a penniless orphan and now has to earn her daily bread."

"Poor Miss Fairfax," cried Harriet. "To be so accomplished and accustomed to living with gentry—to be brought so low..."

Emma was verily humbled. Having never met or known of Jane Fairfax, Harriet was ready to show compassion and true civility. This, indeed, was a moment for self-examination. Why had she never liked Jane? Why did she always wish to do better, to be better, but was never able to see these actions come to fruition?

What makes Isabella and Harriet so good?

"Jane Fairfax is a charming young lady, though she may be a bit too reserved and reticent for my liking. I have no doubt she will fare well in this world, one way or another. And if she does, I shall be happy for her, truly I will—*oh, but, Harriet!*—it has always been difficult for me to be her friend. Do not ask me why; it is simply so!"

"I find that very hard to believe, Miss Woodhouse. Indeed, you have been nothing but charitable with me, and I am of lesser consequence than Miss Fairfax, to be sure!"

"That simply is not true, and besides, Harriet, you are my superior in many ways. I would not change you for the clearest-headed, longest-sighted, best-judging female breathing. Oh! The coldness of a Jane Fairfax! Harriet Smith is worth a hundred such!"

Chapter Twelve

With poor Harriet abed, Emma Woodhouse suddenly found herself in an unfortunate predicament. She had carefully planned the evening, at least in her own mind's eye. Each step and action would have placed Harriet alongside of Mr. Elton or, at the very least, in his view. Mrs. Weston had been a brilliant co-conspiratress and would have seated the pair side by side at her holiday table. But it was all for naught! Poor Harriet was at home, nursing a case of the ague or catarrh, or Heaven only knew what.

The carriage ride to Randalls set the tone for the evening ahead. Her brother by marriage, Mr. John Knightley, had done nothing but complain since he watched his children head off to bed with their nurse. Mr. Elton, whom they had retrieved along the way, was in better spirits.

"I would have much rather stay behind," said Mr. John Knightley, settling back against the squabs after shaking the vicar's hand. "My wife is bound to be anxious all evening, for she quite despairs to leave the children. Her father will surely complain of the cold and wet roads."

"We are sure of excellent fires," replied Mr. Elton. "Mr. and Mrs. Weston will have outdone themselves; on that, you may rely! Good food and better wine."

"Indeed," said Emma. "It is a terrible shame that Miss Smith cannot be one of the party, but Dr. Perry insisted that she remain abed."

"For shame! For shame!" cried Mr. Elton. "On such a night as this! Christmas Eve, a holy night spent with amiable companions and blessed joyfulness—what more could one ask?"

Emma could think of at least one more thing. She would have asked for her friend to be well enough to join the party. She was astonished Mr. Elton was not of the same mind!

Emma could hardly contain her relief when, at length, the three were shown into Mrs. Weston's drawing room. There, in the company of the Westons, she was just as easy as if she were at home. She was welcome in this sanctuary, not only as a friend and neighbor, but as a daughter of sorts. She could do no wrong at Randalls.

Greeting the other guests, Emma explained her sorrow that her friend, Miss Smith, was unable to attend. She was pleased with the reaction her announcement solicited, for it supported her notion that Harriet had been accepted in their society.

"Has Dr. Perry been sent to see Miss Smith?" asked her father.

"Indeed, he has, Papa, and Mrs. Goddard will ensure she follows his recommendations to the letter."

Everyone, it seemed, asked after Harriet—everyone except for Mr. Elton! Emma was perplexed at his lack of concern, for he had been nothing but attentive and charming of late. It seemed that his efforts would continue in this vein, though she could not like his fawning and flattery.

Mr. Elton made himself insufferable with his unending concerns for her father's comfort and admiration for Mrs. Weston's table arrangements. With some effort, Emma managed to preserve her good manners. She would not be rude or petulant, nor would she spoil the evening for herself or the Westons. She would be positively civil though Mr. Elton spoke incessantly about the Weston's artwork (*nothing to yours, naturally, Miss Woodhouse*) or their holiday décor (*Hartfield is sure to be equally arrayed*)!

When Emma heard her host speak his son's name, Frank Weston—known to all as Frank Churchill—she attempted to make her escape, but Mr. Elton would not be deterred and continue with his sycophantic orations.

She did so have an interest in hearing about Mr. Churchill, for his name had often been mentioned in Highbury society for good reason. The gentleman was of an age and quite fortuitously connected, and though she had never had the pleasure of making his acquaintance, Emma was certain that the young man must be clever enough to be handsome—as all young men should. She had every intention to find him pleasant and was certain that he would find favor in her as well. It was only a matter of time before they should meet, but now—thanks to Mr. Elton—Emma was at a loss as to *when* that time would be!

Only when the party sat down to dinner did Mr. Weston raise his glass to toast those who were present and those whose absence was greatly missed.

"We want only two more to celebrate this occasion. We wish your particular friend, Miss Woodhouse, a speedy recovery and my son, Frank, an easy journey. He shall be with us within a fortnight!"

"I thank you, Mr. Weston, for thinking of dear Harriet. I know how much she would have liked to have been here this night." Emma raised her glass to her lips and added, "It will be a great pleasure to welcome your son into Highbury society, sir. I know Mrs. Weston is quite as anxious as I am to meet the gentleman."

Mr. and Mrs. Weston shared a smile, before the young man's father explained the complications that kept his son away. The family that ruled at Enscombe, he said, was very like a Drury Lane spectacle. They were full of drama and ambiguities that no one other than they themselves could decipher or understand.

"Though my son has always been welcome in Highbury, he has not had the liberty to act as he pleased. Frank owes that family his gratitude and his service."

"It is a sad fact," said Mrs. Weston, "but there is no certainty in Frank's coming at all, though he has written to expect him. His aunt and adopted mother, Mrs. Churchill, will grant him leave or she shall not; I am afraid, it still remains to be seen."

"I do hope he comes, Mrs. Weston, if not for you, then for his father. He is missed terribly. I cannot comprehend a young man under such restraint! He ought to be able to come and go as he pleases! One can understand a young woman, who is always under someone's care, but a young man—he is wholly at liberty!"

"It is not fair to judge, Emma dear. I hope I have taught you that, at the very least," said Mrs. Weston. "Every family is a world unto itself. We cannot know or understand what happens under another's roof."

Emma paused to consider the words of her dearest friend and mentor. She was unable to accept, however, that another—a woman, at that—could be so cruel.

"With your sweet temper," Mrs. Weston continued, "you are unable to understand that there are those who care naught for the feelings of others."

Mr. Elton took note of the pretty compliment and could not be happy without showering Emma with several of his own. His need to prove his amiability to her was beginning to grow old.

Oh! If only Harriet had been well enough to attend!

At length, the party continued with the customary rituals; port and cigars were relished by the gentleman, and the drawing room delicacies were equally enjoyed by the ladies. It was then that her father once again began to worry about Harriet's ailments, certain that the whole affair was brought on by the cold and the snow. Emma, who had no real knowledge of how these things came about, silently disagreed. This untimely turn in Harriet's strength and vigor could solely be charged to the state of her heart.

"Promise me, Daughter, until Mr. Perry declares it safe, I would rather you not visit your friend during this holiday season—at the very least until Twelfth Night."

"Oh, yes!" cried Mr. Elton. "Let me persuade you to heed your father's directives. Miss Smith oughtn't receive callers at a time such as this. It would not do for anyone of us to fall ill as well!"

Emma assured her father that she would take good care, but appeasing the vicar was another matter, indeed. What was he about, imploring her to stay away from the sick chamber—the very room where his supposed beloved lay, feverish and all alone?

She was saved from speaking her mind when her brother came bounding into the room, stomping his feet and brushing snowflakes from the shoulders of his greatcoat.

"Mr. Woodhouse," said he, "I believe your coachman, if not your horses, would be most appreciative if we began our journey home."

"I would gladly have you all stay," said Mr. Weston. "You could weather the storm here at Randalls, and return to Hartfield in the morning."

Her father began to worry and fret, and Emma was hard-pressed to make him feel at ease once more.

"We shall go home, Papa, for though Mr. Weston has made a very pretty offer to lodge us all, I know that Mrs. Weston only has two spare rooms. I dare say, sir, we shall all be home and comfortable in no time at all."

"Yes, let us away," said Isabella. "Ring the bell at once

and have them bring the carriages around. The children, John—the children!" She cried as she said her hasty goodbyes and escorted her father to the door.

Emma sighed and turned to her friend, Mrs. Weston. "We hardly had time to catch up on all the news," said she. "I long to hear more about Mr. Churchill's letter, but with Papa and Isabella in such a state, there is nothing for it!"

"We shall make time for tea in a day or two, Emma dearest, but for now, you best make haste. Your father and sister have taken their leave already. Mr. Knightley, along with them!"

"Oh, dear! That means I shall travel alone with Mr. Elton to the vicarage."

Would it be considered bad form to walk instead?

It was all arranged before she knew what was about. Emma had been handed into the carriage, and Mr. Elton climbed aboard, settling against the squabs with some fuss about his coat tails. She felt the awkwardness of the moment exceedingly. It could not be helped; Mr. Elton's suspicious behavior throughout the evening made it impossible to feel otherwise.

Something had to be said, for the silence was unbearable, and rather than allow the gentleman to begin uttering nonsense again, Emma sought a topic that might do for the duration of the ride.

"How sad that the night had to be cut short due to the inclement—"

Emma could not finish her sentence, for in the next moment, her hand was grasped, and Mr. Elton was at her side. He declared sentiments that ought to be given voice only by one violently in love and assured of its return.

"I must take advantage of this opportunity, dear Miss Woodhouse, for I shall perish if you should refuse me! But I know that you shan't, for my ardent attachment could not have failed to impress upon you only my deepest and unequaled love."

Emma could only believe the vicar had had too much of Mr. Weston's good wine. For in this drunken stupor, he believed her to be Harriet—there was no other explanation for such unparalleled passion.

"You forget yourself, Mr. Elton!" she cried. "You are speaking to Miss Woodhouse, not Miss Smith! If your disappointment in not being able to speak with my friend has driven you to drink, I am sorry for it. Pray, let me extend your message to her; I am certain Miss Smith will be happy to receive it."

The look of confusion upon his countenance did not bode well, and Emma prepared herself for the worst.

"Miss Smith!" he cried. "Why should I wish to provide a message to Miss Smith? My words are meant for you, Miss Woodhouse—for you alone!"

This extraordinary conduct was unacceptable, and finding that she had no one to look to for help, Emma assumed her haughty role as the lady of Hartfield, a lady of quality—a lady accustomed to being obeyed.

"Mr. Elton," said she, "take command of yourself immediately, sir. I will endeavor to forget this despicable behavior and shan't say a word of it to anyone, including Miss Smith."

"You may continue to speak of Miss Smith, but I only have thoughts for you, Miss Woodhouse. You may think I am inebriated, but I assure you, madam, I am not. The spirits have only given me courage to speak my heart."

"If it is not the wine that has caused this ungentlemanly-like behavior, sir, then what am I to think? I have only seen you as the suitor of a most beloved friend."

"Good God! Upon my honor, madam, whatever attentions I have paid Miss Smith were only to mark my adoration for you! I have never cared for your friend. I am very sorry to admit it, but I have only ever thought of you! To be sure, Miss Woodhouse, I was certain that my feelings were understood and returned."

Emma was overcome by Mr. Elton's declaration. In remembering his words and actions from the previous weeks, it became all too clear. She had known it, perhaps, but willed it away. Her silence, however, only seemed to provoke the vicar. Grabbing her hand, Mr. Elton expressed his devotion once more.

"Sir!" Emma cried. "I admit that there has been a gross misunderstanding between us. I am very sorry for my part, but I only hoped to recommend you to my friend, Miss Smith."

Desperately wishing to put an end to the conversation, Emma peered behind the curtain and attempted to judge their location along the lane.

Where was the vicarage? Had they not driven the mile from Randalls?

Mr. Elton would not be silenced. He cared not if the snow impeded their passage or if they returned to their homes, safe and sound. He would not be defeated. He would have his say!

"How could you believe I would think seriously of Miss Smith! She is a good sort of girl, very pretty in her own way. I hope that she is happily settled one day—there will be someone, no doubt, who would not object...but, to think that I—madam, I am not so desperate that should make such an alliance!"

"Pray, to what do you refer? Miss Smith is—"

"No, I shan't hear you come to her defense any longer!"

"Her defense, sir? I know naught of any crime committed by my friend. Of what is she accused?"

"Miss Smith is a Jewess! I learned of it while Town, on

the errand I had undertaken to prove my undying love for *you*, madam! I meant to keep the whole sordid affair a secret, but this conversation forces me to bring it to light. Miss Woodhouse, my visits to Hartfield, indeed my every action or effort, has been for yourself only. I find my declaration just, considering the encouragement I have received—"

"Encouragement!" cried Emma. "*I* encouraged *you*! Sir, I have seen you only as the admirer of my friend; however, you have made yourself rightly understood. Your mode of communicating such a salacious report regarding Miss Smith speaks to a vengeful character, one which is quite unbecoming in a clergyman. In any event, I am glad that your intentions have been made known. If my friend is, indeed, a Jewess, she naturally would not be fit to be a vicar's wife. For myself, I can only say that I am not seeking a husband nor do I contemplate marriage in the near future."

It was necessary to continue in this state of mortification, for they had yet to reach their destination. Emma could only think that her father instructed the coachman to go at a snail's pace in order to prevent the carriage from turning over or some such!

When the carriage, at length, turned into Vicarage Lane, they were both able to breathe a sigh of relief. Mr. Elton, continuing to show his bad form, jumped from the carriage without a by your leave. If it had not been for Emma sending him off with a "Good night, Mr. Elton," he would have crossed the threshold of his house without a proper salutation.

Oh! What a wretched business!

Everything had gone wrong, and Emma could not help but find fault with her own actions. Thanks to her encouragement, Harriet had set aside Mr. Martin and developed a *tendre* for Mr. Elton. How could she have misunderstood his attentions? The signs were clear enough!

How would she ever break the news to Harriet? And then there was this nasty report with which to contend. Could Mr. Elton's allegations be true? Was Harriet a Jewess?

"If I had not persuaded Harriet into liking the man, I could have borne anything," she said aloud in the safety of an empty carriage. "But *this*—not only was she born out of wedlock, but to be an Israelite as well!"

Emma contemplated her next steps as the coachman drove up to Hartfield. "There must be someone else good enough for my dear girl, but who? Is there such a thing as a Jew of quality? Oh dear! Perhaps I should give the whole thing up altogether and interfere no more."

At length, another thought came to mind when she blew out the candle and pulled the counterpane close to keep out the chill. There was the matter of Mr. Elton's report. How could one verify such a thing? Perhaps, Emma thought as she drifted off to sleep, Mrs. Goddard could shed some light on the matter.

Chapter Thirteen

She had spent the last six months contriving to repeat her success in match making, as evidenced by the happy union of the Westons. It had all been done with the very best of intentions. Emma Woodhouse meant to do good—she always meant to do good—so why did things turn out so poorly?

Emma thought she would make her way to Mrs. Goddard's in order to call on Harriet, but her father's decree made it nearly impossible. He would not have her visit the sick, not when it meant that she might catch her death! As the days crept by, she grew more and more anxious. The need to confess all to Harriet, to unburden her soul, and to ask for forgiveness weighed heavily upon her spirit.

Clasping the nearest pillow from the sofa, Emma tossed it in frustration, thankfully missing the wassailing bowl, but instead, hitting Mr. Knightley squarely in the center of his well-formed chest.

"'We are not daily beggars that beg from door to door, but we are friendly neighbors whom you have seen before,'" sang Mr. Knightley. "Why do you attack me, Emma?"

She laughed at his teasing, but it did little to soothe her soul.

"I was simply expressing my vexation, sir; it has little to do with you."

"What has provoked your temper at such a time as this?

Should you not be wrapping gifts or dressing the house in greenery?"

"It has all been done! You find me pondering the goings-on from last night. By the way, your absence was noted."

"And what did I miss then? Mrs. Weston, I am certain, provided a fine dinner. Mr. Weston, I have no doubt, spoke of his son that we have yet to meet…"

Emma could not help but roll her eyes at this provocation.

"I am sure I will never understand your poor impression of Mr. Frank Churchill. One would almost think you are jealous of the young man, the way you carry on."

"Jealous? *I*, jealous of that puppy?"

"Is it not rather impolitic to judge a person before making his acquaintance?"

"I could ask the same of you. Have you not already crowned him prince of all Highbury? You have never set eyes upon the man, but you are certain he will meet with everyone's expectations. I would rather wait and judge for myself based on the man's character."

"I will say no more about Frank Churchill, for every word pronounced is altered and made evil. We are both prejudiced; we have no chance of agreeing until he arrives."

"Prejudiced! I am not prejudiced."

"But I am!" cried Emma. "Mr. Weston has become very dear to me, and there are no words to express my feelings for Mrs. Weston. If they think highly of Mr. Churchill, I shall as well. I would prefer, sir, to cease with this pointless argument. My head begins to ache, and I have much yet to do."

"Well, never mind all that," said he. "I have news, and I know how much you like *news*—"

"Oh, yes! Why do you smile? What have you heard? Where did you hear it? Can it be confirmed? Is it about Jane

Fairfax? I have not yet had a moment to call on her—"

Mr. Knightley could not help but laugh, and Emma, for once, did not take offense.

"I was just with Mr. Cole, you see. He received a letter, only a short missive to be precise, from Mr. Elton." Here, Mr. Knightley could not resist but give Emma a sly grin. "It appears there is an announcement to be made."

"Yes, what is it?"

"Well, naturally, I have forgotten the exact words coming from Cole's to Hartfield, but the gist is that Mr. Elton is engaged to be married to a Miss Augusta Hawkins."

"Mr. Elton? Oh dear!" cried Emma. "He will have everybody's wishes for his happiness." *Except for Harriet's!*

"I thought you would enjoy this tittle-tattle, but that does not appear to be the case. There is something you are not telling me, Emma. What is it? What has happened?"

She hesitated momentarily, wondering if she ought to confide in her dearest, oldest friend, but she could not. Indeed, Mr. Knightley *was* her friend, but he was also her adversary. He enjoyed baiting her, pointing out her faults, and criticizing her missteps.

Emma could not admit to misjudging Mr. Elton—not to *him*. She could not confess that she had meddled in Harriet's affairs without knowing—or understanding her friend's true circumstances.

"Nothing, nothing at all," she replied. "You are always ready to point a finger and utter those words: '*I told you so!*'"

"It sounds very much like you *have* done something, and I *will* have to say those exact words, much to my displeasure—and your chagrin."

Emma became prickly under his constant censure and questioning. "I have done trying to meet your expectations, Mr. Knightley. Pray, choose another topic of conversation, or find a good book to keep you company."

The gentleman took a seat in his favorite chair by the fire. It had been his chair these many years, for Hartfield was practically a second home. He had been like a son to her father and a brother to her.

That was not altogether true.

He may have begun neighborly enough—a sibling substitute or a merciless *provocateur*, depending on the occasion—but he had mellowed, and she had matured. Without knowing when the transformation had occurred, Emma could no longer deny that her feelings toward Mr. George Knightley were anything but sisterly.

He had witnessed her flourish from a girl into a young woman. He had encouraged her education, and she enjoyed their debates, as it better helped to improve her mind. But try as she might to prove her newly formed intellect and sensibilities, Mr. Knightley always found reason to admonish. He was quick to judge and firm in his belief that she was up to no good. Perhaps she would yet find a way to convince him otherwise—even if he was ever bent on finding fault.

"I would like us to speak about Harriet..." Emma had thought it necessary to discuss the delicate subject. It pained her to do so, but recent revelations needed to be addressed.

She required his advice.

He would have none of it.

"You have always been equal to any task set before you, Emma," Mr. Knightley began. "But if we are to speak of Miss Smith, Mr. Elton, or Mr. Martin for that matter, I must say that I heartedly disapprove of your interference and refuse to engage in the topic."

"Are we to quarrel about Mr. Martin once again? I will never agree with his being equal to Miss Smith—he is not in her sphere, sir! The disparity of the match leaves one wanting."

"This notion of yours, that every couple must be equally matched in every aspect hasn't always proved successful. Not every relationship is something worthy of a sonnet or romantic novel. Sometimes, it is necessary to examine what hides beyond the surface..."

"Name one couple, sir, one couple that disproves my theory!"

"One couple certainly comes to mind," said he with some confidence. "I name Mr. and Mrs. Bates."

"I do not follow your meaning."

"I am saying that Mrs. Bates, or Miss Graham as was, had a *tendre* for Dr. Martsinkovsky when he first came to Donwell."

"I do not believe you!"

"Nevertheless, it is true. They met by accident one day when the doctor went off wandering in the wood."

Emma was aghast as Mr. Knightley explained a history few were privy to in Highbury.

"It seems Miss Graham and her young brother had gone for a long walk," he began. "The lad strayed away and took a different path—as lads are prone to do. Chasing after some woodland creature, he tripped an old hunter's trap and was ensnared."

The boy, Mr. Knightley explained, was unable to remove his foot from the contraption. His panicked cries reached Miss Graham who was already combing the area in search for her brother. When, at last, she found him, Miss Graham's screams for help brought the doctor to her side. The trap opened, thanks to the doctor's machinations, and he carried the boy back to the house where he treated the wound. Afterward, as the story has been told, the doctor continued to visit the boy, and with each visit, Miss Graham's affections grew.

"Dr. Martsinkovsky told my father about it, for he was

concerned for the young lady's reputation. I share this with you, Emma, in the strictest confidence. Miss Graham had encouraged the doctor to offer for her, but he could not. His faith was such that he could not marry someone outside his community. Miss Graham was devasted and fell ill, such was her grief."

"This is the first I have ever heard of it, Mr. Knightley. How was such a secret kept in our small society," said she. "What happened then?"

Mr. Knightley shrugged his shoulders. "She must have informed her mother, I know naught. She took to her bed, and when her father ascertained the reason behind her melancholy, he became enraged, not because his daughter had been ruined, but because she had fallen in love with a Jew. Mr. Graham had her married off to Mr. Bates as soon as the banns could be read."

"Are you saying that Mr. and Mrs. Bates were not happily wed? That it was an arranged marriage with no affection?"

"No one could tell you for certain; however, I believe both parties were very much wounded." Mr. Knightley ran his hand over his eyes; a sudden exhaustion seemed to come over his countenance. "Emma, a successful match ought to be the coming together of two people who have mutual respect for one another, where there is affection and, yes, even passion—where there are shared goals and an understanding of what God expects of them."

"Mr. Knightley, I have never known you to make such a speech!"

"You know what I am—you hear nothing but truth from me. All I am attempting to say, and failing miserably it would seem, is that one's social sphere ought not play into the equation. I pray you cease this childish interference in the private lives of others. I fear you shall wound many hearts, including your own."

~~

Rushing past the butler and nearly slipping on the marble floor, Harriet Smith ran unchecked to the sitting room, where she nearly collided with the footman opening the double doors.

"Oh! Miss Woodhouse! I left Mrs. Goddard's half an hour ago and got caught in the rain!"

"For heaven's sake, Harriet," cried Emma. "You are soaked through! Come sit by the fire, and I shall ring for tea. We cannot allow you to fall ill again!"

Especially now when there is so much to tell!

Emma sent a footman away for linen to wipe the floor of the mud Harriet dragged through. Taking her friend by the hand, she helped Harriet remove her coat and bonnet; she had half a mind to send the girl upstairs for a long, hot soak, but Harriet would not be moved.

"I have such news, Miss Woodhouse. I must inform you of what occurred just now. I am beside myself!"

"I can see that, dear Harriet. I must also share something with you of great importance, but I suppose it can wait." Coward that she was, Emma could not help but prevaricate and delay speaking of Mr. Elton.

"I had every intention of coming to Hartfield, for I knew that you were expecting me, but the rain began to fall with such a force—and being that I was neither here nor there— I sought shelter at Ford's."

"That was very well done," said Emma. "Why did you not stay there until the storm passed?"

"Oh! I did not think—I was…"

"Yes, dear, I know. You were beside yourself. Pray, what happened to make you so?"

"I was standing near the back of the establishment—you recall the place where Mr. Ford keeps the latest novels newly arrived from London? I believe Mrs. Ford prefers to keep them there so that she may have the opportunity to read them first—"

"Harriet, dear, try to remain on topic. What happened while you were standing in the back of the shop?"

"Yes—well, while perusing the titles, I happened to look up. And who do you think walked in out of the rain?"

"I have no idea!" Emma cried. "You shall have to tell me."

"Miss Elizabeth Martin and her brother! Oh! Miss Woodhouse, I nearly fainted. I was nervous and I knew not what to do! I could not leave without walking past them. And if *he* caught sight of me—which he was about to do, as they kept coming farther and farther to the back of the shop—I did not know what I was to say. Not after that dreadful missive I penned."

"You had every right to respond to his letter, Harriet. Why should you have feared meeting Mr. Martin and his sister? You were in a public setting. There was nothing improper about it."

"No, to be sure. Naturally, there was a general adherence to propriety, but *I* was miserable, Miss Woodhouse. No doubt, my countenance was as white as my gown—at least, as white as it was when I had left the house! And then Elizabeth saw me, and instead of turning away, she came by my side straightaway and asked after my health and extended her hand."

Emma acknowledged that the Martin girl showed proper decorum.

"But she was not herself," cried Harriet. "I could see it in her eyes. The kindness that was always there…oh! I do not know how to explain it, Miss Woodhouse, other than to say that Elizabeth was altered. We used to be such good friends—she said she was very sorry that we never saw each other anymore. Then I asked what brought her to Ford's, and she said that her brother wanted to come to look for a particular book. And that is when I truly began to tremble!"

"Oh, you silly goose! Why should you tremble? You had done nothing wrong."

"No, no, that is not it. I did not tremble in fear or remorse. I trembled when I saw Mr. Martin come toward us. He had a book in his hand. It was *my* book, Miss Woodhouse, or rather the one that I had recommended to him so long ago."

Emma tried desperately not to roll her eyes. What was the girl thinking? This reaction to the farmer did not bode well for anyone.

"Well, what happened next, Harriet? Did he build you an ark and keep you safe from the storm? Apparently not, for you are drenched through and through!"

"Oh, Miss Woodhouse, pray do not make jokes at a time like this! The rain began to let, and I was determined to leave, but Mr. Martin followed me to the door… he leaned in close and whispered ever so softly that I looked well. Imagine! Covered in mud as I was, my hair in such a mess. He said I *looked well*!"

"That was a bit impudent, do you not think?"

"I did not know what to think, if truth be told. I—I thanked him and said I was expected elsewhere and had to take my leave."

"If he were such a gentleman as you say, he ought to have encouraged you to stay, Harriet."

"Oh, but he did! It was only because I insisted—he produced his very own umbrella and held the door for me. He warned me not to go my usual way but to go around

Cole's stables, for the near way was flooded. He bowed then and returned indoors to his sister, and I curtsied and went on my way as he prescribed and…and here I am…and, *Oh, Miss Woodhouse!*"

"Dear Harriet," Emma sighed and halfheartedly patted her friend's hand, "you have had a trying day, to be sure. But you have handled yourself very well. It is obvious that Mr. Martin and his sister are sincere in their affections, and just in their concern for you. Would that everyone in our acquaintance were nearly half as solicitous!"

"What do you mean?" Harriet asked. "Do you speak of anyone in particular?"

"I shall not engage in idle gossip and name names," Emma allowed, "though, upon reflection, it has become clear that I ought to consider everyone's good conduct and honest feelings—no matter their standing or position in society."

Emma thought about her previous conversations with Mr. Knightley and Mr. Elton. Whether she wished it or not, their words weighed heavily upon her spirit, and though it was the proper thing to do, she could not bring herself to address the matter fully. In doing so, acknowledging her culpability would be necessary. Emma was not prepared to own it—at least, not yet.

Chapter Fourteen

Thanks to Mr. Perry for the decoction he prescribed, Harriet had had some relief from the series of megrims that had befallen her. She felt quite herself as she went downstairs, hoping the girls had left some victuals to break her fast. Being a late riser, she would be fortunate to find half a muffin and some scrambled eggs.

But as she made her way to the morning room, she heard Miss Woodhouse's voice in the front parlor. Harriet hoped she had not forgotten an appointment. Try as she might, she could not recall any arrangements for the morning.

Harriet found Mrs. Goddard and her friend seated closely to one another, their whispers barely audible.

"Good morning!" she said, trying to sound cheerful, though she began feeling ill once again. What brought Miss Woodhouse out so early? Why did they both have their heads together as if in some conspiratorial meeting?

"Ah, Harriet, dear," said Mrs. Goddard. "I was just about to have you called down."

"Is anything the matter?" said she. "Pray, is Mr. Woodhouse well?"

Miss Woodhouse smiled and reassured Harriet that all was well at Hartfield.

"I have come to speak with Mrs. Goddard about a matter of great concern. She has been most forthcoming, and I believe…"

Mrs. Goddard arose and held out her hands. The action

only made the matter worse. Harriet began to tremble. What was the news? What were they withholding?

"I shall come out with it, my dear. I can see the alarm in your eyes, and I fear if you do not take a seat, you shall faint straight away."

Miss Woodhouse made room on the sofa, and Harriet managed to make her way there, though her heart raced and her head began to ache.

"My dear girl, there is something you ought to know," Mrs. Goddard began. "I have kept the tale from you all these years, but you are old enough to be told the truth, and I would have you hear it from me rather than from the town gossips."

"I am ready," said Harriet. "Say what you must."

"Very well—oh, how do I begin?" Mrs. Goddard cried and clutched her handkerchief to her breast. "Harriet, child, you were not brought to my door by a stranger all those years ago. I was entrusted with your care by someone near and dear—"

Harriet gasped at this preamble and was prepared to jump out of her seat; the strength of her emotions could hardly be checked.

"You mustn't allow your sensibilities to get the better of you," said the matron. "I pray you listen to the whole of the story, for though it may pain you, it will answer a great many of your concerns."

Clasping her hands together, Harriet awaited Mrs. Goddard's pronouncement with new restraint, praying she would have the courage to manage it well.

"I shall start at the beginning and provide you with the names of those you've longed to know. Your mother is Mrs. Hannah Deutsch, Hannah Weiss as was. At the tender age of seventeen, she believed herself to be betrothed to a Mr. Yaacov Kupperman. They had grown up together—

neighbors, you understand."

"She *believed* herself to be betrothed? How could there be any doubt of such a thing?" asked Harriet.

"Now, my dear, you promised to be patient. I have faithfully kept my vow of silence for nearly two decades. If I am to reveal my secrets—for your benefit, naturally—I pray you allow me the pleasure of unraveling this complicated tale step by step."

"Yes, of course, Mrs. Goddard. I do beg your pardon."

"As I was saying, the young couple were besotted with one another and…as these things happen, they anticipated their wedding vows. Yaacov vowed to speak to Hannah's father and to ask for her hand in marriage. However, he never had the opportunity, for his parents rejected the match outright."

Miss Woodhouse started at this bit of information. Suddenly coming to the realization of what must be discussed, she cautioned the schoolmistress to consider Harriet's delicate nature. But Harriet would have the conversation unfold. She had just learned her parents' names! Mrs. Goddard could not mean to stop now.

"Weeks passed without a word from Yaacov," Mrs. Goddard continued. "When the couple finally met again, Yaacov spoke only of postponing their plans. As you can well imagine, your mother, Hannah, pressed him for an explanation, and he finally acquiesced."

"Tell me all of it at once!" Harriet cried. "I cannot bear it, Mrs. Goddard; truly, I cannot!"

"Yaacov's father had made plans for his son's advancement. And because of this, they sought a more prodigious match, someone with higher connections than a book dealer's daughter."

"Was Yaacov's family so high above in rank?" Miss Woodhouse enquired. *There's happiness!*

"No, quite the opposite. Mr. Kupperman kept books for the tradesmen in their community. The families were of the same sphere; they hailed from the same country and shared the same religion. They were Israelites, you see."

"Then, I fail to understand the impediment to the match," replied Miss Woodhouse.

"Mr. Kupperman had made arrangements with a solicitor of some renown—or at least, the gentleman was prodigiously connected with the Darcys of Pemberley and the Earl of Matlock. I understand the connections were through marriage, but they were significant enough to impress Yaacov's father. This so-called Mr. Phillips was willing to take the young man on. He asked that his apprentice accept a new name; Yaacov became Jacob Cooper."

"How peculiar," said Harriet. "Why would he desire such a thing?"

"It wasn't too long ago that a Christian oath was required of all men who wished to practice law," Mrs. Goddard explained. "Many a patron would walk past a door sign with the name *Yaacov Kupperman* but would not hesitate at a *Mr. Jacob Cooper*, esquire. In any event, Yaacov's father, who believed that this was a golden opportunity, would not countenance any refusal. The young man had no other choice…his family, including his younger sisters, who had no dowry to speak of and slim chances of finding good husbands, were relying on his ascension. Yaacov begged Hannah's forgiveness but explained that it would be years before he could marry, and he could not ensure his parents would relent."

"But my mother was ruined!"

"She was more than that, my dear. She was with child."

"Mrs. Goddard," Miss Woodhouse interjected, "perhaps enough has been said…"

"It is no use to stop now. I would not wish others to use the story to harm my dear Harriet. If she knows the truth of it, she will better manage those too eager to judge."

"Please, continue. What happened?" Harriet pleaded. "However did my poor mother manage?"

"Hannah had no choice but to bring the matter to her mother's attention. You may imagine how difficult it was for the girl to cause such pain to her family. The shame, the fear of being thrown out of her home…"

"Is that how I came to live with you, Mrs. Goddard? Did my grandmother send me away to live with a complete stranger?"

"No, my dear—not quite. Your grandmother, Mrs. Deborah Weiss, had a particular childhood acquaintance— a Miss Miriam Rosen. Your grandmother knew Miss Rosen would come to Hannah's aid because of the support she had given her friend many years ago."

Mrs. Goddard paused to sip her tepid tea and smooth out the imaginary wrinkles in her skirt. The two young ladies waited impatiently, pale and still; their astonished eyes urged her to continue.

"Mrs. Weiss and Miss Rosen had known each other from the old country, as it were. Both families lived together in a cramped, dirty shack in a desolate part of town. Everyone was put to work as soon as they could be of service—it was a matter of survival, you must understand. Miriam's mother found a position for her daughter. She was but twelve years of age when she found herself in the scullery of some well-to-do family's home. Needless to say, it was hard work for such a young thing."

"Did my grandmother help her friend leave this place of employment? Is that why Miss Rosen felt the need to repay her kindness?"

"No," Mrs. Goddard smiled. "I wish it were as simple as

that. A year, or maybe two, passed before the master's son returned from school. Miss Rosen—Miriam—said he began tormenting the upper maids; she knew not what method they employed to escape his abuse. Unwilling to return home and burden her parents, Miram sought assistance from her dear friend, your grandmother. It was she who devised a clever plan to visit the vicar of the parish…"

"But she was a Jewess!"

"Nevertheless, he came to her aid. He knew of a position in Surrey—a man and his wife ran a boarding school and sought a maid of all work. The vicar believed they would accept Miriam—and he was right. Mr. and Mrs. Clark provided a home and hearth as well as the means to earn a living. It was not long after that Miriam met Dr. Martsinkovsky and the two began a quiet courtship. When they married, Miriam left the school and joined her husband. She owed her good fortune, Harriet, to your grandmother's kindness."

"Do you mean to say," Miss Woodhouse interjected, "that Miss Miriam Rosen was *Mrs. Martsinkovsky*?"

"Indeed," Mrs. Goddard replied. "They were one and the same."

"But that is extraordinary! Mr. Knightley never said— well, I suppose he would not have thought to mention it. Just as it would never have occurred to me to ask about the foreigners at Donwell," said Miss Woodhouse, with little remorse. "But you have brought up an interesting matter just now. How, precisely, did Harriet come to live with you?"

"That is a story in and of itself. It was during the period of time when the good doctor was courting Miss Rosen that my own marriage took place."

With all that had already been shared, Harriet could not believe there were further secrets to reveal. Neither she nor any of the girls had heard tell of their mistress's courtship with Mr. Goddard. She attempted to regulate her breathing and calm her nerves for whatever else was forthcoming, Harriet knew it would be difficult to hear.

"Upon marrying, Mr. Goddard and I rented a small piece of land that bordered the Clarks' school. We were quite friendly with the elderly couple. I was alone when my James went away—he served the Crown as an ensign in Colonel Knightley's battalion. I began spending more and more time with Mrs. Clark. Miriam would drop by occasionally, and we would enjoy tea and cakes and, of course, a bit of neighborly gossip.

Two missives were received one terrible day. The information they contained changed everything. Miriam received news from Mrs. Weiss who shared that her unwed daughter was with child—and I received news of a different nature altogether. That was when I learned that my James would not be coming home."

Harriet's eyes filled with tears. With all that had befallen her, she had always been a naturally happy child. And, though she knew naught of her family and had been cast aside by those who ought to have loved her, Harriet began to realize that she had been spared a life of misery. Perhaps that had been Mrs. Goddard's lesson all along.

Everything happened for a reason.

How often had Harriet heard that refrain? Perhaps God had planned to remove her from an unhappy home to be raised by someone who could nurture and care for her. But who cared for Mrs. Goddard? Harriet's heart felt as if it would burst with compassion—and, if she were truthful, with not a little shame.

"How did you manage?" asked she. "Were you very much afraid?"

"I must admit, my dear, I was anxious about my

situation. My friends looked after me and ensured that I was well cared for. Mr. Woodhouse and Colonel Knightley were very kind, to be sure."

"Indeed," said Miss Woodhouse. "They are the best of men."

"It was they who helped secure my position as proprietress of this school. You see, the Clarks had long desired to live by the sea. After consulting with the leaders of the community, namely your father, Miss Woodhouse, and the Colonel, they retired and left everything to my name!"

"Dear Papa! He never let on."

"Soon after, Hannah Weiss arrived at the Martsinkovsky's doorstep, just as the London letter had foretold, and she remained at Donwell Cottage throughout her confinement. Your mother's labor was short and sweet, and upon hearing your first cry, she named you *Hadarit*, for a crown of golden curls adorned your sweet face."

"But I am known as Harriet…"

"It is a custom that has followed your people in the diaspora. Your mother explained it all, though I cannot say that I shall recall the full of it these many years later," Mrs. Goddard admitted.

"I am afraid I do not follow; forgive me…" Miss Woodhouse asked. "Diaspora?"

"From the time that the Israelites were forcibly removed from Judea, they have been living in the diaspora," Mrs. Goddard informed. "Yes—I do recall it now. Whether they lived in England, Spain, Germany, or Imperial Russia, they survived their displacement but have not been *home*. It became a tradition to provide the babe with a name in colloquial language, which is how you came to be known as *Harriet*. However, it is customary to name the child in their biblical language, to honor a deceased loved one—at least that is the tradition amongst your mother's people. I remember that lesson as well!"

Harriet was eager to hear whom her mother chose to honor. Perhaps a grandmother or a biblical matriarch? But as Mrs. Goddard continued her tale, Harriet learned the truth of the matter.

"Your mother was grieving, my dear. I pray you never know such pain," said Mrs. Goddard. "She chose *Hadarit* because it would forever signify what you meant to her—a precious jewel to adorn and bring beauty into her life. A life that she would have to live without you."

It was far too much—too much to bear, too much to comprehend. Such needless suffering. Emotions that Harriet had battled for years were threatening to overtake her weakened state. Yes—she was grateful to know, at long last, the painful truth. But did it follow that she was ready to forgive? To forget? She could not credit the notion!

She had grown accustomed to sorrow and yearning, but there was something new—something that perhaps had been lingering, just waiting for the appropriate moment to rear its ugly face. It was Anger.

If only her mother had been prudent and secured her position as a beloved wife before that of an unwed mother. If only her father had acted in a more gentlemanly-like fashion, and safeguarded his true love's virtue and character. But it was done. Just like the pages in a cherished book, she could not return to the beginning and attempt to craft a different ending simply because she did not favor the author's conclusion.

Miss Woodhouse spoke first, returning Harriet's focus to the present conversation.

"There appears to be more to the story, for I cannot comprehend how Harriet came to live with you, Mrs. Goddard. Hannah Weiss was delivered of her daughter at

Donwell. When or how did you come to have guardianship over our dear girl?"

"That is another sorrowful tale, I am afraid. You see, Mrs. Martsinkovsky had contracted a disease of the lungs when she was a child. She never fully recovered. Every winter was a struggle, for she became dreadfully weak, and it was difficult for her to draw breath." Mrs. Goddard paused and allowed the familiar sensation of grief wash over her heart.

"When you were nearly three years old, Harriet, the doctor appeared at my doorstep. You were holding his hand and carrying a small reticule fashioned by Miriam herself. I knew then my friend was no longer of this world."

"Do you not recall anything, Harriet?" Miss Woodhouse enquired. "Do you not have any memory of these events?"

"Not a bit of it…though, there are times when something seems familiar, a tune or a particular taste—or a lingering scent," said she. "I never could quite put my finger on it. It was so long ago."

"Well, there you have it, "said Miss Woodhouse. "Miss Harriet Smith is the daughter of foreign merchants. "Naturally, no one could fault *my* astonishment, for my friend is everything charming. One would never have guessed the truth! But do tell, Mrs. Goddard, if this Mr. Kupperman, or Mr. Cooper as he wishes to be known, did not acknowledge his daughter and pay her board and care, who did?"

"Oh yes! Pray, do not withhold any detail, no matter how small," Harriet cried. "I must know to whom I owe my deepest gratitude. It is the final piece of the puzzle, you see. I dare not hope that my father managed to do his duty."

"No—I never had a word about your father again. But did I not address this earlier, my dear? I thought I mentioned it was a gentleman who saw to your needs."

"Then it must have been *my* father," said Miss

Woodhouse, "or, perhaps, the Colonel..."

"I beg your pardon," Mrs. Goddard replied, "but your assumption is incorrect. "It was none other than Dr. Martsinkovsky himself. The day he escorted you to my home, Harriet, he reminded me of his wife's wishes. She had gladly accepted the position of being your patroness. It was a testament to the cruel turn of events that kept you from your parents—and those events that made *her* run from her own."

"Mrs. Martsinkovsky and the doctor would have seen to your upbringing, Harriet, had the lady lived," Miss Woodhouse said. "You might have remained with the doctor—certainly, there were nurses and servants to see to your needs. You would have known Donwell in all its glory."

"Perhaps, but I believe the doctor chose the best course of action," replied Harriet. "I might not have been raised in the lap of luxury, but I have known a mother's love in many ways. I have had Mrs. Goddard by my side."

"Ah, my dear, I did my Christian duty. After the Seven Years' War, we grew accustomed to horrific stories. Families were torn apart, men never returned—or worse yet, they returned home unable to resume their places as husbands and fathers. I could not bear thinking of all those children, orphaned or left to starve in the streets. I could not tend to everyone, but I *could* do right by you. And you have been happy here, Harriet, have you not—with me and the other girls?"

"Yes, of course, Mrs. Goddard, and I thank you. But tell me, if you can, what happened to my mother? Did she return to London, or did she follow in the footsteps of her friend, Mrs. Martsinkovsky, and run from home?"

"No, indeed. Hannah remained by your side for nearly three months before receiving a missive from London. It seemed your grandmother had been busy all the while; she had made a fine match for her, Hannah. I understood that the groom, a Mr. Deutsch, was a kind and generous man. I believe he was a woodworker of sorts."

"I can attest to that," said Miss Woodhouse. "You see, I have a tale that must be told…"

For the second time that morning, Harriet was set upon by a dear friend who clearly meant well; nonetheless, was unable to suspend her mortification. She sat perfectly still, her hands clasped in her lap, her back pressed against Mrs. Goddard's paisley cushioned chair.

Miss Woodhouse had a penchant for speaking with decorum; she often reprimanded Harriet for not enunciating properly or rambling on without the pleasure of taking a breath. Therefore, her current method of hurriedly communicating what had transpired on the night of the Weston's Christmas party only gave rise to Harriet's increased humiliation.

She learned that Mr. Elton never held a *tendre* for her. No—his every action and thought had been for Miss Emma Woodhouse. Harriet learned that it was Mr. Elton himself who discovered that she, Miss Harriet Smith, was no better than the scullery maid he had in his employ—no, that was not quite right. The scullery maid was very likely *not* a bastard. Harriet's disgrace was complete.

Her head ached, overwhelmed by violent emotions, so powerful, so fierce! It was as if each sensation had suddenly become a sentient being—each one battled for recognition. Each one demanded that she look it in the eye and acknowledge the power it held over her. She had no other recourse but to surrender. Perhaps that was part of the Divine plan. Perhaps she was meant *to feel…*

The shame of being rejected for another.

The fear of not being worthy.

The sense of disappointment within herself, for she knew—deep in her soul—that she did not love Mr. Elton.

Harriet knew, at once, that Miss Woodhouse was being kind. She had come to understand her friend. She understood her strengths and weaknesses, and Harriet knew, without compunction, that Miss Woodhouse was not telling the full of it. Undoubtedly, there were details too cruel to share.

But what did it matter now?

Mr. Elton had used them ill. Everything in his manner had seemed to indicate that his feelings were true, that his goodwill and gallant gestures were meant for a Miss Smith and not a Miss Woodhouse. It was all well and good. Harriet found that she held no remorse for him, nor did she fault her friend who had encouraged the match. She felt another sensation altogether. It was Pity; pity for Miss Augusta Hawkins, who believed she was first in her betrothed's affections when, in reality, her pocketbook held that coveted position.

"Pray, Miss Woodhouse," said Harriet, now the consoler rather than the consoled. "Do not blame yourself. How could you have known? It is a testament to your own goodness, that you could not see his duplicity. I dare say you had more faith in me than was warranted. What would a gentleman such as Mr. Elton want with someone like me? A girl with neither dowry nor connections."

Harriet began to laugh, not the laughter of one who knows joy, but the nervous laughter of one who is now willing to face the truth.

"Ah, but there is the rub." She winced at her attempt at levity in quoting Shakespeare at such a time. "Mr. Elton *knows* my connections. I am illegitimate, born out of wedlock to a fallen woman and a heartless man! All of Highbury will soon know that I am a Jewess. They shall judge me and proselytize—as if I had not been a good Christian the whole of my life. I know naught of my mother's faith, but it shall be as if I had engraved across my forehead. No other gentleman will offer for me now."

Miss Woodhouse glanced at Mrs. Goddard, who cried quietly into her handkerchief. "Mr. Elton shall not divulge this information, for he will fear the stain to own social standing and reputation." She reached to take her friend's hand. "You need not tell anyone of your circumstances or any future plans. Indeed, I would encourage you to keep your own counsel. Leave it to me, dear Harriet. I shall not abandon you."

Chapter Fifteen

Quiet understanding and earnest compassion comes naturally to those who, for years, have been seeing to the needs of others. Mrs. Goddard excused Harriet from school the following day, knowing she was not in the proper state of mind to stand before her class. Indeed, upon taking her leave—after *The Tale That Must Be Told* was disclosed—Miss Woodhouse made mention that Harriet was too pale and withdrawn for her liking. It made her anxious.

Funny that!

Here she was, the person at the center of the imbroglio, but Miss Woodhouse was discomforted. Even in her present state, Harriet overheard Mrs. Goddard's assurances, as Miss Woodhouse prepared to depart, that she would look after her dear friend's well-being. However, for the rest of the day and throughout the evening, Harriet preferred to keep to herself.

Instead of letting loose with a string of questions, there was silence. Instead of cries of indignation and despondency, there was silence. Harriet neither desired conversation nor refreshment. The girls thought her ill, and Mrs. Goddard did her utmost to keep them at bay.

Was her comportment so astonishing, then?

After all, Mrs. Goddard had had nearly fifteen years to ruminate over the matter. She, on the other hand, had only just discovered the truth.

After a fitful night, Harriet awoke with a sense of urgency. There was an ache in her stomach, an emptiness that had not been there before. For years, she had dreamt of her parents, picturing all sorts of fanciful scenarios that would explain how a babe could be abandoned and never reclaimed. She no longer needed to fabricate stories as she had in her youth.

When she was a girl of eleven or twelve, Mrs. Goddard had told her students of England's attempt to invade a Spanish colony far away in the Americas. There had been other lessons, of course. Trekking across the Continent, Napoleon and his mighty army were always being discussed; however, this particular historical event was different, for England had been shamed in the Viceroyalty of Río de la Plata. Stories of their wretched failure, coupled with the humiliating loss of their colors, and devastating casualties only helped Harriet's vivid imagination to take flight.

In her mind's eye, she saw her father sailing away to Spanish America, a handsome officer in His Majesty's navy. She had envisioned her mother, a lovely, delicate creature, waving goodbye with a small babe in her arms. Of course, the story was doomed to end tragically, for the officer never returned to England's shores. His sweet wife would die of a broken heart, and the poor child would be sent away to be raised by another.

The tale, conceived in innocence, provided the resolution Harriet desperately craved. It was the only ending that made sense. Why else would her parents give her away? It brought her peace for some time, but as she grew, it did not suffice to take away the emptiness and longing. Now the ache had been replaced. Instead of longing, she had the truth.

Harriet dressed with purpose that morning. Donning a favorite sprigged muslin gown and clutching her wrap and bonnet, she set out toward the town square. There, near the post office on Broadway Lane and across the way from Wallis' bakery, was an unremarkable building. She had passed it countless times, going hither and dither from Mrs. Goddard's school to Ford's or the circulating library, but she had never thought to enter. Why would she? It held no interest for her—until today.

Today, Harriet would visit Highbury's synagogue.

Arriving at her chosen destination, Harriet took note of the whitewashed brick and stone structure. Tucked away on the side street, nothing about the austere building distinguished it from other meeting houses. No symbols or icons told one and all: *Here is a House of Israelites*! Yet, Harriet knew where she stood. She had seen the Martins enter, along with others in the village, on Saturday mornings and throughout the year.

Her hand hesitated but a moment as she reached for the door's handle. What would she find inside? Would it be very different from visiting the church? A worse thought came to mind. Would she be sent away to be—once again and forever—alone in the world?

Harriet resolved to confront the worst of her fears. Opening the door, she found herself immediately in the vestibule. A wooden table, roughly hewn, held a multitude of books stacked alongside a supply of striped linen, folded and piled high. On the wall, she observed a prayer board with two sections. One side contained the foreign lettering she had first witnessed in a book found at Abbey-Mill Farm. There was nothing for it; she could not make heads or tails of the script. The other side, however, contained a prayer written in English, and, in such becoming lettering, Harriet could not help but read the whole of it.

May he that dispentheth Salvation unto Kings and Dominion unto Princes; whose Kingdom is an everlasting Kingdom, that delivered his Servant David from the destructive Sword; that maketh a Way in the Sea, and a Path through the mighty Waters Bless, preserve, guard, and assist, our most gracious Sovereign Lord, King George, our gracious Queen Charlotte, their Royal Highnesses George Prince of Wales, the Princess Dowager of Wales, and all the Royal Family. May the supreme King of Kings, through his infinite Mercies preserve them, and grant them Life and deliver them from all Manner of Trouble and Danger. May the supreme King of Kings aggrandize and highly exalt our Sovereign Lord the King, and grant him long and prosperously to reign. May the supreme King of Kings inspire him, and his Council, and the States of his Kingdoms, with Benevolence towards us, and all Israel, our Brethren. In his, and our Days, may Jehudah be saved, and Israel dwell in Safety And may the Redeemer come unto Tzion: Which God of his infinite Mercies grant; and let us say, Amen.

Harriet's half-boots announced her entrance as she crossed the wooden floor, though she heard no other sound. Without any certainty of whom she might find, she called out a greeting, hoping that a caretaker, if not the clergyman himself, would appear.

Walking into the nave, her eyes were drawn to an upstairs gallery, and she could not help but wonder if the congregation was so large that they needed two separate spaces to hold its members. She continued to move forward, walking past several rows of wooden pews toward the chancel on the eastern wall. There, behind a tall table draped in white linen worked with fine embroidery, stood an elaborate piece of cabinetry adorned with carvings and foreign lettering. Two candelabras were placed on either side of the cupboard as if standing guard. Though these were not lit, Harriet recognized a chancel lamp strung from above and burning brightly.

The tightness in her chest began to subside, and she just began to believe that the Israelites were not all so different when, all at once, Harriet heard the soft footfall of someone's approach. Coming from a side room that had gone previously unnoticed, Harriet immediately recognized the man as the same who had visited the Martins.

What did they call him? Parson? No, the honorific began with an "R." Reverand? No! Rabbi—Rabbi Kolman.

The clergyman smiled upon meeting her eyes. Harriet saw that he recognized her as well, but it appeared that he could not recall where they met. She quickly moved to put the man at ease and provided her name and the occasion of their previous introduction.

"Of course," said he. "I recall now. It was a sorrowful occasion, to be sure."

An uncomfortable moment passed while he waited for the young lady to state the reason for her visit. When Harriet did not offer an explanation, the clergyman took charge. He asked that she make herself comfortable and showed her to the nearest pew.

"What can I do for you, Miss Smith? Are the Martins quite well?"

"Oh, yes!" she cried. "They are quite well; at least, they were the last time I saw them. I do not bring bad tidings, sir."

An awkward moment passed as Harriet found she could not put two words together! She had come seeking advice; she had come seeking answers to questions she had never once previously considered. But how did one begin? Ought she start with the fact that she was a bastard child, or ought she inform the clergyman that she was a Jewess raised in the Anglican church?

Harriet was at a loss on how to broach such a delicate subject! Instead, she turned her mind back to its natural state of continual inquisitiveness.

"I—I have passed this building on numerous occasions,"

she began, "but never realized its many delights. I flatter myself, sir, and say I am a student of history. Has this House of Prayer been established for very long?"

The man stroked his bristly beard and smiled. "Why, yes. The structure has been in this very place going on a hundred years, maybe more. However, it was Colonel Knightley who made a gift of it to my father, the previous leader of this congregation, some fifty years ago. The Colonel saw a need amongst the residents in both the Donwell parish and Highbury; or rather, his friend, Dr. Martsinkovsky, brought the matter to the Colonel's attention on the occasion of his marriage. By combining our two small communities, we have flourished in this *Beit Tefillah*—or House of Prayer, as you say. But you have not come to discuss history. How may I be of service, Miss Smith?"

"How perceptive of you, sir." Harriet pulled a handkerchief from her reticule and immediately began to wind it about her fingers. "I am come—that is to say, I have discovered…I have been told—"

"Pray, child, do not make yourself uneasy. You may speak to me without fear. I am no different than the parson, at least in one important respect. I am a man of God—I am a teacher. It is my deepest wish to serve His children by any means at my disposal."

These few words, spoken gently and so sincere, gave Harriet pause. They served as a balm, quieting her misgivings, and allowing her to speak plainly.

"Thank you, sir. You are very kind. I shall begin at the beginning, as any storyteller ought, and will gladly accept your counsel when I have done."

Harriet repeated what she had learned from Mrs. Goddard, not leaving out any detail, no matter her shame or apprehension. To his credit, Harriet did not observe judgment or repugnance upon the clergyman's face. He nodded his head occasionally, his countenance one of condolence and empathy.

"Having had the story complete, sir, I have one question to put to you—well, that is not wholly true, for I have many, but this *main* question must be the first one to resolve." She put aside her abused handkerchief and quieted her hands. On her next breath, she asked what she needed most to know:

"Am I a Jewess?"

The rabbi smiled at the simple yet profound inquiry. "I can readily understand your present emotional state. You have lived these seventeen years as a Christian, only to discover your Israelite ancestry. Let me share this fundamental principle with you, Miss Smith. Our code of law dictates that anyone born of a Jewess is a member of our community."

Harriet gasped at this decree. "I am accepted, such as I am?"

"Are there further considerations to bear in mind? Of course! We do not have the luxury of viewing your parent's *ketubah* or wedding contract, as they did not marry. We do not have any credible proof from the midwife or the local rabbinical court. That being said, in this day and age of reform and liberal application of the law, I have it within my authority to pass judgment over your claim. But I must put it to you to settle other points—your own feelings being my main concern. What care you if *I* call you a Jewess if *you* wish to remain an Anglican? Have you been christened, Miss Smith? Do you know?"

"Why, I had never thought to ask!"

"You may wish to confirm that one way or another; nonetheless, you must reflect upon your heart's desire. I can offer instruction on how to live as we do, I can teach precepts and principles. My wife can instruct you on the ways of the *mikvah*, a practice not unsimilar to the Christian baptism but used in our faith for various reasons and seasons."

"It appears that I have not given this much thought."

"My dear! You have only just discovered the truth of your origins!" He exclaimed. "You cannot be expected to make such a decision without proper reflection. To align yourself with our people is to take on a heavy yoke. Though we have been blessed in this country for several generations, it has not always been the case. And even in this day, when we are granted many privileges, we, as a people, are still maligned and seen as foreigners."

The rabbi was correct. Harriet had not thought of that aspect.

"Your friends may counsel you to distance yourself—to disavow your ancestry. If you were a true convert, I, as the rabbi, would be obliged to turn you away until you had sufficient time to consider your choice."

Astonished to hear such a declaration, Harriet was brought to tears. "I cannot comprehend why this has happened to me. I am an innocent in this matter. I am prohibited the guidance and the indulgence of a mother and father; I am wholly without a family. I am asked to choose between a God and a church that I know—one that is accepted by all good people of conscience—and one that is foreign to me and to much of the world! Pray forgive me, sir, for I do not mean to offend—but why *me*? Why would God punish me so?"

"My daughter," he said, "it is perfectly normal to question God, blessed be He, but tell me this: do you believe in Divine Providence?"

Harriet shrugged. "I suppose—"

"We may never know the answers, we may never understand the reasons, but I believe that nothing happens without cause. He alone understands His plan. It is said in our liturgy that some of the most precious sparks of holiness are hidden in the darkest, deepest corners of our daily lives. We each of us are tasked with discovering these Truths and helping to bring Light into this world. Perhaps your task is harder than others, though one can never truly appreciate what one's neighbor is asked to endure. This may not make your burden any lighter, but perhaps it can help you understand that you are not being punished, as you say."

Harriet sat quietly for a moment and closed her eyes. The rabbi allowed her time to regulate her breath and to dry her tears. She could hear a clock ticking somewhere in a nearby room; Harriet felt as if Life itself was speaking out to her. It was time to set aside her childhood complaints. It was time to mature and become the woman she wished to be.

Upon opening her eyes, Harriet's gaze fell upon the eastern wall with its adornments and displays. "Sir, pray tell me, what does the inscription say—the one above the cabinet just there?"

"That cabinet is known to us as the *Aron Hakodesh*. It is our holy ark. Our Torah scrolls, the Five Books of Moses, are kept within. It is customary to decorate the ark with words from scripture. In fact, our congregation took several months to decide on just the right phrase. Their indecision tested my patience, but that is another story for another day!"

The rabbi smiled as he translated the words: "'Let all come and occupy themselves with the ark, in order that they may merit the Torah.' In truth, Miss Smith, those words have never meant as much to me as they do today. Here we have a true testament to *emunah* and *bitachon*, two words that mean faith and trust."

Harriet swallowed her growing sense of despair. She could not comprehend the lesson. The rabbi's words only seemed to prove her fears. The puzzle pieces would not fit; she was lost between two worlds.

Noting her silence, the rabbi sought to explain his thoughts further. "By placing one's trust in the Lord and having faith in His plan, our burdens are lightened, Miss Smith. When we do not question the obstacles in our path, but instead attempt to learn the lessons they bring, we improve our connection with the Divine."

"Forgive me, but I struggle to understand how these ancient words—words you have read over and over throughout the years—have taken on a new meaning simply because I have come to call."

Once again, the rabbi stroked his beard and thought for a moment. "Because the study of Torah is the heritage of *all* Israel, Miss Smith, whether they be learned or not. Could this message have come at a better time? One of our greatest scholars, a man we call Maimonides, said that three crowns were conferred upon Israel. Aaron, the brother of Moses, merited the crown of the priesthood. David, the shepherd, merited the crown of royalty. But the crown of Torah was set aside. It waits and is ready for each and every *Yehudi*, every person of Judea. It is our inheritance as the descendants of Abraham, Isaac, and Jacob. The words over this ark imply that whosoever desires the Torah, may come and take it! You see, Miss Smith, the choice is up to *you*. Will you take it?"

Chapter Sixteen

With her mind fraught with such heavy concerns, Harriet begged off from attending Miss Woodhouse for several days. She would have made it a week complete had Mrs. Goddard not insisted. An afternoon out of the house would do wonders, she had said. It would have been more to the point, and closer to the truth, if Mrs. G. had admitted to wanting to hear the latest tittle-tattle.

The new Mrs. Elton had made sure that the whole of Highbury were aware that her brother and sister, Mr. and Mrs. Suckling of Maple Grove, were expected to visit quite soon. A trip to Box Hill was being organized on their behalf. Would they arrive in time for the outing?

Mrs. Goddard wished to know.

Then, of course, there was a bit of cheerful news coming from Randalls. It seemed that the Westons would be welcoming an addition to their little family. All of their neighbors were giddy with anticipation. Would the babe come at Michaelmas?

Mrs. Goddard wished to know.

These matters were of little interest to Harriet at this moment in time, for her mind was otherwise engaged. However, Mrs. Goddard would not take no for an answer, and she shooed Harriet out the door.

Miss Woodhouse welcomed her to Hartfield in her usual manner—if not with a bit more solicitude. Every consideration was taken to ensure Harriet's comfort and pleasure. Her favorite iced cakes were at the ready, green tea had been prepared instead of black. Indeed, Harriet felt as if she were a noblewoman who came to call in a coach and four rather than a young girl of no consequence who arrived on foot.

Every attempt was made to engage in easy conversation; recent developments concerning Harriet's home life—let alone her love life—were deemed too raw to address. In this manner, Box Hill became the subject of choice, and, needless to say, Miss Woodhouse had plenty to opine. She went on for a quarter of an hour complaining about Mrs. Elton and her Maple Grove relations.

"If the lady does not desist relating stories of their summer adventures, I fear I shall do something to shame my dear father! Truly, Harriet, I am at my wit's end!"

"You are the epitome of elegance and grace, Miss Woodhouse," said Harriet. "No doubt, when introduced to Mrs. Elton's relatives, you will make your father—and all of Highbury—proud."

Miss Woodhouse sighed, accepting the compliment with aplomb. "In fact, they are *not* to attend the picnic, Harriet! Mr. Weston had decided to make a go of it, even without the visitors from Maple Grove, for Frank Churchill is expected."

"Then all is well. We shall make a merry party, to be sure."

"No, indeed," said Miss Woodhouse. "For the outing was postponed. And I *did* so want to see Box Hill! I have never been, and I believe the Woodhouses should be familiar with all the nearby delights."

Harriet was at a loss. There were so many twists and turns to the story. How had a simple outing in the countryside become so complex?

"Mrs. Weston, in her delicate condition, was to remain at home," Miss Woodhouse explained, "but Mr. Weston had planned every detail—down to the pigeon pies and cold lamb. These are Mr. Churchill's favorites, or so I was told. All was proceeding accordingly, when, suddenly, the Westons declared another impediment!"

"I am sorry to hear it," said Harriet. "Whatever happened?"

"Mrs. Weston sent a note—something about their carriage horse going lame. All plans for the event have been suspended."

Harriet could not help but notice her friend's annoyance. Indeed, Miss Woodhouse was quite put out! It was now the middle of June, and, naturally, she wished to enjoy the good weather while it lasted.

"Is there nothing to be done? Can we not picnic elsewhere?"

"Indeed, we shall, for Mr. Knightley has invited the party to Donwell. His strawberries are ready for harvest; we shall pick the choicest fruits and eat our fill. Of course, he will provide a luncheon meal and see to our every comfort. Papa will be glad to be out of the sun and away from any possible drafts. Mr. Knightley is very thoughtful in that way."

"If we are not to go to Box Hill," said Harriet, "I shall beg off." She had not said a word of her visit to the synagogue. Neither Mrs. Goddard nor Miss Woodhouse knew what she was about, but here was an opportunity to visit the Kolmans once again—and she would take it!

"Oh, no! I shan't allow it. I shan't allow you to become overwrought and depressed. No one is aware of Mr. Elton's findings, Harriet. He will not dare speak a word of it. He knows not to make an enemy of Hartfield. Papa would be most displeased."

"I am not afraid of Mr. Elton, Miss Woodhouse. I simply wish for time to think—"

"I will not hear of it! What you need is a day of sun, good food, and friends. And, if I am not mistaken, it is nearly your birthday. You *shall* come be one with the party, and we shall have cause to celebrate."

And so it came to pass, a few days later, that the Eltons and the Westons made their way to Donwell by their own accord. Harriet walked to Hartfield, but joined the party as they were comfortably conveyed to the famed strawberry beds. It was a hot, summer's day, but—almost at once—Mr. Woodhouse was escorted indoors, where everything had been prepared for his pleasure, including a small fire and a cup of warm gruel.

The rest of the party were shown to the gardens. Footmen stood by with pillows, baskets, and all manner of necessities to ensure the enjoyment of all. Harriet sat apart from the others and studied Mr. Knightley's estate with renewed appreciation. Indeed, she was glad she had come after all.

Her mother had lived somewhere on this very property for three months' time. Hannah Weiss had given birth to her, *here* at Donwell. Harriet had not the courage to ask where the cottage was located and had to make do with admiring the abbey proper.

The building was of respectable size and style, though the east wing must have been centuries old. She was drawn to the ancient keep and bell tower. What stories must be held within those stones? The estate was much larger than Hartfield and happily situated among ample gardens and a small lake in its center; a nearby stream rambled around a row of timber. It was altogether lovely, Harriet thought, bringing a ripe berry to her lips.

Turning her attention to the other guests, she suddenly realized Mr. Frank Churchill was not of the party. He had planned to visit Highbury on numerous occasions; she had lost count of his comings and goings, not to mention his failed attempts! It was of no concern to her, though she thought, perhaps, Miss Woodhouse would have appreciated his attendance today. Miss Bates seemed to be enjoying herself, but that was her way. Miss Jane Fairfax was another matter. It was always difficult to tell how she fared. Her eyes were frequently downcast, as if she wished to shield herself in some manner. Today was no different. Mrs. Elton, however, was in her element, making quite a pretty picture in her becoming bonnet and wicker basket.

Sitting upon a pillow, Mrs. Elton's skirts fluttered in the breeze in a sort of feminine disarray. The lady seemed, in every way, ready to lead the conversation, which naturally centered around strawberries. Mrs. Elton declared that everyone's favorite fruit must be strawberries, but it did not end there. She instructed the party on where one ought to *grow* strawberries, how to *pick* strawberries, how to *prepare* strawberries—it was a wonder that Mr. Knightley did not put a stop to the conversation, but he was much too much a gentleman to take that course of action!

Once the subject of fruit had been thoroughly examined, Mrs. Elton broached a new topic concerning Miss Jane Fairfax and her prospects for employment. Though it seemed to Harriet that the young lady did not care to discuss the matter, Mrs. Elton went on and on about a Mrs. Bragge, a lady known in Maple Grove. She declared her to be everything charming and delightful, a woman of first circles who would not find offense in Miss Fairfax's situation and would gladly take her on—for a trial basis, of course.

"I thank you, madam," said Miss Fairfax, surprising the party for getting in a word edgewise. "I do not wish to engage in a new situation at present. Pray, relay my gratitude to Mrs. Bragge for her kind consideration."

"Now, my dear, you *must* authorize me to act on your behalf! It is plain to see that your previous experience with the Campbells will not open many doors. As to your connections," the vicar's wife allowed her gaze to fall upon

Miss Bates before settling upon Harriet, "well—I will simply say that you will not find a better situation, and will leave it at that."

It may have been the oppressive weather or Mrs. Elton's persistence to reign supreme over one and all, but Harriet could bear it no longer. She arose from her secluded corner in the garden, and, without calling needless attention to herself, Harriet made her way along a verdant path that led to who knew where. The shade was refreshing, as was the act of removing certain people from her present sphere. The constant need to smile sweetly and to respond to every inquiry or demand in an acquiescent manner was, at times, fatiguing.

Oh! The comfort of being sometimes alone!

Her ramblings took Harriet across Donwell's gardens; she followed one path insensibly and without much care, until reaching a low stone wall that allowed for a charming view of Abbey-Mill Farm. Harriet's heart seemed to cinch, and her hand went to her breast as if to calm the pain there.

Her eyes followed the sloped, tree-lined grounds to spy the charming meadow that sheltered her friends' home. She had been happy there. She had been made to feel part of the family, and if her heart betrayed her with stronger feelings for Mr. Martin than she ought to have had, they were hers alone. Mr. Martin had taken the blame, but she was just as much at fault.

What a pitiful creature she was!

Her need to be loved and accepted was stronger than her need to be sensible and prudent. Perhaps Miss Woodhouse was correct after all. Perhaps she required her friend's strong, upper hand, for she understood the ways of the world better than Harriet ever could.

Turning away from the idyllic setting, so verdant and lush, Harriet walked toward the main house. She would check on Mr. Woodhouse, if someone stopped and asked what she was about, for she knew that he would appreciate her company and she would find comfort in his.

Upon entering the grand foyer, Harriet became overwhelmed and had to ask a footman to direct her. She found Mr. Woodhouse seated by a small fire, and though she was quite warm from her walk, Harriet removed her bonnet and accepted a chair by his side.

"Thank goodness you have come, Miss Smith," said he. "You look overheated, my dear. Won't you have some refreshment?" Mr. Woodhouse signaled to the footman, who quickly provided a fresh glass of lemonade.

They sat together in quiet companionship, sipping their drinks and enjoying the birdsong filtering in from a half-opened window until the gentleman fell fast asleep. At length, when the warmth from the fire began to overwhelm, and Mr. Woodhouse's soft snores caused her own eyes to close, Harriet arose and began taking a turn about the room.

From floor to ceiling, the walls were lined with shelves filled with books from all ages. She read a few titles and was not surprised to find Shakespeare, Milton, and Voltaire among Mr. Knightley's prized possessions. Included in the collection, however, were numerous books delving into the sciences and history. Harriet felt her heart race, here was true happiness!

Gently, she withdrew a book from its place in between, *An Essay of Man* and *An Account of the Ancient Feudal Government of England.* Settling nearer the window to better benefit from the refreshing breeze, Harriet turned the delicate vellum and sighed with pleasure. She remained thus for a quarter of an hour until being stirred from this comfortable state.

"What do you do there?" Mr. Woodhouse coughed and cleared his throat. "You shall catch a chill! The draft, Miss

Smith, remember the draft!"

"Please, sir, do not be anxious on my account," she replied. "See, I have my wrap and am quite cozy."

"As you say. Tell me, which of Mr. Knightley's novels has caught your eye? Do you favor Arthurian tales—complete with chivalrous knights and damsels in distress? Or do you prefer Shakespeare? *Romeo and Juliet*, perhaps?"

"No, indeed, sir!" Setting the tome aside, Harriet understood she would likely not be at liberty to read it now that Mr. Woodhouse was ready for conversation. The gentleman had always been kind and considerate of her feelings; she was happy to return the attention.

"I must then congratulate you, Miss Smith. I cannot agree with fairy tales and the like. It serves no purpose to glorify the days of yore, what with the lack of proper food and sanitation," said Mr. Woodhouse. "It is a wonder that mankind has survived thus far!"

"I do not a read a novel, sir, but a work of history. It is entitled, *The Cathedrall and Conventvall Churches of England and Wales*." Having always lived with Mrs. Goddard, Harriet knew so very little of the world. Her curiosity and wanderlust had led her to books at an early age. History, she explained, had always been a favorite subject in school. She did not add that it would have been a dream come true to attend university or, at the very least, to have had a tutor to provide that which Mrs. G. found impossibly beyond her scope.

Mr. Woodhouse raised a bushy brow at her declaration. "Indeed. I often wonder if young people today consider their good fortune. What say you, Miss Smith? Do young people acknowledge that their very lives are built on the sacrifices of countless souls throughout these many generations?"

Unable to think of a proper response, Harriet shrugged

her shoulders in a miniscule display of uncertainty. As it was a topic of great importance to the gentleman, she could do naught other than listen attentively while he spoke of war and illness and all manner of misery.

"We raise our sons to be gallant knights, but do we speak of the atrocities of the crusades?"

"I cannot say, sir. In my experience, the subject was not deemed an appropriate course of study for young ladies."

"Indeed! That is my point, precisely!" Mr. Woodhouse exclaimed. "We teach our daughters to be obedient and chaste. Demure damsels, always in need of rescue; we expect our daughters to be keepers of hearth and home, while waiting for their knights in shining armor to return. We speak of Camelot and castles, but never mention the horrors of battle, of prejudice and hatred, of the unnatural deaths brought about by the spread of disease."

"I fear you are correct, sir." Harriet replied. "Perhaps these topics are discussed by gentlemen at university—"

"No doubt, *no doubt*." Mr. Woodhouse agreed. "But they are only taught to glorify the victories, there is no true debate on the costs incurred by such veneration of aggression and brutality."

Harriet became startled at the turn of the conversation. Would Mr. Woodhouse now expound on his own personal experiences as a prisoner of war? Would she be privy to details that should only be relayed to his most intimate family members? Uncertain what had prompted the gentleman to recall such dark memories in the first place, Harriet was hesitant to speak. She hoped her silence would encourage Mr. Woodhouse to reconsider his audience, but that was not to be.

"When I met Doctor Martsinkovsky," Mr. Woodhouse began, "I was not...I was not well, Miss Smith. I had seen numerous experts, all professing to have *the* cure for my ongoing—and ever worsening—malaise. No one was of any help, no one understood what ailed me. I, myself, did not understand. All hope was gone."

"Until you met Doctor Martsinkovsky," Harriet supplied.

"Precisely. He possessed worldly knowledge, but it was more than that. He possessed an understanding of the natural course of things. I am not a religious man, Miss Smith, not in a traditional sense; nonetheless, I do believe in God. I believe He created this world with Good and Evil. There is no escaping sickness or suffering, but we are offered a chance for healing. I believe that my friend, Doctor Martsinkovsky worked in partnership with the Lord. I believe that his people, the Israelites or Hebrews or however you wish to call them, were appointed 'the chosen ones' *not* because they are better than any of us, but because they chose to accept the yoke that God had offered them."

Now this was interesting!

Mr. Woodhouse could not know that he had touched upon a subject that was naturally intriguing to Harriet. She would not be persuaded to quit the room or encourage another topic of conversation if her life depended upon it!

The gentleman begged her pardon for rambling on for the better part of an hour, but she urged him to be at ease— to speak to his heart's content—and he did just that. Though he jumped from one era to another, Harriet managed to follow his train of thought as Mr. Woodhouse spoke of the Black Plague.

"While countless numbers were dying throughout Europe, Israelite communities seemed to be able to hold their own," he informed. "As a people, they follow dietary restrictions that keep them from eating certain animals— many of which are often diseased. They are required to wash themselves before blessing and consuming food or wine. There is a blessing for the act of washing their hands, Miss Smith! Homes are to be cleaned prior to receiving the Sabbath. Less dirt, means less vermin, you see. There are even practices that govern how and when they bury their dead. For these reasons, and Heaven knows how many more, their communities were not as affected by the plague."

"I would think that their neighbors would have followed suit!" Harriet had thought as much while visiting the Martins. Many of their practices seemed to be regulated by logic and common sense.

"That would have been reasonable, my dear; however, their neighbors were beyond any rational thought. The prospect of death and the loss of their loved ones caused suspicion to rule the day. The Israelites were blamed for the onslaught of the disease, rather than consulted on how to prevent it. History tells us that these innocent lives were put to death in the most abhorrent and evil ways. Out of ignorance. Out of fear. Humanity has learned but a little since then. It is only because of men such like Martsinkovsky that we seem to be able to move forward in the smallest of increments."

"Do you compare yourself to the doctor only to find fault, sir? Surely, no one who lives in this world is perfect."

"I do not say that he was a better man than I, only that he was stronger. He placed his faith in the Lord. When hardship struck, he did not bemoan the fact; rather, he sought to be an instrument in the Hand of God, and to do His will. I, on the other hand, am a weak. I cry out in anger. I question. *I fear.* I want desperately to believe, but find it difficult to trust that all will be well in the end. I have seen much, my dear Miss Smith, and have lost much. And—" Mr. Woodhouse paused, hearing a clock chime in the distance. "And, it would appear, that I have taken up far too much of your time. You should have said! I have kept you from your book—what was it? Something about medieval architecture?"

"It is a book on English convents and cathedrals, sir. And you are greatly mistaken. I have enjoyed our conversation. It has been a pleasure and my honor." Harriet assured the gentleman she could not have asked for a better companion for a lazy summer afternoon. She conveyed her appreciation for all things deeply rooted in antiquity. The library, with its shelves full of literature and history, was an added blessing.

"Then you are fortunate, indeed, Miss Smith, to find yourself in this very place," said Mr. Woodhouse. "The abbey dates back to the 16th century, not this part of the house, to be sure, but the east wing for certain."

"Imagine!" she cried. "Imagine belonging to a place for *hundreds* and *hundreds* of years. Mr. Knightley is blessed in ways that fortune itself cannot compare. His ancestors have left a priceless legacy, to my way of thinking, simply by ensuring stability—continuity." Harriet felt herself blush, for who was she to voice such an opinion? But in the next instant, Mr. Woodhouse put her mind at ease.

"Ancestors interest you, eh? I believe you would enjoy perusing Mr. Knightley's gallery. You may look upon the Donwell's dynasties in all their glory there. Tell the footman to show you the way, my dear, but be sure to take your wrap, for it is drafty in the hallways."

"Will you be quite well on your own, sir?"

"Most certainly, dear Miss Smith, and Emma shall check on me soon enough, I think."

Harriet returned the book to its proper place and gathered her things. The footman, who had been present all the while, opened the library's door and led her to the staircase, where another footman took up the task to act as a guide. She followed the servant up two flights of stairs, and upon arriving at the hall of portraits, he took his leave with a silent bow.

Finding herself, at once, all on her own, Harriet felt much like a child fresh off of leading strings. She peered down the long hallway with its striking crimson carpeted floor. The walls were covered in paper of the palest shade of yellow. Sunbeams splintered between heavy draperies, causing a fanciful dance of dust and light across the many generations of Knightleys. Their faces taunted her; they seemed to say:

I once lived. I once loved.

I once belonged—and I still do.

Each portrait held her interest; they were not all handsome, nor were they all beautifully attired; nonetheless, they each had a story to tell. She was enthralled; she was completely taken into another world. So much so that when the blissful silence was broken by a cacophony of sneezing, Harriet cried out in fright.

"Oh! Pardon me, miss," said a maid, struggling to stand erect. "I had no notion that anyone was here, save me." The woman finally arose, retrieving a basket of dusters and cleaning utensils. She attempted to bob a curtsy, but her knee gave out, and stayed her course of escape.

"Will you not sit?" asked Harriet. "I have interrupted your work, though it appears that you may need to rest."

"Oh no, miss!" she cried. "I just need a moment to steady my old bones. Mrs. Hodges would never let me hear the end of it. She already believes I am too old for my position…says I ought to be put out to pasture."

Harriet shortened the distance between the two until she was at the maid's side. "Pray, sit, do. I shan't say a word of it to Mrs. Hodges."

"I oughtn't be here, miss, not at this time of day," said the maid, laying a clean cloth upon a chair before taking a seat. "The dusting is supposed to be done first thing in the morning, but my knee was swollen like a summer melon, and Mrs. Hodges allowed me to put it up for a bit."

"See, now?" said Harriet. "It sounds like the housekeeper is a kind woman, after all. She won't begrudge you a short respite. I shall join you, if you like, while you catch your breath."

"Much obliged, miss. You are kindness itself."

"I am Miss Smith, by the way. I have come on Mr. Knightley's invitation—although he does not know I have invaded the upstairs hallway to view his family portraits. I dare say that no one in the party has even detected my absence! Now, tell me, what is your name?"

"Me? My name can be of no consequence, miss!"

The maid fluttered a piece of linen across a side table, capturing a few specks of dust there. Her quick movement, so simple a task, filled the air with the scent of lemon and beeswax, and …Harriet knew not what.

"I suppose 'tis no harm in sharing my name. I am Sofia, Sofia Bereznickas."

The woman's response, coupled with the familiar scent that tickled her nose, gave rise to a haunting memory. It was right *there*—right at the edge between knowledge and recognition, but Harriet could not place it.

"It is a pleasure to meet you," said she. "Tell me, am I mistaken, or do I hear a bit of an accent in your speech?"

"Yes, miss. I am from a faraway country, though I have lived most of my life here in Donwell. It is strange, no? We are taught many things in the first few years of life, and though we leave our motherland, some things remain with us—*always*. We may move far away, we may speak another language, and learn new ways of doing even the most menial things, but we are essentially that same person who walked those first few steps, holding on to Mama's hand—

oh!" Sofia brought her fingers to her lips in shame. "Listen to me go on!"

"Please," Harriet implored, "I would hear more of your tale. I have never been away from this place. Surrey has been my entire world. Why did you leave home? Had you always dreamt of traveling to faraway places?"

"No, miss, not a bit of it. I would have lived and died at home, if I had been given a chance to opine. I had a happy childhood. My life was idyllic. Mama insisted that my sister and I go to the city to study. She had always said we would have an education, something which she had always wished for herself."

"It sounds like quite an adventure! Your mama was very wise, then."

"She was the very best of women, miss. But then came a time of great upheaval, and my people were caught in a dangerous game of power and greed. My sister and I were safe, for the time being, but the people of my village were not so fortunate. Our friend, Doctor Martsinkovsky, brought us the news one spring day. The village had been viciously attacked...Mama and Papa did not survive the *pogrom.*"

Whatever Harriet was expecting, it certainly was not this declaration, and when she was able to draw her next breath, she apologized for insisting on hearing the painful story.

"I must always ask questions! It is a terrible trait," said she.

"Questions are not a bad thing, miss. Indeed, if no one ever asked, no one would ever learn. I have lived many years in this country and have told the tale but once or twice. It is better to tell one's story—perhaps it will lead to a better understanding amongst all peoples."

Harriet was brought to tears and took the maid's hand into her own. It was wrinkled, like Mrs. Goddard's, but rough and calloused. "How did you come to live at Donwell?"

"It is a long tale with many twists and turns. Suffice it to say that it was Doctor Martsinkovsky himself who saved me—my sister and cousin, too—when our country became a nightmare for the Jews!" Sofia exclaimed.

She spoke of the doctor in glowing terms, he had been a Godsend, an angel of mercy. When he found he was to accompany Colonel Knightley to England, the doctor intervened on her family's behalf. The three were now orphans, though none of them were of age.

"The Colonel engaged the three of us at once. My sister and I were placed in the scullery to learn how to be in service. Our cousin was sent to work with the stablemaster. We have thanked the good doctor and the Colonel every day since then. Coming to England saved our lives."

Could it be possible?

Had she misunderstood?

"Do you mean to say that you have lived here, in Donwell Abbey, all this time—with Doctor Martsinkovsky?"

"That is correct." Noting the young lady's sudden change in demeanor, Sofia qualified her reply. "Well—in truth, miss, we lived in the abbey until the doctor took a wife. When he and the missus moved to Donwell Cottage, we followed and served them there. My sister came along as an undercook, and my cousin saw to the grounds and the stables. Our hearts were broken when the missus died. The doctor, the poor man, was utterly distraught!"

"Had they no children?" Harriet whispered.

"Indeed, they were blessed with a son; Jonathan was his name. Soon after, a babe arrived from who knew where—a ward of the missus, we were told. The little girl remained in the house for nearly three years; Harriet was her name. She was a treasure, she was. I used to bathe her and feed her, and if time permitted, we would play with a poppet I crafted for the little mite. We never knew what had become of Harriet after the missus died. Neither Doctor Martsinkovsky nor the Colonel ever said a word, and of course, we would never pry."

"Sofia," said she, bringing the maid's wrinkled hand to her lips, "I shall tell you what happened to that little mite. *I am she*. I am Harriet."

Chapter Seventeen

There had been much talk of a ball from the time Mr. Frank Churchill had made his appearance in Highbury; however, the date had changed on numerous occasions for one reason or another. Though there was a general sense of disappointment, Harriet believed Miss Woodhouse was vexed, far and beyond the others, with each postponement of the anticipated event.

Upon a little reflection, Harriet was convinced that her friend was forming an attachment to Mr. Churchill. It was another matter altogether to detect any such feeling from the gentleman himself. One moment, he was everything a young man should be: elegant, attentive, and clever. The next moment, he was aloof and ill-mannered—seemingly attesting to the fact that Mr. Churchill lacked even the most basic of essentials.

And yet…there *was* something that had drawn Miss Woodhouse to the gentleman. Harriet found it difficult to accept that her friend believed herself to be in love. It was a strange turn of events, to be sure, for Miss Woodhouse had often said she would never marry.

Harriet sometimes could not find fault with Mr. Churchill's changeable character, for he was always coming and going—always at his aunt's beck and call. It was difficult to ascertain if the young man had the liberty to determine his own heart's desires upon any matter, let alone the marriage state. When Frank Church did finally return to

Highbury, there could be no doubt—at least to Harriet's way of thinking—that he did, indeed, take great pleasure in seeing Miss Woodhouse.

But now, what was this?

Miss Woodhouse did not appear to exude the same tender feelings as witnessed before. Had she had a change of heart? Had Mr. Churchill's impertinence offended her friend one too many times?

There would be more opportunities to see the two of them together, as Mrs. Churchill, the great and mighty aunt, had moved herself and her household to Richmond—only nine miles away! For two months, while his aunt was under an eminent physician's care, Mr. Churchill would be free to make calls, go on picnics, and, at last, attend a ball. Harriet would be sure to observe from afar and take note of any tender feelings.

Mr. Weston had planned the ball at The Crown, but, in truth, all of Highbury was a flutter what with the many details that needed addressing! Someone needed to oversee the menu, someone had to hire the musicians. Decorations, flowers, and candles…it was a miracle that the day of the event arrived without any misfortune or mishap.

Harriet was relieved that her only duty was to dress in accordance with her newly established position in society. Miss Woodhouse had been quite generous with her time and suggestions on how to prepare for the event. Harriet had thought her yellow gown would be appropriate, but Miss Woodhouse deemed it too youthful and altogether too plain.

"That gown would suit a Miss Bickerton or a Miss Martin, but a Miss Smith," said Miss Woodhouse, "requires something that speaks to her inherent elegance and beauty."

A white silk was chosen from Ford's, and Miss Woodhouse oversaw the design and trimmings, the selection of gloves and slippers, and even how Harriet dressed her hair. Every detail had been carefully considered.

Nothing was left to chance or doubt. However, when the day of the event arrived, Harriet's nerves would not settle—there was nothing for it, though Mrs. Goddard did her best to soothe and reassure. Harriet awaited Hartfield's carriage in the parlor, allowing the younger girls to sit with her in companionable silence—after securing their promise to cease asking questions or professing their approval of Harriet's new frock.

They arrived at the Crown before the set time, for Mr. Weston requested that Miss Woodhouse look over the rooms and give her approval. Indeed, Mr. Weston himself was there to help them alight from the conveyance. There was a certain amount of pride in knowing one's friend was so highly regarded. Never in her dreams had Harriet envisioned herself to be in such a position.

She walked shoulder to shoulder with Hartfield's mistress, inspecting this and admiring that. It was obvious that Miss Woodhouse was enjoying her power. But as they began to tour the hall, it was evident that others had been invited to come early—in order that they, too, opine.

"It seems as if half the company is here!" Miss Woodhouse declared. "I needn't have rushed my poor maid to complete my *toilette* in such haste."

"But it is your opinion," said Mr. Weston, "that is most valued!"

Harriet smiled as Miss Woodhouse blushed. The whole party walked about and praised Mr. Weston's choices and declared the evening a success when, in fact, it had barely begun!

At last, the other attendees began to arrive. A long line of carriages had queued up at the front of The Crown; well-turned-out gentlemen handed down ladies dressed in their finery, and the room was soon filled with all of Highbury in their best looks.

Only when Mr. and Mrs. Elton arrived did Harriet feel a familiar tightness in her chest. Though she had not injured the lady—in any form or fashion known to her—Harriet felt Mrs. Elton's contempt. Her true feelings were displayed in the lady's countenance, even as she smiled at everyone— everyone except Harriet.

The couple proceeded to promenade to the center of the floor while Mrs. Elton bowed her head in a regal manner, greeting and welcoming all as if *she* were the event's hostess. It was then that Mr. Frank Churchill asked after Miss Bates and Miss Fairfax. It seemed that the Eltons were supposed to have conveyed the ladies in their carriage—yet they were still at home!

"Poor Miss Fairfax!" said Miss Woodhouse. "And it has started to rain! Oh dear!"

Harriet witnessed her friend's smile behind her fan and would have questioned her wicked actions, but Mr. Churchill raised such a fuss just then that Mrs. Elton sent her coachman back to fetch their missing friends. It was all put to rights by the time Mr. Knightley arrived. Miss Bates and Miss Fairfax were safely delivered, and everyone was quite pleased with themselves and each other.

Except for Mrs. Elton, who only seemed to look at a person to find fault with this one's *coiffure* or that one's trimmings. Harriet was quite taken aback, for in her little corner—she had stepped back and allowed her elders their place—compliments abounded amongst the other guests. The vicar's wife was not all she should be. Harriet struggled not to form opinions of a lady so clearly in need of a lesson in humility and charity.

The musicians played a few notes to call the dancers to the floor. It seemed that Mrs. Elton would be given the honor of opening the ball, though most thought the honor should have gone to Miss Woodhouse. Harriet had had high hopes of seeing her friend paired with Frank Churchill, for they made a handsome couple, but would he be partnered with the vicar's wife instead? It seemed, for a moment, that that was the plan, but in the very next instant, Mr. Weston led Mrs. Elton to the center of the room, and Mr. Churchill was able to claim Miss Woodhouse. That pairing brought smiles across the room, Harriet the happiest, for her friend appeared to blush as the set began to form.

Not having been asked to dance, Harriet found a seat and tapped her slippered feet to keep with the rhythm.

Surely, someone will ask for my hand with the next set!

The ball proceeded pleasantly enough, and Harriet was soon asked to stand with a Mr. Fullerton, an anxious young man who hailed from Richmond. Sadly, he was not a skillful partner. Though his clumsy performance caused some embarrassment—and injured her delicate slippers—Harriet would not complain.

As the couples performed their steps—whirling and gliding and reeling down the line—their baubles and other adornments caught the flickering candlelight, causing a magical glow about the room. The musicians were tireless, playing one tune after another; their joy in making the music was equal to the couples enjoying the dance.

Having completed a set, Harriet was escorted to her seat, where she, once again, observed the couples on the floor. She knew she ought to have been grateful for being asked at all, but she was eager for more. Unable to restrain her tapping feet, Harriet hummed along with the current tune and hoped Mrs. Weston—who stood by her side—would take note. Perhaps she would help Harriet find a partner before supper was announced.

It was then that Mr. Elton crossed the lady's path, and Mrs. Weston called upon his service.

"I am happy to dance with Mrs. Gilbert or yourself, madam," said Mr. Elton.

"Mrs. Gilbert does not mean to dance, sir. Nor am I in want of a partner."

Mrs. Weston's hand delicately signaled in Harriet's direction, and when the lady said Miss Smith was in need of partner, Mr. Elton emphatically declined.

Harriet was mortified as his declaration was heard above the din of dancers and musicians at play. As the vicar turned his back, Harriet saw Mr. Knightley walking toward her direction. She turned her eyes away—she could not bear to see pity in his gaze. But she was mistaken in his intent, for Mr. Knightley did not mean to gloat at her insult; he meant to redeem her from this moment of shame.

Taking her hand, Mr. Knightley escorted Harriet to the floor. They performed the first few steps in silence, but when the opportunity arose to speak, he made use of the time.

"Why did Mr. Elton mean to slight you, Miss Smith?"

"I cannot say, Mr. Knightley!" she replied when next they met in the formation. Gratified to be on the floor with such a gentleman, Harriet did not wish to diminish the joy of the moment with thoughts of Miss Woodhouse's previous matchmaking schemes.

Nonetheless, Harriet had not been truthful to Mr. Knightley. It was evident that both Mr. and Mrs. Elton aimed to wound her and Miss Woodhouse alike. She believed that Mr. Elton held a grudge, though it was not very Christian-like behavior—and he was a happily married man besides! Why should he *still* resent Miss Woodhouse for rejecting his proposal? Surely, he would not have mentioned the whole affair to this wife! It was all a misunderstanding, certainly nothing to hold against one another for a lifetime of antipathy.

She felt it necessary to say *something* to Mr. Knightley. The thought of his finding out her secret made her ill, for he, above everyone else in Highbury, knew most of the players of her never-ending drama. Colonel Knightley and Dr. Martsinkovsky would have known her, or of her, from birth. Mr. Knightley continued to employ servants who were well acquainted with her story.

When she spied Mr. Knightley walking toward the cards room, Harriet stayed his course.

"I *do* have something to confess, sir," said she. "I fear you may be quite astonished as I was when I first heard the tale."

Having a particular talent for babbling—without pausing or taking unnecessary breaths—had never come in so handy until this very moment. Harriet knew she had little time to waste, particularly because Miss Woodhouse would soon enquire after their conversation. She explained what Mr. Elton had discovered while in London without revealing the minor details of his unexpected, and unwelcome, marriage proposal to Miss Woodhouse.

Mr. Knightley, for his part, listened intently, never saying a word until Harriet mentioned Sofia and her family.

"You are the child that was sent away? You are *that* Harriet?"

"To be sure, sir. I am. Did you know me then?"

"I was at school, Miss Smith. I knew of you, but I was a young man of twenty or thereabouts. What with attending university and the social season, you may very well imagine that my thoughts were otherwise engaged."

Naturally, Mr. Knightley would not have given her a second thought. Who was she to garner any consideration—some chit that had long ago been abandoned? Who was her father? Certainly not the landed gentleman of Miss Woodhouse's imagination!

"I understand, sir," said Harriet, "I did not mean to

insinuate that you ought to have been concerned for my welfare or my whereabouts for that matter. To be sure, you have shown me great kindness. It has been my honor to be in your company; but now that my ancestry has been made known to you, sir, I would not wish to impose on your generosity any further."

"There must be some misunderstanding, Miss Smith, for I am delighted to know you are not lost or alone in the world! Though I was young and a bit of a Corinthian, it does not follow that I was heartless or insensible to the goings on at Donwell Cottage. The household was in sixes and sevens when that precocious little girl was sent away. Dr. Martsinkovsky was inconsolable, for he had just lost his wife. He insisted that no one ever speak of their ward; he said it was a delicate matter. A promise of secrecy had been made, and he aimed to honor that promise in his wife's memory."

"That is very kind of you to say, sir. I wish I could remember the doctor and Mrs. Martsinkovsky," said she, "but I must be satisfied with only the shadowy images that come to visit me in my dreams."

"But what of this nonsense you speak of—what is this about imposing on my generosity? I have done nothing…"

"You have done much, sir!" she cried. "You have been a true gentleman. You have honored your father's wishes and have seen to the well-being of people in your care. Would that my own father could have been such a person. Mr. Knightley, I must beg you to keep my secret a little longer, for I fear my future is not certain."

"Why should you say that?"

"Society does not take kindly to those born out of wedlock." A poignant pause followed before Harriet made her final point. "And, let us not forget, my people are Israelites."

Mr. Knightley shook his head, muttering something under his breath. "And what of it? Did not my father befriend the doctor and his wife? I have never known such a bond; their mutual respect and admiration for one another served as an example to this young man just starting out in the world." Mr. Knightley bent his head and whispered, "You can depend on me. I shan't say a word of this to anyone, but pray allow me this piece of advice, Miss Smith. Do not let small-minded people charter the course of your life."

Harriet gasped at the gentleman's breath on her cheek. Her eyes scanned the company, hoping no one witnessed their little tête à tête.

"What will you do now?" Mr. Knightley asked, seemingly unaware of her apprehension.

It was Harriet's turn to shake her head and mumble. "It depends very much on Miss Woodhouse and her plans."

Harriet slept away the next morning, unable to rouse herself before noon. Not having attended the ball, Emily Bickerton had waited since the morning light for Harriet to open her eyes—and she did so, thanks, in no small part, to Miss Bickerton drawing back the curtains.

"I want to hear all about it, Harriet! Get up, do!"

It took another half hour of tossing, turning, and throwing a pillow at her roommate before Harriet could be persuaded to see to her *morning* ablutions. Then, there was the matter of coming down to break her fast. Finally, when Miss Bickerton could not stand it any longer, both young ladies grabbed their bonnets and went out for a long walk. Harriet had wished for privacy to discuss all that occurred; she certainly had no desire to speak in front of the younger girls.

They walked through the center of Highbury, passing neighbors and merchants without paying much mind. With all the chattering, giggling, and rolling of eyes, the young women had walked to the edge of town without noticing that they were now on Richmond Road, nearly half a mile beyond the safety of shops, stalls, and family homes. Harriet took Emily Bickerton's arm and led her down the road, recognizing the path she and Miss Woodhouse had previously taken when they came across Mr. Martin in the wood.

The road was heavily shaded, and tall elm trees lined each side. Harriet had run out of conversation and, Miss Bickerton, of questions. The pair walked in companionable silence until noticing a horse, unbridled, grazing near a large and unusual wagon. Emily clutched at Harriet's arm.

"Gypsies!" she cried. "We must away!"

But Harriet did not sense any alarm nor need to flee. From their distance, she spied what appeared to be a happy family: A father, a mother, and possibly a grandmama or two. A boy was strumming a guitar, and the older women sang a sad song of yearning in some minor key. The mama stood, her colorful patched skirt fluttering in the breeze, and walked toward a small firepit. A black pot hung from above, and she stirred what Harriet presumed to be the family's dinner.

"Harriet, what do you do there? Come away at once!" declared Miss Bickerton.

"There can be no harm in continuing our walk. They are a family, like any other, enjoying a picnic on a summer's day."

Miss Bickerton would have none of it. Excessively frightened, she shook off Harriet's arm, made a sudden turn, and ran back to Highbury. The family witnessed the entire episode and waved their welcome. In truth, Harriet was ready to rest her weary feet; the previous night's dancing and the excessive walking out of town had taken their toll. She waved back and decided to head toward the family's camp, but as she made her way, her foot cramped, and she cried out as she fell to the ground.

A child came dashing through the trees. Her father soon followed. Though he spoke little English, he offered to assist Harriet and managed to say that his mother was a healer. She would look at her foot if Harriet would permit her care.

Harriet felt powerless; and, in this state, she was obliged to remain. In a matter of moments, the woman had ascertained the damage, dabbed a bit of liniment retrieved from a glass vial, and wrapped her ankle.

While a child brought Harriet a cool glass of water, the family shared their story and explained where they were from and where they were going. They must have spent a quarter of an hour in this manner when Harriet believed herself able to walk. She arose slowly and began voicing her heartfelt gratitude when she reached for a coin in her reticule. The father would not accept it, the mother would not hear of it. Harriet insisted.

"For the children," she said, placing the shilling in the healer's hand. "Buy them some sweets for the journey."

She said her goodbyes and made her way to Hartfield, having almost forgotten entirely that Miss Woodhouse awaited her there. As Harriet retraced the very steps she had taken when coming upon Mr. Martin, her ankle began to throb. She cried out in pain when it gave out, and she found herself on the ground once more.

Regretting how far she had allowed herself to walk out, she considered the plan for returning home when a horse and rider cut through the thicket of trees. Oh, dear! Harriet felt Miss Bickerton's fear, contemplating what stranger would set upon her, but in the next moment, she sighed in relief.

Mr. Frank Churchill! Praise God!

Harriet told her sorry tale as Mr. Churchill quickly dismounted and ascertained the extent of her injury. Through hiccups and tears, she assured him that her foot was not broken, though it pained her to walk. She informed the gentleman that she was expected at Hartfield and was now quite late.

Nothing further needed to be said, though Mr. Churchill seemed a bit perturbed and checked his fob for the time. He helped her mount his great beast of a horse, and in an instant, he jumped up behind her. Harriet was all afire, feeling his arms come around her waist, but someone had to hold the reins, and she was surely about to swoon.

Fretting about Miss Woodhouse and the spectacle that she and Mr. Churchill were sure to present—she with a tear-stained face and wrapped ankle—Harriet prayed that Miss Woodhouse was not situated near a window that looked out upon the drive. But it was not meant to be, for Miss Woodhouse *did* see the pair approach and watched as Mr. Churchill gently helped Harriet dismount.

"Whatever happened?" cried Miss Woodhouse. "Are you quite well, Harriet?"

"Indeed," said she. "Pray, do not fret. It looks far worse than it is."

Mr. Churchill made his bow. "It appears to be a sprain, Miss Woodhouse, nothing more. I do apologize, but I cannot stay. I am expected…I am expected elsewhere."

Another bow and he was off, handing Harriet off for Miss Woodhouse to support as if she were a side of pork or a sack of potatoes.

"Come inside, dear Harriet! Tell me what has occurred!"

In typical form that Harriet had come to know and admire, Miss Woodhouse had her comfortable and cozy with her foot upon a pillow and a cup of tea in her hand in a matter of minutes. There, by a small fire—that was never necessary but always lit—Harriet once again told her story.

"Gypsies!" Miss Woodhouse cried. "Here? I must alert Mr. Knightley at once!" Without wasting another moment, she picked up her quill and pulled a fresh sheet of paper from her desk. Jotting a few words down, she sealed the missive and sent it off with a footman. "I shall inform Mrs. Goddard as well. You shall stay the night, Harriet."

Harriet sipped her tea and watched as Miss Woodhouse did what she did best. Organize and prepare, see to the needs of her guests, and most importantly, ensure that her father learned as little as possible of the dangers lurking in the wood.

"Truly, Miss Woodhouse, I was not troubled whatsoever by the gypsies. My friend, Miss Bickerton, did not have the opportunity to meet them and judge for herself. They were kind and ever so friendly. Indeed, they would not accept compensation for wrapping my ankle."

"Compensation! Do you mean you displayed the contents of your reticule? You are fortunate they did not rob you of all your coin! Miss Bickerton had the right of it, Harriet. You should have fled immediately."

"You are mistaken. My injury was of my own doing. They offered me refreshment and told me a bit about themselves. They lead such an interesting sort of life; they travel—"

"Nay! I shall not hear another word, Harriet. You are fortunate that Mr. Churchill arrived when he did. Such gallantry! His service to you conveys a great deal. If only he had arrived a few minutes sooner—he might have dispersed the troublesome gang altogether from Donwell lands! This is not to be borne!"

Harriet saw that any further commentary would be lost on Miss Woodhouse. She had made up her mind to dislike these people—this *troublesome gang*—where Harriet could only see a family. A family that preferred to remain together, no matter the inconvenience, no matter how poor.

"We never spoke of the dance last evening, Miss Woodhouse," said Harriet, attempting to lighten the mood and change the subject entirely. "You appeared to enjoy yourself."

"Indeed, I believe it was a great success for both of us. Mr. Knightley spoke very highly of you. He approved of your dress and said you were very pretty indeed. He also mentioned that you were a delightful dancing partner."

"I too enjoyed our dance immensely and shall never forget his kindness," Harriet replied. She wondered if any mention would be made of their prolonged discourse, but it appeared that she would be spared having to explain her conversation with Mr. Knightley—at least, for the time being. "And what of Mr. Churchill?"

"What of him? He was courteous, to be sure, very handsome and gracious. Do not forget, it was he who had proposed having a ball in the first place. Mr. Weston wished to please his son—and rightly so."

"Yes, but did you enjoy his company, Miss Woodhouse?" Harriet asked.

"I suppose I did, though he did not seem to enjoy *mine*! He flittered about from one lady to another, acting more like the host than the honored guest. He even had a dance or two with Jane Fairfax. But what say you about the Eltons? They seemed bound and determined to spoil it all!" Miss Woodhouse cried. "Whatever did the vicar mean by refusing to stand up with you? I hope you no longer feel the injury of Mr. Elton's false representation."

"No, of course not. I feared *you* felt the injured party, after all; his deception was geared more toward you than me, Miss Woodhouse. He had no notion of my existence other than being your friend. I cannot fault you for wanting to make the match, nor can I fault him for his preference."

"You are too good, Harriet. I led you to believe that you had captured his heart. I was so certain of it!"

"I shan't say I was wholly untouched by the whole affair. I wanted so much to form an attachment—I suppose one cannot force these emotions, no matter how much one longs for it, or holds on to the illusion. I may as well confess something to you now, Miss Woodhouse, for I have been ashamed for some time."

"I cannot imagine anything you could have done that would cause shame!"

"I have kept some items of Mr. Elton's as treasures, nothing of value, to be sure. They were simple things—things that a child would have stored in a keepsake box. In truth, it is precisely where I placed them, along with that old rag doll that I brought to Mrs. G.'s so long ago."

"Oh, Harriet…"

"No—pray, be at ease. That is what I wished to say. I have discarded them, one and all. What care I about a bit of bandage or a useless pencil, the bit without any lead? They are meaningless, as a match between myself and Mr. Elton would have been."

"I begin to see that you may be right. There is a littleness about him, and I had not realized it before."

Harriet nodded her agreement. "There would have been no understanding between us; he would have been the lord of the household, my superior in every way. We have no shared history or heritage. In short, we have nothing in common, and where there is no friendship and mutual respect, there can be no love."

Harriet observed Miss Woodhouse carefully and hoped that her countenance would show compassion and understanding. When she was confident that her friend was not vexed, Harriet continued her speech, taking advantage of the present situation that held them in seclusion.

"I fully comprehend your fear of the people I met with today," said she, "but I would have you consider my opinion on the matter. There was something to their story that touched me, Miss Woodhouse. I imagined how they felt, being so far from home, strangers in this land—everyone suspicious of them and wishing them away."

"But *you* are not a stranger, you are not some foreign person who needs to explain or defend herself to the residents of Highbury."

"That is precisely who I am!" cried Harriet. "Mr. Elton has discovered the truth about me and mine. When the rest of our friends and neighbors hear of it, I will be no different than those who live on the edge of society."

Miss Woodhouse shook her head in disagreement, but Harriet saw something in her eyes, and that silent agreement gave her courage to continue. She spoke of meeting Sofia, an Israelite living at the abbey. Harriet shared the maid's story, divulging the horrific tale of the woman's murdered family. She explained how Sofia, her sister, and her cousin came to live at Donwell.

"They were in residence, *in the abbey*, when my mother gave birth to me. These foreigners may have heard my first cries, they may have seen my first steps, or heard me utter my first words."

"But Harriet," Miss Woodhouse whispered, "they are servants."

"They are more my family than my own flesh and blood. They are Israelites, like my own people. They *are* my people."

Chapter Eighteen

The summer months offered many opportunities for reading and writing, picking flowers, creating memories— all in all, a time for appreciating the beauty of one's surroundings and gathering one's thoughts. As most of the girls were at their homes for the season, Harriet was at her leisure and had time to partake in all and sundry.

She had great admiration for Miss Woodhouse; having benefited from her kindness and generosity for nearly a year complete. Ever since she had unburdened her heart to her friend, Harriet had felt a sense of relief. Perhaps now Miss Woodhouse would truly see her for herself—and not as a project or a pleasant diversion.

That being said, there were certain subjects that were delicate and required prodigious consideration. They required a perspective that Miss Woodhouse could not afford. Harriet had not ceased to admire her friend, nor did she find fault in her character. She merely applied a lesson learned from Mrs. Goddard's practices. '*Each child is precious to God*'—it was up to the teacher to find the student's strengths, and not to concentrate on undesirable attributes. Understanding Harriet's predicament simply was not one of Miss Woodhouse's strengths.

Midweek, on a bright and sunny afternoon, Harriet found herself again in Rabbi Kolman's company. If the gentleman was surprised to see her, he was kind enough not to let on. His wife, the *rebbetzin*, had prepared tea and cakes as was her wont for this time of day. It was their custom to sit together and review the congregation's needs once a week—which family had been blessed with a new child, which family prepared for a loved one's passing. While enjoying a cup of tea, a bit of cake or *mandelbroit*, they reviewed the calendar for holy days and discussed the upcoming Torah portions. The rabbi relished including his wife's perspective in his weekly sermons.

Mrs. Kolman set another place at the table as her husband extended the invitation. Timid at first, Harriet had begun to think of an excuse to beg off, but some deeper feeling prompted her to accept the kind offer. She would allow herself this opportunity to form a new acquaintance.

"It is a pleasure to meet you, Mrs. Kolman," Harriet said as the rabbi offered her a seat. "Pray forgive me, I did not mean to interrupt your afternoon. My thoughts are only for myself these days; I tend to forget that others have their own needs and wants to attend."

"You are very welcome," said the rabbi's wife. "I can confer with my husband at another time if you would prefer to speak with him about a private matter—"

"No, indeed. Pray, do not leave on my account. I am certain to ramble on indefinitely. You see, I do not have the privilege of having my own mother and father to guide me, and there are certain thoughts that keep me awake and fill my days and, well…I would prefer not speaking with Mrs. Goddard or Miss Woodhouse—oh! You are most likely not acquainted with either…and, you see, I *am* rambling."

Husband and wife shared a smile while tea was poured and cake was sliced and plated. The rabbi asked Harriet to proceed with any matter of concern. He and Mrs. Kolman would be glad to be of service when and if it was required.

Setting down her plate, Harriet began telling the couple about the ball at The Crown. She began with the fact that poor, old Mr. Woodhouse remained at home, for he would not journey out of doors in the evening, unless it was absolutely necessary. She told them about kind Mrs. Bates and Miss Bates and Mr. and Mrs. Weston.

Harriet spoke of Miss Woodhouse for over a quarter of an hour, explaining their friendship in the best possible light. She expressed, however, a growing desire to merit recognition of her own—yearning for the day she would not live in Hartfield's shadow. That conversation led to the embarrassing scenario created with Mr. Elton, leading to *Mrs. Elton's* dissatisfaction and contempt.

"Their behavior is quite astonishing, and I should be ashamed of myself if I were they. Mrs. Elton is a lady of quality! Oughtn't she know how to conduct herself appropriately rather than insulting this person and that person and taking on airs?"

Harriet went on to discuss Mr. Frank Churchill, who had lived with his aunt for the vast majority of his life. Harriet explained that half the town believed Mr. Churchill and Miss Woodhouse would make a perfect match, but she had begun to believe that something odd was afoot!

"I do confess, I cannot say that Miss Woodhouse cares for the young man, and he now appears to care for someone else entirely! Only, he will not come out and say—and it certainly is not my place to mention it."

Speaking of matches and perfect couples could only bring one person to mind. Harriet timidly mentioned Mr. Martin and how their friendship grew during her visit last summer.

"But then he wrote a letter and apologized for giving rise to feelings that oughtn't be felt…and—and Miss Woodhouse did not approve the match, though I believe Mr. Knightley would not have minded it so much!"

Having mentioned Mr. Knightley, Harriet felt it only

right to continue with her explanation—though Mr. George Knightley, whom everybody admired and respected—needed no introduction. The gentleman was attentive to the Bateses, Miss Fairfax, Mr. Woodhouse, and even to herself.

"He danced with me at the ball and saved me from being the talk of the town! He danced with Miss Woodhouse afterward. I was very pleased to see them together. They are such dear friends—so much like brother and sister—yet, on the other hand, not at all."

When she finally took a breath, Mrs. Kolman poured a fresh cup of hot tea, expecting Harriet's throat to be parched and sore. Seeing his chance, Rabbi Kolman removed his glasses, wiped them with a piece of linen, and began speaking.

"Miss Smith, you have provided us with some interesting knowledge, and I must say, it may take me a day or two to review it and understand it and provide you with guidance, if indeed it is necessary. However, one bit of your soliloquy caught my attention. What is this about Mr. Martin?"

Before Harriet could reply, Mrs. Kolman shook her head and said, "No."

She stood, pushing her chair away from the table and moving to her husband's side.

"Yosef, I believe duty calls." She shuffled his papers together and gathered his books. "You will let me know what needs doing afterward. Now is not the time, for I have decided to have a nice coze with Miss Smith."

"But the young lady came to see me!" The rabbi laughed as he followed his wife's directives.

"Husband, as the saying goes: you are smart, smart, smart—but you are not *so* smart!"

Mrs. Kolman poured herself another cup of tea, sliced another piece of cake, and bade Harriet to commence where she had left off. With such an invitation, it was nearly impossible for Harriet to do otherwise—and why would she?

She started at the very beginning, explaining how she came to stay with the Martins last summer. She spoke of her growing admiration for Mr. Martin and his gentle, considerate manner. Harriet closed her eyes and recalled all the precious moments spent in Mrs. Martin's kitchen. The laughter, the aromas—some familiar, some tantalizingly new. She recalled observing the family while they welcomed the Sabbath on Friday evenings—a multitude of questions went unanswered, for there was never sufficient time on the farm.

Unable to hold back her emotions, tears flowed freely when she finally told the story about her birth.

"Perhaps the rabbi already shared this with you, Mrs. Kolman," said she, "but it does feel better saying it aloud once more. It seems the more I affirm it, the more it feels...intimate—*familiar*. I am a Jewess."

"My dear Miss Smith, my husband does not discuss private conversations with me or anyone else for that matter. I am honored to hear your story from your own lips and will be pleased to help you—not only as the rabbi's wife, but as a friend."

Mrs. Kolman picked up her husband's writing instruments and a fresh sheet of paper. "We shall make a list, you and I. We shall write down all of your questions about Shabbat, about recipes—about love and marriage—and I will happily answer the best I can." She smiled as she numbered and lined the page.

Harriet began to express her gratitude, but this, the rebbetzin would not allow.

"Before you thank me, Miss Smith, I shall share the first lesson. You will find that in Judaism, for every question answered, another two questions take its place."

"How ever will I learn it all, Mrs. Kolman? I have started too late in life!"

The lady shook her head and laughed. "One is never too young or too old to learn, and if you think you may be able to *learn it all*, as you say, you are bound to be disappointed, my dear. Even the greatest rabbis do not know everything, though they would like us all to think they do! Now, let us get to work, shall we?"

~ヒ

The following Saturday, Harriet and the others gathered for the morning meal as was their custom. She had not made mention of her plans. There was no need to disclose the information. Those at school were accustomed to Harriet spending her days at Hartfield whenever time allowed. However, she had dressed in her finest Sunday clothes, and the girls thought she had confused the days on the calendar. It took a bit of fibbing, for Harriet did not want to reveal her true destination. She would eventually have to own up to it, but for now, the newness of it all, and her own insecurities and doubts, would not allow Harriet to be... *Harriet.*

She smiled, bobbed a curtsy, and dashed out the door, leaving Mrs. G. to manage the questions and teasing. Harriet made quick work of her walk to the synagogue. It was early yet, few people were on the streets; nonetheless, she was anxious as she took the staircase to the upper gallery—hoping that she had not been spied.

Mrs. Kolman had explained that the women of the congregation sat in a separate section. They were allowed, of course, to enter the main hall or sanctuary, but during prayer or services, the men sat below while the women sat above. The rabbi's wife could read the questions in Harriet's eyes and provided answers to the best of her abilities.

"You will find, Miss Smith, that there are varying interpretations to most everything in Judaism. We are children of Jacob, who, you will recall, struggled with an angel and God changed his name to Israel. It is within our nature to struggle, to question to offer different interpretations…but that is not the matter at hand, is it? We were speaking of the *mechitzah*, the separation between men and women in the synagogue. Some sanctuaries provide a curtain or some sort of shelving or barrier. Others, like ours, provide a balcony or upper gallery."

"Yes, but why? Why must we not sit with our family members or friends? Are we, as women, not invited to participate in the service?"

"No specific law requires the division, Harriet, but the tradition stems from our sacred text. Some sages say that the separation is needed to maintain morality. Others say that males come to this world at a spiritual disadvantage; their souls need greater instruction. Rabbi Kolman believes that prayer allows us to connect with our souls. Our souls, in turn, communicate with our God. It follows that this union between ourselves and the Holy One, the Supreme King of kings, leaves no room for a third—neither a wife, husband, teacher, nor a friend. We ought not be preoccupied with worldly distractions."

Harriet nodded her comprehension. In truth, she would not wish to sit amongst the men, for she feared seeing Mr. Martin in the congregation. Mrs. Kolman was correct. She *would* be distracted beyond measure. But sitting in the women's gallery had its own set of problems. Mrs. Martin and her daughters were certain to be there.

"You shall sit by me, Miss Smith," said the rebbetzin. "Perhaps if everyone keeps their eyes on their prayer books, there shan't be too much time for socializing until after services are over. At which time, you may try to escape the Martins' notice, or not, as you prefer."

It all started well and good. Harriet took the seat furthest from the other women and was gratified to see that the mothers kept their little ones close by and the older girls kept their eyes on their prayers in front of them—or closed as they listened to the chanting from below.

This contentment was short-lived, however.

No sooner than the chanting stopped, Harriet felt someone tugging on her wrap. She turned ever so slightly and saw that Miss Elizabeth Martin and her sister had exchanged seats and were now situated directly behind her place next to the rabbi's wife.

"Does Mrs. Goddard know of your whereabouts?" whispered Elizabeth Martin.

"No," Harriet whispered over her shoulder. "But I shall inform her soon enough."

Judith Martin would have questioned her next, but the chanting began again, and they were all to rise as the scrolls were removed from the ark.

Harriet took notice of each and every action. It was as if the men were completing a dance formation. One was instructed to remove the tapestry covering the scroll, another was instructed to chant some sort of blessing, for Harriet heard a resounding *amen* when the gentleman had concluded. Others swayed as they wrapped themselves, covered almost completely in their fringed prayer shawls.

Taking a long instrument fashioned in the shape of a hand with a pointed finger, the rabbi read from the scroll. The language was foreign to her ears, but not so unfamiliar that she could not recognize it as the same spoken in the Martins' house for their Sabbath celebrations.

Harriet recognized Mr. Trahtermann, the local bookbinder, as he joined the other men by the rabbi's side.

"Yes," confirmed Mrs. Kolman, "however, he was called to the *bimah*—the podium—by his Hebrew name: Reuven ben Yosef, or Ruben, son of Joseph."

"Why is that?"

"It is an honor to be called up to the *bimah*. It symbolizes an ascension from the mundane to the sacred; therefore, the colloquial name is set aside to give the occasion its due."

"It sounds a bit like being introduced to royalty," said Harriet, recalling stories of the knights of the realm.

"Precisely. When Mr. Trahtermann became a Bar Mitzvah, a Son of the Commandments, he read from the Torah as Reuven ben Yosef. He also used this name when he stood with his bride beneath the *chuppah*, the wedding canopy. Do you see, my dear?"

Harriet nodded. In some ways, it was similar to a christening; it sanctified one's entry into the community.

She kept still for over a quarter of an hour and witnessed as the scroll was rolled up and covered once again. There was another moment of silence—or rather, a moment when quiet murmurings commenced, for no one was truly silent—while the men continued their orchestrated ancient maneuverings. Another tug on Harriet's wrap had her peering over her shoulder.

"What do you do here?" Elizabeth persisted.

Something had to be said; it was solely a matter of saying as little as possible. Harriet glanced at the rebbetzin who nodded her acquiescence. "You know my nature. I am always curious."

"If you wished to indulge your *curiosity*, why did you not say?"

The question was one not easily answered. Her friendship with Elizabeth must suffer the consequences of her muddled relationship with Mr. Martin; and, undoubtedly, her newly formed acquaintance with the Rabbi and his wife must arouse curiosity. "I am here on Mrs. Kolman's invitation," Harriet replied. "Do me the courtesy of not informing your brother, I beg you."

With the rabbi's wife now in a private conversation with another congregant, Harriet risked addressing her friends once again.

"Since you are full of questions," she whispered, "I shall ask one of my own—pray, do not respond by asking *why*!" With their acquiescence, she proceeded to ask after their Hebrew names.

Elizabeth was first to reply. "I am named Elisheva bas Ruchel, after my great-grandmother."

"And I am Yehudit bas Ruchel," said her sister with some pride. "I am named for the great heroine of the Chanukkah story, and well—also for my mother's great aunt who lived in Plymouth."

"What is the meaning of *bas Ruchel*?" asked Harriet.

"It signifies that we are daughters of Rachel, our mother's name."

"I see. I once knew someone named Hannah. Her mother was Deborah," Harriet offered with not a little trepidation.

"Hannah was another brave heroine from the Chanukkah story," said Judith.

Harriet tucked that information away for another time. She would ask the rabbi, or look up the information herself, and would come to know this biblical Hannah. It was very likely she would never know *her* Hannah.

She was resigned to the truth now. Its acceptance made her stronger, for it had been the act of denial that had made her weak. Her mother would never be a part of her life. The cut was deep, but it was not as painful as before.

Perhaps, in some ways, there was healing in coming to the synagogue and hearing the words of her ancestors. Perhaps, like ascending to the *bimah*, her attendance today was a form of surmounting her past anguish. In this holy space, she honored her heritage, and it was good.

Chapter Nineteen

Having finally settled on a day for the picnic, with all the arrangements and accommodations handled by Mr. Weston, Harriet, along with Miss Woodhouse, were conveyed from Hartfield to Box Hill. Though it was a fine day, and it was only a seven-mile carriage ride, the general sentiment of the party was not equal to the occasion.

With recent events still fresh and tender, Harriet was not prepared to be in society; however, Miss Woodhouse refused to allow her to remain alone at home. After enduring a well-intended lecture on the perils of too much ruminating, Harriet was forced to acquiesce. However, she could not help but note that Miss Woodhouse had little enthusiasm for being one of the party herself. This alteration in demeanor gave Harriet pause.

For all that Miss Woodhouse was and for all that she represented, it was evident to Harriet that she was relied upon for more than just companionship. Miss Woodhouse relied upon her as a vehicle to promote her own courage, intelligence, influence, elegance, and who knows what! Harriet would not go so far as to say that Miss Woodhouse was disingenuous, but…*heavens*! She always seemed to get her own way.

They arrived on time, or more to the point, they arrived in a caravan, for Mr. and Mrs. Elton followed from the vicarage—Miss Bates and Miss Fairfax had not been forgotten this time. Mr. Weston, Mr. Churchill, and Mr.

Knightley came along on horseback, and as the gentlemen dismounted and the ladies were handed down, smiles and greetings were exchanged with great alacrity—but little feeling.

Harriet wondered at the entire expedition, the cost and the planning, the servants who had been discharged to feed and care for them...and yet, as she looked from one face to another, it was clear that no one was pleased. Mr. Weston took everyone to task for their lack of spirit. It was only due to his own jovial personality that the party attempted to be light and gay; but everyone, thought Harriet, was very dull indeed.

Miss Woodhouse and Mr. Churchill were downright insufferable, and she could not comprehend why either of them chose to attend. Was it possible that they had had a falling out? But that would have meant they had previously come to an understanding, and Harriet was certain she would have been told!

The servants provided blankets and shades and every manner of comfort. As the ladies settled their skirts and opened their parasols, Mr. Frank Churchill—the charming and attentive gentleman, not the irrational and unsatisfied gentleman—made an appearance. He flirted with everyone, made jokes, and offered riddles. He chose Miss Woodhouse as his particular muse, and they began to flirt excessively.

It was thought-provoking, to say the least. The rest of the party seemed equally needled by their infantile behavior—though no one would voice such an opinion. Harriet supposed it would have to be borne, for it was Miss Woodhouse and Mr. Churchill taking the lead, and Mr. Weston quite approved.

"Come now!" Mr. Churchill suddenly exclaimed. "We must do something to liven up this company! What say you, Miss Woodhouse? Shall we order everyone to talk?"

"Talk of what?" said she.

"You decide, madam; simply command, and we shall obey!"

Miss Bates, of course, laughed and approved at once, for she admired Miss Woodhouse above all. Mr. Knightley, Harriet observed, rolled his eyes, but it was Mrs. Elton who was most enflamed by the remark.

"I believed, as the vicar's wife—the only married lady of the party—I was to be chaperon, and I would have the authority, nay, the right, to organize appropriate entertainment."

"Quite right, Augusta!" Mr. Elton exclaimed.

Mr. Churchill would not give way and continued pestering and poking until he achieved the reaction he sought.

"I am ordered by Miss Woodhouse to speak in her stead. She requires that each of you share one very entertaining tidbit, two moderately clever things, or three very dull things in order that we all enjoy a hearty laugh."

It was originally understood to be a joke, but to continue in that way, suggesting that Miss Woodhouse was indeed the preferred lady of consequence, put everyone ill at ease. Harriet was uncomfortable, unable to understand the tension among people she thought to know. The playacting between Mr. Churchill and Miss Woodhouse was difficult to observe; it was unnatural, so forced.

Hoping to appease them both and lighten the mood, Harriet determined to say something that might be considered, if not moderately clever, at least moderately interesting.

"During my stay at Abbey-Mill Farm last summer, I learned something that you might consider entertaining," said she. "To be sure, I found it excessively diverting—at the time. You see, I learned that Israelites do not consume bacon."

"What, *never?*" cried Miss Bates. "I cannot recall the many times Mr. and Miss Woodhouse have blessed our humble household with a side of pork, Hartfield's finest, to be sure! Why, Mama and I would have to go without if not for their generosity. Perhaps the Martins have never had a proper piece of pork...oh dear! *That* is quite entertaining in and of itself—A *p*roper *p*iece of *p*ork!"

"It is not a matter of quality or cut, Miss Bates," Harriet replied. "They do not eat sausage, hock, or loin. Imagine not having bacon at breakfast or a nice slice of cold ham! Neither do they partake of meat of any kind with dairy, which I thought an oddity as well, but kind Mrs. Martin only had to mention her sweet Welch cow, whom she named Bronwyn. She said, 'Harriet, would it not be cruel to boil Bronwyn's calf in her mother's milk?' I still cannot countenance consuming cheese in my sandwich."

With not a little pride, Harriet believed she had fulfilled the request for something entertaining, but as she looked around the party, she found that none were engrossed by her comments. She sought Miss Woodhouse's gaze, hoping to find a modicum of approval, but only witnessed a sad smile.

"What a silly creature you are, Miss Smith. Imagine any one of us caring a whit what those people consume!" exclaimed Mrs. Elton.

"Your astonishment in this matter," Mr. Elton interjected, "reveals a shocking want of piety, Miss Smith. Does not Leviticus explain, in great detail, what the Israelites may or may not consume? Perhaps you ought to dedicate more attention to the scriptures."

"Never mind that now, vicar! Who shall be next?" Mr. Churchill demanded. "Come now, do not over-worry. Miss Woodhouse vows to be receptive to any and all!"

"I must be excused," said Mrs. Elton, "for I have nothing to compare with Miss Smith's Hebrews. I cannot attempt it—I am not fond of that sort of thing. *Miss Woodhouse* must excuse me."

It was not the first time, nor would it be the last, Harriet feared Mrs. Elton would attempt to give a cut-direct with one of her acerbic remarks. The lady expounded that, while her vivacity and brilliant conversation were always appreciated at Maple Grove, she ought not be expected to exhibit on demand, *particularly* in present company.

Closing her parasol and giving her gloved hand to her husband, she arose and prepared to quit the party.

"Jane, dear," she said, "would you care to join us? Miss Bates? We shall go for a short stroll while we await luncheon to be served. Let the *children* play as they will!"

With that, Mr. Weston signaled for the servants to prepare the meal. At least, they were guaranteed to have the choicest cuts of cold meats and the finest fruits. The bustle of plates, utensils, and tablecloths allowed for the appearance of a joyful time; however, the air was thick and tense, and Miss Woodhouse looked quite vexed.

When the Eltons returned, with Miss Bates and Miss Fairfax in tow, the remaining party endeavored to continue with the charade of being cheerful excursionists. They ate and drank Mr. Weston's good wine with great alacrity— anything to appear occupied and diverted! One and all would later say, '*A finer day had never been spent,*' but that would be to appease Mr. Weston alone.

Harriet hoped she would never be invited again to such a party and in such company. She was thankful she had only mentioned the Martins and said naught of the rabbi and his wife. She could only imagine what cruel and hurtful things Mr. and Mrs. Elton would have said then.

Harriet had only meant to share a harmless bit of

knowledge; it was her way—a coward's way, truth be told—to test the waters. She had been curious to know what the others would think of the Martins' customs, for in the course of time, it would be a commentary on what they would think of her.

~

In two days' time, it was arranged that Harriet should accompany Miss Woodhouse on her morning calls. Never mind that she had other plans, Mrs. G. encouraged Harriet to go along, for every moment spent in good company was well spent.

As if one's worth would greatly improve simply by accompanying Miss Woodhouse on her errands!

Whatever else, Harriet was dutiful and, for the most part, eager to please. She followed the familiar path to Hartfield, where she paid her respects to Mr. Woodhouse and complimented the gentleman on his new backgammon set. Then it was off to visit Miss Bates and her relatives, Harriet carrying a bouquet of freshly picked flowers from the Hartfield gardens and Miss Woodhouse with her basket of baked goods and jams.

Mrs. Bates greeted them as they were granted entry by Patty, the maid of all work. It was an unusual circumstance, to be sure. Neither Miss Fairfax nor Miss Bates were anywhere to be found, for Miss Fairfax was not feeling well enough to receive visitors, and Miss Bates was attempting to provide her niece comfort. Therefore, unlikely as it seemed, Mrs. Bates beckoned them upstairs and offered refreshment.

The lady ensured that the tea things were brought out, and while she poured, Mrs. Bates passed along the latest news along with slices of lemon seed cake.

"It seems we are to lose our Jane," said she. "She has accepted a position with a Mrs. Smallridge, a friend of a friend of Mrs. Elton's, I gather. It will have to do, for her other prospects have not come to fruition."

It was the longest speech Harriet had ever heard come from the widow's mouth. Here she thought Mrs. Bates was hard of hearing and unwilling to participate in conversation, but apparently, it was not so.

"Jane will be only four miles from Maple Grove, home to Mrs. Suckling and Mrs. Bragge and, of course, to Mrs. Elton, to whom we owe a debt of gratitude. Jane will have charge of three little girls and will be comfortable there, I am sure. Naturally, we shall miss her, but it is to her advantage, as I have insisted all the while. She oughtn't remain in Highbury under the present circumstances."

"We shall miss her, Mrs. Bates," said Miss Woodhouse and hushed Harriet when she whispered: *What circumstances?* "I am certain that Miss Fairfax will be successful; she is an extremely talented young lady. And who knows," Miss Woodhouse continued, "the future may have other plans for us all. Do we not always say, 'All good things come for those who wait'?"

"Our poor Jane has waited long enough, Miss Woodhouse," said Mrs. Bates.

Harriet sipped her tea and kept her counsel. She knew not how to add to the conversation. It was peculiar in more ways than one. Here sat Mrs. Bates, all a chatter and full of news. Miss Woodhouse was showering compliments upon the very woman who had always been a thorn in her side. Both Miss Bates and Miss Fairfax were nowhere to be seen, but their voices could be heard behind a closed door. Though originally Harriet had not wished to accompany Miss Woodhouse, it turned out to be an extraordinary morning after all.

The next instant, Patty entered the parlor and announced Mr. Churchill. Harriet spied on Miss Woodhouse to see if she blushed in anticipation but noted no anxious behavior. Harriet must have been wrong about the pair. She could detect no fine feeling between them.

"Good morning to all!" Mr. Churchill exclaimed. He removed his hat and bowed low to all the ladies, particularly Mrs. Bates. "I bring news!" Looking about the room, he noticed missing members from the party. "Where is Miss Fairfax? Miss Bates?"

Explanations were quickly provided, and a chair and cup of tea were offered, but Mr. Churchill would have none.

"I cannot stay. I am wanted at Randalls immediately, but I thought to stop by and share the ...*the news.*"

They waited for his next words, Mrs. Bates, Miss Woodhouse, and Harriet all. Would he not speak? Was it good news, or did he bring bad tidings? Perhaps he wished to spare their delicate feelings and was reconsidering his thoughts.

"I received an express from Richmond," said he, now crestfallen. "It was about my aunt. Mrs. Churchill is no more. Some sort of seizure has taken her from this life—I know not all the particulars."

There was a great cry of condolence, each lady offering her heartfelt sympathy to the young man, though he did not seem to hear.

"I—I must be away. Please inform Miss Fairfax—and Miss Bates, of course—for I will be off quite soon. I simply wished to pay my respects before leaving Highbury."

He departed as quickly as he descended upon them moments ago.

"Well, well. The great Mrs. Churchill is no more," said Mrs. Bates. "'*A good name is better than precious ointment, and the day of death than the day of birth.*'"

"Indeed," Miss Woodhouse replied. She arose, fixing her gloves and replacing her reticule upon her arm.

Harriet was not taken aback at this abrupt departure, for she knew her friend had little patience when one began quoting scripture. It was not that scripture made Miss Woodhouse uncomfortable; it was the fear of being expected to cite the reference and committing a grievous error in judgment.

"Pray," continued Miss Woodhouse, "send our regards to Miss Bates and Miss Fairfax. Miss Smith is expected elsewhere this morning, and I am certain you will have other callers. We shan't keep you."

"Please stay awhile, do," said Mrs. Bates. "No doubt, Jane and Hetty will keep to their beds, and we shan't have more company today, not now—now that Frank Churchill has come and gone. He will not call again today."

"Mr. Churchill is very attentive, is he?" said Miss Woodhouse.

"Oh yes, indeed. It is a shame that he has not been free to act as his heart dictates, but now that his aunt has died—"

"Mrs. Bates! I do not have the pleasure of understanding your meaning."

"Oh my, oh my!" The widow's eyes grew wide.

Astonished, Harriet gripped her cup and saucer, fearing she would let them fall. Mrs. Bates had spoken out of turn! Miss Woodhouse would not allow fresh gossip to go unheard and bade her to continue.

Bringing her weathered fingers to her lips, Mrs. Bates leaned over the tea things. "We must not be overheard," said she. "It is fortunate that Hetty knows nothing of the entire imbroglio, but Jane will be furious with me! Jane, of course, does not know that *I* know…"

"What?" Harriet insisted. "What is it that you know?"

"You must promise not to divulge the secret, at least not

until they make it publicly known, and then, of course, it shan't be a secret any longer!"

"Yes, yes, of course," said Miss Woodhouse. "What do you have to tell us?"

And then Mrs. Bates revealed the full of it.

"Our Jane and Frank Churchill have been secretly engaged these past months—since October!"

Her wrinkled eyes, usually dull and fixed upon some random feature, were fairly twinkling as Mrs. Bates told the story that was not hers to tell.

"They used *you*, Miss Woodhouse, as a distraction so that no one would suspect. It had been planned since Weymouth, in order to keep the truth from Mrs. Churchill. She would not have approved the match, you must understand."

"Good God!" Miss Woodhouse cried. "They have used us ill indeed!"

"Oh, Miss Woodhouse," said Harriet. "I ought to have said—" If only she had trusted her suspicions. If only she had held her own instincts in as high regard as she held the opinions of others "I had a notion that something was not quite right, but I had not thought it was my place to say..."

"How indelicate!" Miss Woodhouse exclaimed, showing no evidence of being attentive. "How cruel! And poor Jane! To suffer his attentions to another young lady all the while!"

"And Mr. Churchill! He too must have suffered, knowing that Mrs. Elton was securing a position for Miss Fairfax—and he, unable to prevent it, for fear of his aunt," said Harriet.

Mrs. Bates concurred with a girlish giggle. She affirmed that the pair were in misery for the most part—always in a state of concealment.

"No one knew," she divulged. "I found them out only because they believed I was asleep, or that I was inattentive to their scheming. But now, they have done. More's the pity, I say, for their little charade was the most diversion I have had in some time! *'All the world's a stage'*, as Shakespeare wrote long ago, *'and all the men and women merely players; They have their exits and their entrances...'"* The lady was overcome with laughter at her cleverness.

"Mrs. Bates," said Harriet, "are you quite well? I fear the excitement has you confused..."

"Not at all," said she. "I am fully aware of my own sensibilities—or lack thereof! I simply meant to say, with the advent of Mrs. Churchill's demise, I fear the play is over."

Unexpectedly and without preamble, Miss Woodhouse prepared to leave once more, and if Mrs. Bates was saddened by this sudden departure, she did not convey these sentiments to either young lady. Indeed, Harriet was ready to believe that Mrs. Bates was relieved at their departure, for she would now be able to prepare for the drama that was sure to unfold.

They had not yet reached the final step in the stairwell when Miss Woodhouse began to protest; however, rather than denouncing Mr. Frank Churchill—as Harriet believed to be the most rational target—Miss Woodhouse chose to rebuke the *least* provocative.

"That nerve of Mrs. Bates! She ought to be on stage. Why, she is a natural for Drury Lane! Always quiet and woolgathering—always pretending not to capture one's meaning or, worse yet, not hearing one's conversation. I cannot credit it," said Miss Woodhouse. "It has all been an act! She must have devised the plan years ago, in order not to have to listen to her ridiculous daughter speak nonsense!"

"Oh no!" cried Harriet. "That cannot be. Perhaps, it is only a matter of her age—something not of her doing, but rather, a symptom of her dotage."

"As you say. I am sure I have done with the lot of them.

They do not deserve another moment's consideration, not with their scheming ways and machinations."

"But, Miss Woodhouse, they are your friends…"

"Not another word, Harriet! I shall speak with Mrs. Weston regarding her step-son, for I am overwrought by deceptions just now."

"Very well. Where do we go from here?"

"I believe I shall leave off visiting the tenants for another day. Did you not have an engagement of your own? Shall I accompany you?"

For all that she complained earlier, Harriet would have preferred it if they had completed their rounds as planned. In that way, they would have returned to Hartfield, and she would have said her goodbyes. As it was, Harriet would have to be truthful and inform Miss Woodhouse of her arrangements.

"Indeed, and you are welcome to join me if you should like. I am for the synagogue to visit with the Kolmans."

"I cannot credit that announcement, Harriet. Truly, I am astonished!"

"Is it so very wrong? They are leaders of their community and have been nothing but kind and welcoming. I am certain they would be pleased to have you join us."

But Miss Woodhouse suddenly recalled another appointment and begged off. Kissing Harriet first on one check and then the other, she wished her friend a pleasant day and asked her to come to Hartfield on the morrow.

Adjusting her bonnet and fixing a smile upon her face, Harriet turned again to Broadway Lane. There, she was sure of excellent conversation and every comfort that could be afforded. Their affection, the warm attachment of Mrs. Kolman in particular, was all the more pleasing— considering the circumstances of Harriet's questionable upbringing. Indeed, she began to look upon the couple as her kinsmen—in truth, they were much like her godparents. *Naturally*, Harriet was drawn away by her engagements with Kolmans. Her newfound personage, her history and ancestry required further study and understanding, and if the result was a lessening of intimacy between herself and Miss Woodhouse, it would be for the best.

Their friendship would change in the most gradual, natural manner. Miss Woodhouse would no longer always be the superior advisor, and Harriet would no longer always be the eager apprentice. She did not wish to seem ungracious, for Miss Woodhouse had been a good friend when all was said and done. Harriet thought it not quite proper to reproach her; indeed, it was not her way, nor her right. Still, there was something desirable about an agreed-upon separation—if only that meant not spending every free moment with one another.

Chapter Twenty

"Poor woman!" cried Harriet. "Everyone was always vexed with Mrs. Churchill and, as it happens, always wishing her gone! Now that she is no longer of this world, they will mourn her and sing her praise. Never mind that her family only spoke ill of the woman for five and twenty years. I find it disheartening. Worse than that, I find it dishonorable!"

Rabbi Kolman and his wife could only nod their heads, for they were still in a state of confusion as of the moment Harriet came through their door. It was evident that something unsettling had occurred, but the young lady hadn't taken a breath for a quarter of an hour, and they had never heard anything like the story before.

"Now Mr. Churchill is free to marry, and everyone seems concerned for Frank and how *he* suffered, but will no one say that he and Miss Fairfax were heartless and uncharitable? Are they not to suffer the consequences for their inconsiderate behavior?"

"Forgive me, Miss Smith, but I am not altogether certain who the couple has harmed?" said the rabbi.

"To begin with, *Miss Woodhouse*! Her family and friends were ready to wish her joy for contracting such a match. Certainly, Mr. and Mrs. Weston favored bringing the two together. And just now, when we first learned the news, I believe Miss Woodhouse was too astonished for words! She refused to discuss the subject, which is so very unlike her. If there is something that Miss Woodhouse enjoys, it is speculating and measuring individuals, their preferences, and their circumstances."

"Was the young lady very much attached to this Mr. Churchill?" asked Mrs. Kolman.

Harriet paused. "I believe Miss Woodhouse might have longed to experience an attachment more than she wished to be attached to the gentleman himself."

"Perhaps, Miss Smith, it is a matter of hurt pride rather than an injury to her reputation or, Heaven forfend, her person."

Harriet nodded, biting her lip to hold back further banter. She would have to consider all that had occurred, for she was overwhelmed with emotion. Mrs. Kolman may have the right of it; yet the deception still needled her! Why should Mr. Churchill be acquitted simply because he had no victim? Were they all not *his victims*? Were they all not deceived?

Unable to hold her tongue, Harriet posed another question. "Mr. Churchill could not have known if he had won a young lady's heart with his charm and attentiveness. Miss Woodhouse, or, even I, could have found ourselves utterly at his mercy! What would he have said to Mr. Woodhouse if the gentleman challenged him for giving rise to certain expectations?"

"There are many stories in the Torah—or the Bible if you will—that speak of deception," said Rabbi Kolman. "Think of the Tree of Knowledge and the snake's trickery; think of Esau and Jacob's story or that of Laban and Jacob. We have been warned against *lashon hara*–the evil tongue of gossip— and the evil of telling falsehoods."

"*A lying spirit practices unrighteousness,*" Harriet recited.

"That is correct. I fear we risk committing such a sin by continuing this conversation, and yet—"

Mrs. Kolman laughed. "As I have said, Miss Smith, in the

study of Judaism, there is always another point to be made, another view to be considered."

"Wife," said the rabbi, "pray allow me to continue before I forget what I meant to say! The great sages have said there are certain times when it is permissible to lie. If, and I must emphasize the word, *if* the ultimate goal for the deception will allow a positive outcome, then, *and only then*, a falsehood may be permitted."

"In marrying Mr. Churchill, Miss Fairfax is saved from a life of penury," murmured Harriet. "And she marries for love."

"That would be a positive outcome, to be sure," said Rabbi Kolman, "though I am not certain it is sufficient justification—"

"Just so. They tricked us all!" Harriet exclaimed. "More importantly, Mr. Churchill deceived his aunt by hiding his true affections. He was *not* honorable."

"What need was there to deceive this woman? What hold did she have over the young man?"

"I would presume it was his inheritance. He was adopted by the Churchills as a babe when his own mother died. When Frank Churchill first came to Highbury, Miss Woodhouse explained the matter. He was brought up as his uncle's heir; thus, he took that family's name rather than keeping his own."

"Then, it would seem, this story revolves around more than just the young man's deception. There was also intimidation and coercion on the part of those who were meant to care for him. Would it have been honorable for Mrs. Churchill to withhold what was promised to the young man after a lifetime of commitment and devotion to the family?"

"I suppose that is a valid point, Rabbi. I had not thought of it in that light."

"My dear," said Mrs. Kolman, "it is only natural to feel these emotions. It has come as a great shock, to be sure. You are a young lady of remarkable character. Your Mrs. Goddard is to be commended, for it is not common to have faced such hardships and yet have such a pure and open heart."

With lips trembling and tears threatening to flow down her cheeks, Harriet could not utter a word. It had been a difficult morning—nay, it had been *difficult* for several months passed. She had enjoyed coming to see the Kolmans. They had received her with warmth and compassion, always ready to answer her questions and to encourage, but never to compel her in one direction or another.

"I do not deserve such praise, for I have been unjust," she murmured. "I have held strong feelings against Miss Fairfax and Mr. Churchill but have misnamed the sentiment. It is not anger. It must be given its true name: Envy."

"Why, Miss Smith!" exclaimed the rabbi. "That is rather harsh. Why should you say such a thing?"

"Because it is true! How fortunate they are; she is a beautiful and talented young lady, and he is a charming and handsome young man. It is a love match, and what is more, there is no impediment to their future happiness—not now, in any event."

"Do *you* wish to marry, Miss Smith?" asked the rabbi.

Harriet nodded her reply.

"And what impedes your future happiness, my child?"

"Mr. Martin will not offer for me. Indeed, he reproaches himself for feelings that, he believes, are better set aside and forgotten. Though it cannot be denied that we care for one another, Mr. Martin has made it necessary for us to suffer the loss of an attachment without ever enjoying its advantages."

"You have not told him of your recent discoveries?" Mrs. Kolman asked.

Unable to speak, Harriet shook her head with the smallest possible motion. Her reply was too painful even for this acknowledgment.

Rabbi Kolman raised his bushy brow to his wife. "Miss Smith, you have been studying with us for some time. I have questioned you and have been quite satisfied with how you have replied. Certainly, if you would wish it, my wife may supervise the ritual ceremony of purification in the *mikveh*. We may even request that the rabbinical court in London review and make a determination of your case. However, dear girl, the decision of whether or not you are a Jewess is yours to make."

"Dear Miss Smith—Harriet," said Mrs. Kolman, "choose your path carefully, not for Mr. Martin's sake, but for your own connection with your God."

"And, if I do choose this path," said Harriet, "how will I explain it all to Mr. Martin? I have kept this great secret from him. I have nothing but second-hand stories to offer as evidence of my birth. What if he questions the validity of my claim?"

"King David's lineage was also questioned…"

"King David! *Always King David!*" Mrs. Kolman exclaimed. "Miss Smith, have you never read *The Book of Ruth*? I encourage you to read the passage. Be courageous and follow Ruth's example."

The rabbi smiled and took his wife's hand in his. "Sound advice, Rabbi Kolman—that is to say, *Mrs. Kolman*."

Chapter Twenty-One

With her heart pounding and matching the determination of her rushed footsteps, Harriet arrived at Hartfield. There had been much left unsaid yesterday morning, allowing for unnecessary speculation between the two women. Had they not learned that, left unaddressed, these wild imaginings always ended badly. Certainly, the tangled web of deception and matrimonial machinations had caused enough grief and humiliation. All things being equal, Harriet would rather deal with ten hard truths than just one lie. More than anything, she wished for comprehension. She wished to clear the air.

"Well, Miss Woodhouse!" cried Harriet, coming eagerly into the room. "Have you had sufficient time to reflect on yesterday's scandalous tittle-tattle? Was it not the oddest news that ever was?"

"If yesterday's news was odd, as you say," Miss Woodhouse replied, "I believe *your* reaction to the entire situation is odder still!"

Having carefully examined her behavior, Harriet hadn't found fault with her actions the previous day, certainly nothing of note or particular concern. She gazed upon Miss Woodhouse and encouraged her to provide further elucidation. Yet, none was offered.

"Had you any idea, Miss Woodhouse?" Harriet asked with some trepidation. "You have the talent of seeing into everybody's heart. I thought, perhaps, you knew more about Mr. Churchill and Miss Fairfax than you let on."

But Miss Woodhouse remained silent. She made for the tea things, busily arranging plates and napkins and feeling if the pot had cooled to the point where she would have to call for another. Finally, she looked back at Harriet, who awaited her reply.

"My dear, I have no such talent! I believe Mr. Knightley was correct when he stated as much so many months passed. I was certain that you and Mr. Elton would suit. I was wrong. I encouraged you to set aside your feelings, not once, but twice. I was wrong, and I am sorry for it."

"Twice?" said Harriet. "I cannot blame you for wanting to see me happily settled. Mr. Elton seemed the ideal candidate though he proved to be unworthy and duplicitous. Pray, who might the other be?"

"You know very well that I speak of Mr. Churchill!" Miss Woodhouse cried. "You had every reason to care for him. Indeed, I had it from your own lips when you spoke of his service to you."

What was the meaning of this new misunderstanding? Were they never to understand one another?

"Dear Miss Woodhouse! Let us speak plainly, for I am astonished that you could have mistaken me on this point. I never meant to give rise—to *insinuate* that I cared for Frank Churchill!"

"Mistake you? To whom were you referring then?"

"We agreed never to name *him*—you made yourself quite clear on that subject—but I should not have thought it possible that I could be supposed to mean any other person! I feel that he and I are meant for each other, just as Mrs. Bates once said: it was *bashert*. Do you remember that night we were all here at Hartfield? Mrs. Bates surprised the party when she said one simple word in reference to Dr.

Martsinkovsky and his bride. They were meant to be!"

"Please, Harriet!" cried Miss Woodhouse. "You and I have failed miserably to communicate in English, let alone some foreign language. Let us understand each other now without using idioms that may or might not be known to Mrs. Bates. Tell me at once. Is it possible—or am I mistaken once again—that you are speaking of Mr. Martin?"

"To be sure! Indeed, I never truly could have thought of anybody else. I thought you understood, especially when we last spoke of him. I thought it was quite clear!"

"No, not *quite clear* by any means," replied Miss Woodhouse. "If anything, I was certain that you spoke of his gallant service—the service that Frank Churchill provided when you were injured."

Miss Woodhouse recreated the scene as if she were at her easel painting a picture, reminding Harriet of what was witnessed through the drawing room window that day. Frank Churchill held her gently in his arms upon his noble steed. He appeared to be a knight of old, and Harriet was the injured damsel, laying her head upon his broad shoulder.

"I remember it perfectly. He assisted you to dismount, never taking his eyes from your countenance, ashen with shock and fear. You, with tears overflowing, thanked him again and again. Harriet, you trembled in his arms!"

"It was a natural emotion! The tears were due to the pain that I had endured, the trembling was from the fright of sitting atop such a large animal! Your memory is correct, but you have mistaken any connection between myself and Mr. Churchill!"

"As you say." Miss Woodhouse paused in the attempt to regain her composure. "You have made your point, Harriet, but tell me now, to what service were you referring with regard to Mr. Martin?"

It seemed worth repeating, once and hopefully, for the last time. Harriet would bear her soul and pray that this time, Miss Woodhouse would have the courtesy of not trampling over it. Harriet's memories of Mr. Martin were precious. She had kept each and every kindness in her heart; every action, every attention were safely stored away to think upon and cherish whenever she had the need.

Harriet spoke of that fateful day when she had walked to Ford's and got caught in a torrential storm.

"I came upon Mr. Martin; he was nothing short of courteous and attentive. He was genuinely concerned for my well-being. Though he teased me for being caught unprepared in the rain, he took the time to ensure my safe return home. Mr. Churchill did perform a service, that much is true, but it was forced, and he was inconvenienced by it. I felt it exceedingly! He brought me to Hartfield and fairly dropped me by your side before running away! His actions are nothing to Mr. Martin's. *His* is the service I treasure; his actions were noble benevolence and showed a generosity of spirit. He cared not if I had moved into a different sphere—into your circle and society. It mattered not that I was now always at my leisure with exalted friends, enjoying dinners, dances, and picnics—while he toiled to earn his daily bread. Believing we could never marry, he still honored me with kindness and respect. That service made me feel how superior he was to every other man."

"Gracious!" cried Miss Woodhouse. "I should have been a better friend to you, Harriet. If you had accepted Mr. Elton or Mr. Churchill, I see now that you would have done so for the wrong reasons. You would have done so to please me while your heart was held by another! Had I suggested *Mr. Knightley* himself as a potential suitor, you might have capitulated, but he would not have been first in your affections."

Harriet laughed, imagining a time when that gentleman would ever come in second best.

"It is rather ridiculous to believe Mr. Knightley and I would ever suit!"

"Come, come now," said Miss Woodhouse, "I saw the two of you speaking quite intimately on several occasions. We have spoken of every topic imaginable, yet you have not said a word about your conversations with Mr. Knightley. I shall not hold it against you, Harriet—heaven knows, I have failed you in many ways—is there something you wish to confess?"

Harriet was ill prepared for the accusation but rallied quickly once she realized that sharing the truth would not be impolitic.

"There is nothing to confess, Miss Woodhouse, for in speaking with Mr. Knightley, I harmed no one. The information I shared was mine to do with what I liked. After some consideration, I thought it best to come forward and inform Mr. Knightley of my news. After all, he was a member of the household when I came to Donwell. I—I wanted him to know the truth from me, and I promised myself that I would accept whatever judgment he imposed."

"Judgment? Why should Mr. Knightley judge you? You are an innocent in this matter. And as far as your…heritage, nothing need be done. Mr. Knightley is a gentleman; he will not betray your trust and will not speak of the matter."

"Of that, there is no doubt. Mr. Knightley's superior education in the ways of the world, his gentility and gentlemanly manners permit him to show respect and kindness to those that others may scorn."

"I am humbled by your admonishment, Harriet, even if you try to dissemble your meaning. I own I have been too proud. I have been uncaring for those beneath my social standing. Mr. Knightley has often pointed out the error of my ways. In your defense of the gentleman, I cannot help but imagine that you hold a *tendre* for him."

"Even if there were the slightest possibility that Mr. Knightley would offer for me—and he would not, for his heart belongs to another—I could not accept him!" Pausing to moderate her tone, Harriet carefully considered her next words. She would have her friend understand.

"I have come to learn what matters most in life, Miss Woodhouse," said she. "Love of family, roots, connection—I would have those things with Mr. Martin and his family. There is no need to dissemble; I am firm and resolved to settle the question."

"What question is that, Harriet? I promise I will endeavor to provide my full support."

"After many months of attentive study with the Kolmans, I have come to terms with my past—and my future. You see, I have forgiven my mother and father. I am no longer angry or resentful but have decided to be grateful for the many blessings I have received instead. I attempted it once, but did not pursue the task. If I were to begin again, to list all those who have cared for me and ensured my health, happiness, and well-being, I would soon run out of paper and ruin my pen!"

"Pray ensure my name is not included on your list, Harriet. I fear I do not deserve it."

"That is nonsense. You have taught me many things, and without your introduction into Highbury society, I would have never experienced a world that was wholly out of my reach."

"And yet, you are happiest in entering the marital state with Mr. Martin—never minding the great disparity of the match."

"If Mr. Martin accepts my offer of marriage, I should count myself fortunate indeed. We are equally paired, and—if you would allow me to try my hand at match-making, I believe you and Mr. Knightley are equally so. As I referenced earlier, I believe you already have his heart."

"Oh, Harriet! Now *you* are speaking nonsense!"

"I think not," said she. "You are not so much like brother and sister after all. I believe there is true affection between you—if only you would set aside your list of *disparities* and reasons that you would not suit."

"Name them if you dare!"

"To start with, you would list your father as the first *contra*. You would not wish to leave him, for he would feel abandoned. Little Henry would be next on your list, for you would not wish him to lose his place as heir apparent. I think the next reason might hit the hardest, and I pray that you forgive my impertinence. You have said few women are half as much mistress of their husbands' homes as you are of Hartfield. You admitted to never expecting to be so truly beloved as you are now in your father's eyes. In marrying Mr. Knightley, you shall have to learn to compromise; you shall have to accept that his tenants, the harvest, or any number of problems may need to come first in his attentions."

"These are all truths," murmured Miss Woodhouse. "I cannot deny it."

"Nay, they are only obstacles you have secured into place, most likely to protect your heart and much-beleaguered spirit. If I have learned anything these many months past, it is that we are not alone in our struggles. Divine Providence plans everything and oversees *everything*, but the choice to be happy and strive to fulfill one's dreams is left up to us."

"You once said that you feared being ridiculous. Do you recall the conversation?" Seeing Harriet's nod, Miss Woodhouse continued with fierce determination. "You said you should be an old maid, quite like Miss Bates one day, for no one would wish to marry a chatterbox such as yourself. In *my infinite wisdom,* I thought I was the appropriate person to encourage your growth, both in character and with your social connections. I believed myself superior in all the essentials." Miss Woodhouse took her young companion's hands and held fast." Harriet, I was wrong."

Chapter Twenty-Two

Though she had never traveled outside the county, Harriet believed Surrey to be the most magical of places, as the autumn colors began to paint its wooded areas in shades of orange, yellow, and red. Rain had fallen during the night, the wind scattering leaves that were not ready to fall. She stepped carefully, avoiding puddles and slippery stones, as she made her way through town when Donwell Abbey came into view.

She crossed the meadow and followed alongside the stream, its waters glistening in the sun like so many precious gems. Standing majestically to one side, the folly announced she was near, but Harriet did not require a sign or marker to know her way about. Abbey-Mill Farm lay just beyond the low stone wall.

Harriet had asked for a sign from above in her morning prayers, a sign to indicate that her plans had met with His approval. She hadn't asked for a dove, a rainbow, or even a bolt of lightning, only that she may be able to recognize it— to feel it within her soul. Harriet had walked only a few steps upon the farmland when she saw Mr. Martin in the fields. He was alone; neither sister accompanied him nor fieldhand or shepherd. Here was Harriet's sign. She knew it; she felt it as she waved her greeting to the man she loved.

Upon seeing her approach, Mr. Martin made to meet her. Removing his hat, he smiled and bowed low as she reached his side. "Good morning, Miss Smith. What do you do here? Is something amiss?"

"Not at all! It is a lovely day for a walk, and I—no, I shan't make any excuses!"

Mr. Martin fumbled with his hat, his hands seeking an occupation though there was no clear understanding of what was wanted.

"Certainly, you do not require an excuse to come to call, Miss Smith," said he. "My sisters and mother are always glad to receive you."

"Oh, if you knew how much I love everything that is decided and open!" She cried.

Mr. Martin's countenance reflected his confusion and disappointment; Harriet had to paused to collect her thoughts. She meant no disrespect to Elizabeth or any members of his dear family, but her words for solely for him.

"I have done us both a great disservice," said she. "If you would but grant me a few moments of your time, I mean to rectify the situation at once."

"I do not have the pleasure of following your meaning, Miss Smith," he replied.

Harriet felt herself blush under his gaze but would not allow herself to falter. There has been so much secrecy, so blatant and contrived. No longer would she live this life of deceit.

"I have done with being ashamed and worrying about my place in society, Mr. Martin. I shan't be swayed by my history or my circumstances any longer. If nothing else, Mr. Frank Churchill has shown me that I must take the reins to secure my own happiness."

"Mr. Churchill? Pray, forgive me, Miss Smith. He is not a person I think about from one minute to another."

"He is to be married, sir."

"He, then, is a most fortunate man!" cried Mr. Martin. "We are of an age, I believe, but that is where our similarities end. He chooses a wife, and she accepts. There are no complaints or criticisms to stay their progress. Everything is in his favor!"

"You speak as if you envied him."

"And I do, Miss Smith, I do envy him."

"Then hear me, Mr. Martin, for I shall tell you why you ought not."

Harriet waited for him to acquiesce, to ask her for further explanation but he remained silent, abusing his hat with his restless hands.

"You will not ask me, sir? Are you so determined to allow envy to wallow in your soul? You believe yourself to be wise, to allow things to remain as they are? Well, I am determined to speak, Mr. Martin!"

"I pray you do not. I fear you shall tell me that you are to marry. I fear that I shall be obliged to wish you joy! Pray, take a little time to consider your words before you wound me in such a harsh a manner."

She realized then that Mr. Martin had misaligned the pieces of the puzzle. Given the circumstances, he took the information and managed to come up with the only conceivable solution.

And it pained him.

He did not yet know that Harriet held the answer to their prayers; it was in her power to solve the riddle, to make the puzzle complete.

"Will you listen, sir?" Harriet entreated.

"Speak openly, Miss Smith," he murmured then. "You and I used to be able to converse about a great many things. I often recall the time you were with us on the farm; those memories are precious to me. In honor of that shared history, I shall hear whatever you wish to say."

"I thank you, Mr. Martin. I fear I may, indeed, wound you, but it will not be long lasting! You see, I have been carrying on in perfect secrecy for many months. Something of great importance was revealed, but I had not the courage to share it. I, who at all times cries out for openness and simplicity, have been in league with someone of superior experience who asked me to shield the truth of my birth. In short, Mr. Martin, I know the names of my parents. And what is more, I know that I am a Jewess, for my mother Hannah is a Jewess, as was her mother before her."

"But—but, why did you not say?"

"Because I was uncertain of how it would be perceived by Highbury society. Because Miss Woodhouse insisted that I seek advancement and make a good match. Because I did not know if I would be accepted by the congregation or— more importantly—by you."

"My dear Miss Smith! Can you be in earnest? But what of your upbringing? You have been an Anglican the whole of your life."

"This is true; I have been living amongst Gentiles and following the ways of their church. I have known kindness and goodness and absolute forgiveness. However, I am what I am. Rabbi Kolman and his wife have explained many things to me. I have celebrated the Sabbath with your sisters on several occasions. I have even experienced the *mikveh* with Mrs. Kolman's help."

"You have been studying all this time? The *mikveh* as well? I—I do not understand. Have you undergone a conversion?"

"No, a conversion was not necessary. The rabbi was satisfied with the evidence provided, thanks to Mrs. Goddard and the Jews of Donwell Abbey. However, I wanted to experience a separation of sorts—something that marked my return...*home*."

She wished to take hold of his hand, but believed it to be too forward. Mr. Martin appeared to have the same desire; however, he would not move. He appeared utterly astounded. Harriet began to fear that she had waited too long to speak her truth. Had she lost her chance at happiness?

No! I shall not give up now.

"Let me say this plainly, Mr. Martin," she began. "Once, not so long ago, you expressed some tender feelings for me. However, you spoke only of impediments. I say to you now: there are no impediments to our happiness. That is if you would have me."

"*You* are offering for *me*?"

"Indeed, just as Ruth did in days of old. She would not wait until Boaz made up his mind to act. Like Ruth, I do not wish to go another day without being my true self. If you will have me, I shall gladly be your wife. Your people shall be my people, and your God shall be my God."

Being a man so much in love, Mr. Martin could do naught but accept.

Mrs. Goddard had prepared her best parlor for the day's event. Though it was near winter, she filled the room with marigolds, sweet violets, and even some Jerusalem sage. The guest of honor had been kept away until all was made ready; silverware was polished, the prettiest linens were prepared, and only the best tea service would be laid out.

Harriet had asked permission to host a gathering, and Mrs. Goddard was only too pleased to open her home to whomever the bride wished to invite. One of her girls was to be wed! Mrs. Goddard would not have it said that she did not provide a proper send-off.

When it was nearly time for the guests to arrive, Harriet was called down. She wore her best gown, one that Miss Woodhouse had declared her most attractive. Emily Bickerton helped her with her hair and arranged Harriet's fair curls just so. She wished to be in her best looks this day. Mrs. Martin was coming to call, along with her daughters. Harriet had invited Sofia Bereznickas and her elder sister, along with Mrs. Kolman. Harriet hoped to unite this circle of women who had played a tremendous role in her life. Miss Woodhouse's invitation had been the first one penned, but Harriet was not at all certain she would attend.

"You shall be in the company of Mrs. Goddard," Harriet had said when they met the other day at Ford's. "Miss Nash and Miss Bickerton shall be there as well."

"I thank you for the invitation, Harriet, dear. I shall have to check my agenda."

Of course, Harriet understood her meaning. She knew very well that Miss Woodhouse did not require an agenda to keep up with her social activities. But she would not allow her happiness to depend on her friend's approbation. If she could not—or would not—accept her new family, then Harriet would know how to act.

The women began arriving, and soon, the tea things were brought out, along with the delectable treats that Cook had been lovingly prepared. Mrs. Goddard made everyone feel quite at home, and soon, the elders were seated together, sharing recipes and condoling with one another for this pain or that. The younger girls spoke of Harriet's plans.

"Miss Jane Fairfax and Mr. Frank Churchill have had the banns read in the Campbell's parish," said Miss Nash. "When shall your banns be read, Harriet?"

Though it may have been uncomfortable to own it, Harriet explained that the time-honored tradition was not practiced in her new congregation. Indeed, it was not a requirement for Jews, for they were considered dissidents by the Crown. Harriet looked to Mrs. Kolman for help, but the lady did not appear eager to intercede.

Perhaps Mrs. Kolman was uncomfortable in *mixed* company, thought Harriet. Perhaps Miss Woodhouse was right all along. Perhaps it was best for all to remain in one's circles of acquaintances and be at ease. *Perhaps* that was so, but that knowledge did not remove the sting of Miss Woodhouse's absence.

Just then, when Harriet had begun to second guess her campaign to unite this all and sundry assembly, another guest was announced. Miss Woodhouse arrived in her best walking dress and pelisse, carrying an umbrella on one arm and a large, wrapped box in another.

"Pray, forgive my tardiness! I was just on my way hither when an express arrived from London." Placing the package on a near table, Miss Woodhouse took a seat alongside Harriet. "What did I hear upon entering the foyer?" said she. "Am I mistaken, or did I hear the word *dissident* spoken in Mrs. Goddard's house?"

Harriet had hoped that that particular conversation would have been set aside with the lady's unexpected entrance.

"We were speaking of different marriage rituals," said Elizabeth Martin. "You see, certain regulations do not apply to Jews."

"Neither do they apply to Quakers nor any other group of nonconformists. Jane and Mr. Churchill, Harriet, and Mr. Martin—and, if I may add myself and Mr. Knightley to the growing list of brides and grooms—each of us, in our own unique way, have behaved the *enfant terrible*. Clandestine engagements, concealed emotions—we have proven to be quite unconventional."

"'But love is blind, and lovers cannot see, the pretty follies that *themselves commit, for if they could Cupid himself would blush.'"* Mrs. Goddard recited. "Shakespeare understood this business of love better than we ever could."

"Precisely," Miss Woodhouse continued. "No matter our so-called *pretty follies* or unorthodox courtship, we three couples shall declare our love in front of God and our chosen congregations. There ought to be no question of our faith or our commitment. The word *dissident* has no place here. Am I right, Mrs. Kolman?"

Nonplussed, the rabbi's wife could only nod in silence; Mrs. Martin's teacup was held in midair, not quite close to her lips, not near enough to set down. Harriet had no notion what had transpired to make Miss Woodhouse speak in such a manner, but she was pleased. She was very pleased indeed!

"Now, Harriet," said Miss Woodhouse, "you may take your pretty package up to your room and open it at your leisure, but if you do so, you shall have a room full of wounded women when you return."

"I have no idea what it could be. I didn't send away for anything. I know no one in London!"

"I received a brief note from the sender, for it was delivered to my attention at Hartfield. I shall not hold it against you if you prefer to read it privately—and perhaps, you ought, now that I have made a blunder of it all."

"No, I thank you, Miss Woodhouse, but I have done with secrets and mysteries. Everyone in this room is near and dear to my heart. I know that you care a great deal for me. It follows that whatever the letter states, whatever is wrapped up in that box, you shall either rejoice with me or condole with me. Pray, may I see the missive you received?"

Miss Woodhouse looked about the room until she found Mrs. Goddard's concerned gaze. She nodded her assurance that it was for the best before reaching into her reticule and retrieving the note.

"I shall read it aloud," Harriet declared.

Dear Miss Woodhouse,

I pray you forgive my impudence in writing without the benefit of a proper introduction.

Not long ago, a gentleman transacted business in my husband's shop. I shan't go into all the details, but suffice it to say, Mr. Elton made it known that a Miss Harriet Smith was under your mentorship. I pray God that you be blessed with long life, health, and happiness for the kindness you have bestowed upon my daughter.

I have accepted my lot in life; I have made mistakes and have paid the consequences. But bringing my precious daughter into this world was not a mistake. If God ordained it, He must have had a reason. I shall continue to pray and have faith in His mercy.

Mr. Elton informed me that my daughter was happy, healthy, and well cared for—a prayer answered. It has been a lifetime since I parted with my babe, a lifetime of worrying and wondering in whose hands she has been placed. What sort of woman looks after her wellbeing? What sort of home has she been provided? Does she know she is the daughter of a King? Does she guard her dignity? Does she know her worth?

When the time comes for my Hannahleh to wed, I would ask a favor of you, Miss Woodhouse. Your assistance would afford me a great honor, for it would ensure the continuation of a family tradition—that I would not have broken the chain. I ask that you give my daughter the enclosed. It must be known, however, that though it comes from my hands, the gift does not stem from me.

For many generations, this chanukkiah, this ancient candelabra, has been given to the eldest daughter in my family on the occasion of her wedding. It is my daughter's birthright—the only legacy I am able to give. It has been in the homes of courageous women, of nurturing women, of women who have fallen, who have been forgiven, and who have had the fortitude to go on.

I pray that when she kindles these lights, she will know that my love for her and our shared heritage burns eternally in my heart. May she know she is loved—that she has always been loved, and will be loved forever more.

With sincere gratitude,
Hannah Weiss Deutsch

The letter fell from her hands just as her tears fell unrestrained. Harriet was uncertain if the power of movement would ever be restored to her; she sat motionless as a piece of petrified wood that had turned to stone.

"Shall I open it for you, Harriet?" asked Elizabeth Martin.

As her soon-to-be sister tore back each layer of thick paper, the item within began to take shape. Harriet had seen a similar object in the Martins' house. It held a place of honor among the keepsakes and ritual pieces.

"What a treasure," said Mrs. Kolman.

"Indeed," replied Mrs. Martin. "It must go back hundreds of years, Harriet. Highbury's silversmith will take great delight in inspecting the craftsmanship."

"I shall have to be taught the prayers and the meaning of the nine branches," Harriet murmured as she ran her hand across the intricate workings. "I shall want to recite the words properly."

"My dear girl," said Mrs. Goddard, "you have always striven to do things *properly*. It has always been your belief that you were inferior in some way; that if you did not measure up to the expectation, love would be withheld, that home or security would be denied you."

"Harriet—daughter, look around this room," said Mrs. Martin. "Look at what you have accomplished. You have brought us together, a group of women who may have never had the opportunity to meet. You have started a circle of friends, both Christian and Jew, to learn from one another, to share life's trials, to rejoice in glad tidings. This is precisely your gift to us, to those who love you."

Her cheeks flushed, and Harriet felt a yearning for *something*, though she knew not what. She had dreamt her whole life of knowing her mother's love, of knowing her place in the world, of knowing—come what may—that she was not adrift, floating from one circumstance to another.

Now, she understood, the time for yearning was no longer. There was no need to be afraid, no need to be anxious. She looked upon Sofia's face and then gazed upon Mrs. Goddard's countenance. She had been blessed in being placed in their care. She turned her gaze upon the Martin girls and recognized in them a true sisterhood. They had been her first teachers, educating by example, eventually leading her to Mrs. Kolman. Lastly, Harriet took Miss Woodhouse's hand in her own.

"We have had quite the adventure, you and I," said Harriet. "I believe our places were transposed, for, at times, I was the clearheaded one who knew what was what, while your head was filled with fanciful designs. Despite these things, or perhaps because of them, the wishes, the hopes, the predictions of our small band of true friends shall be fully answered in the perfect happiness of our unions and matrimonial bliss."

And as she gazed upon her mother's legacy, Harriet knew without compunction that she was anchored to tradition, affixed to a good husband and a loving family. In truth, she owned it was more than that. It was something akin to *emunah* and *bitachon*—she had faith and trust. She need no longer fear the journey. She need no longer question her path. Here was the constancy she desperately sought; here was the purposeful life she so long desired. Harriet Smith was no longer alone, *Hadarit bas Hannah* was home.

Author's Notes

Before she began what was to be the last novel published in her lifetime, Austen wrote, "I am going to take a heroine whom no one but myself will much like." I believe the author *was* successful in that endeavor. To befriend Miss Emma Woodhouse, one truly needs to understand her upbringing and surrounding circumstances, but rather than focusing on Austen's lead heroine and her *tsures* (her troubles), I chose to shine the light on Miss Harriet Smith. I hope you've enjoyed the storyline I've created for this young lady.

One of my beta-readers was drawn to the few sentences I dedicated to the Viceroyalty of Río de la Plata in Chapter Fifteen. I want to take the opportunity to expand on Harriet's school lesson. Most Regency fans are familiar with the Napoleonic Wars, its impact on the Austen family and her fictional characters. England, after all, was at war almost continually throughout the author's lifetime.

Mostly, these battles remained on the Continent, with brief mentions of the West Indies and the Caribbean. But in the course of Harriet's story, I took you further south, all the way to South America, *Spanish America* as was. Some readers may believe I chose that location at random, but they would be incorrect. The Viceroyalty of Río de la Plata came to be known as the Republic of Argentina, and it is my native homeland.

England was very much a part of the viceroyalty's growth. Whalers, farmers, engineers, bankers, and second sons journeyed there to make their fortunes. Things got a little heated; however, when in 1806 and again in 1807, the English decided to invade the territory. Remember— England's resources had been spread thin, what with those pesky American colonists, not to mention the French! The Crown needed to expand its reach to fill its emptying coffers.

In the Viceroyalty, the *criollos* (those born in the New World but of European ancestry) were contemplating their freedom from Spain—much like their brethren up north had done—when the English decided to attack. Sir Home Popham captured Buenos Aires. But when he tried to impose an oath of loyalty, the citizens refused to obey. The *criollos* fought and took back their city. The Redcoats were unsuccessful, having been repulsed by a ragtag colonial militia.

A few months later, England sent more troops to engage with the Spanish colony; however, they soon found themselves fighting in the streets and negotiating an evacuation! Their shame was complete.

Jane Austen was a fervent supporter of the Navy. In a letter dated April 1807, we find a poem penned by her own hand in homage to Sir Home Popham.

Of a Ministry pitiful, angry, mean,
A gallant commander the victim is seen.
For promptitude, vigour, success, does he stand,
Condemn'd to receive a severe reprimand!
To his foes I could wish a resemblance in fate:
That they, too, may suffer themselves, soon or late,
The injustice they warrant. But vain is my spite,
They cannot so suffer who never do right.

Credit: http://www.theloiterer.org/essays/warspart5.html

Understandably, Austen would be sympathetic to that officer; she had two brothers in the Navy and would, naturally, support the cause. Nonetheless, there was a large population of English in the Viceroyalty; many had married and raised their families in the New World. They did not support the English invasion, nor did they support the Spanish crown.

In 1807, Napoleon invaded Spain, and the king was removed from power. Living an ocean away, the *criollos* believed they had the right to govern themselves until the lawful king was restored to the throne. In January 1809, Napoleon crowned his brother, Joseph, King of Spain. This act was the perfect excuse for those in the Viceroyalty to fight for secession—in addition to being the perfect fodder for another book of mine entitled *Celestial Persuasion* ~ a *Persuasion* prequel.

Another reader questioned the Jewish population of Regency England. Did Jews exist in large numbers? Would they have lived outside of London, particularly in Surrey, the prime location for this novel? I found many answers on Jewishgen.org, where history and genealogical records abound!

Credit: https://www.jewishgen.org/jcr-uk/England.htm

Jews followed William the Conqueror from Normandy into England. Their communities are well-recorded throughout the land and date back to the year 1066. A medieval synagogue was discovered in the county of Surrey—home to Austen's fictional Donwell Abbey. It dates back to the twelfth century and appears to be the oldest remaining Jewish structure in Western Europe.

The synagogue would have been abandoned when the entire Jewish population was expelled by a royal edict in 1290. It wasn't until September of 1655, when Oliver Cromwell, lord protector of England, Scotland, and Ireland invited Rabbi Menasseh Ben Israel of Amsterdam, along with three other colleagues, to discuss the readmittance of the Jewish population. It was during England's civil war, that political and economic situations allowed for the Jews (mostly Sephardi) to be *informally* welcomed back to the country.

Sephardic Jews, people from the Iberian Peninsula, founded the first modern congregation in England in 1657. These

Spanish and Portuguese Jews went on to build the Bevis Marks Synagogue in 1701. It is still functioning today.

Closer to this novel's timeframe, *The Surrey Quarter Sessions* of the late 18th and early 19th centuries contain several references to Jews living in Bermondsey, Newington, and Southwark. During this period, Surrey was home to several prominent Jewish families, including the Sassoon family of Ashley Park and the De Worms family of Pirbright and Egham.

Sir Moses Haim Montefiore and his wife, Lady Judith Montefiore née Barent Cohen were arguably the most influential Jewish couple throughout the Georgian and Victorian eras. Their roles in society are showcased in my novel, *The Meyersons of Meryton*, a *Pride and Prejudice* variation.

Montefiore (a Sephardic Jew) collaborated with the Duke of Norfolk (a Catholic) by working on removing religious prejudice from areas of national life. By the time Montefiore served as a captain in the 3rd Surrey Local Militia in 1810, he was not required to pledge an oath on the true faith of a Christian. After retiring from the business world in 1824, Montefiore devoted his time to community and civic affairs. He was named Sheriff of London in 1837 and was knighted by Queen Victoria the following year. In 1846, he received a baronetcy in recognition of his services to humanitarian causes on behalf of the Jewish people.

The "First Lady of Anglo Jewry," Judith Montefiore (an Ashkenazi Jew), was known for her philanthropic work and devotion to the Jewish community. She was highly educated, spoke several languages and assisted her husband in his communal affairs and public activities. Lady Judith wrote of their experiences when she and Sir Moses visited Damascus, Rome, St. Petersburg and the Holy Land, but more than travel logs; these works were later hailed as spiritually inspiring and educational. In addition, she wrote *A Jewish Manual; or Practical Information in Jewish & Modern Cookery, with a Collection of Valuable Recipes & Hints Relating to the Toilette.* This "how-to" book included adapted recipes that conformed to Jewish dietary laws, replacing ingredients such as lard, so much used in English kitchens, and eliminating shellfish and forbidden meats. Lady Judith recommended simplicity in dress and considered delicate hands a mark of elegance and refinement. On the other hand, she had strong beliefs regarding a woman's mind and spirit. She said, "Let those females, therefore, who are the most solicitous about their beauty and the most eager to produce a favorable impression, cultivate the *moral, religious* and *intellectual* attributes, and in this advice consists the recipe for the finest cosmetic in the world."

The point I am attempting to make, of course, is that Jews were part of the tapestry that made up English society—and not solely in the stereotypical fashion we have been given to imagine. Yes, there were peddlers and loan brokers, but these occupations were *imposed* on the immigrants. There were restrictions regarding owning property, as there were restrictions on attending certain universities or obtaining certain licenses and certifications. Yet, there *were* Jews in the middle and upper classes, such as the families mentioned above.

As noted by Montefiore's success, and other well-known Jewish entrepreneurs, such as his brother-in-law, Nathan Mayer Rothschild, the British Parliament loosened some of their discriminatory controls by the mid-1800s. For example, The Reform Act of 1867 granted every adult male householder the right to vote. The Universities Tests Act of 1871 removed various obstacles for Jews to become scholars or fellows in an English university. In 1885, Sir Nathaniel de

Rothschild was raised to the upper house as Lord Rothschild, the first Jewish peer.

By 1890, all restrictions for every position in the British Empire were removed for Jews and Roman Catholics, except for that of the monarch.

Another question posed by my wonderful beta readers was regarding the various words used to describe followers of Judaism. The Hebrew word *yehudi* signifies a member of the tribe of Judah or a member of the Kingdom of Judah. After numerous conquests, and the after effects of the diaspora, the word "Jew" came into use. Of course, variants depended upon its translation in the older versions of the French, German and English languages.

The term "Israelite" was used in reference to Jews of antiquity and throughout the ages, well into the mid twentieth century. I can attest to this fact from personal experience. In Argentina, it is common to see *Hospital Israelita* or *Club Israelita* rather than seeing the word *judío* in the name. It was deemed more genteel—more elegant.

Due to the disparaging manner that *Jew* had been used by antisemites promoting stereotypical caricatures, it was often avoided in polite conversation. To avoid using a slur, the term "Hebrew" became a popular option. Even today, people are wary of using the word Jew. Some people, even Jews themselves, prefer to use *Jewish*.

The Book of Esther refers to a man named *Mordechai Hayehudi*—Mordechai the Jew (10:3). It's probably the first place we see this appellation. And while it has been used in a derogatory fashion since that time, I personally take ownership of the word and wear it as a badge of honor. I *am* a Hebrew, an Israelite—*a Jew*; and, like the Harriet Smith of my novel, I am rooted in this history.

Acknowledgements

My fascination with Jewish history and genealogy, coupled with an obsession for all things Georgian, Victorian, and Edwardian, has long been the inspiration to write Jewish Historical Fiction or Jewish Regency Romance. I have also been inspired by my grandparents—my *bobes* and *zeides*. Their foresight, courage, and determination, along with others of their generation, must be remembered and praised. Surviving tragedies and hardships, they planted seeds of hope and tenacity. My parents continued in this same vein, instilling a sense of pride in my heritage and culture. I thank them all, knowing I stand on the shoulders of giants!

I want to acknowledge my husband and children, who have been my greatest champions. Thanks to my army of volunteer beta-readers, including Delia Athey, Pamela Brown, and Reah N, who gave of themselves and provided invaluable input and feedback. A special note of gratitude goes to Debbie Stone Brown. Her generous spirit, her passion and editor's eagle eye are very much appreciated. Lastly, thank you, dear reader, for your interest and support of this work. Connecting with every one of you has been the greatest gift of all.

If you are so inclined, please leave a rating and a review on Amazon and Goodreads. As an "indie" author, I rely on your kind words on these websites and social media outlets. Your feedback is most appreciated!

For more information, please visit me on Facebook, BookBub, Goodreads, Amazon, or follow my blog: http://www.mirtainestruppauthor.com.

Also by
Mirta Ines Trupp

From Meidelach to Matriarchs ~ A Journal
~Jewish Women of Yesteryear to Inspire your Today

Celestial Persuasion

The Meyersons of Meryton

Destiny By Design: Leah's Journey

Becoming Malka

With Love, The Argentina Family~
Memories of Tango and Kugel, Maté with Knishes

27704293R00152